JAHAJIN

Peggy Mohan began life in Trinidad, West Indies, and her first career was as a linguist, specializing in Trinidad Bhojpuri. After moving to India she dabbled in linguistics, television programmes for children and cartoon animation. She now teaches music at Vasant Valley School, New Delhi.

JAHAJIN

Peggy Mohan

HarperCollins *Publishers* India
a joint venture with

New Delhi

First published in India in 2007 by
HarperCollins *Publishers* India
a joint venture with
The India Today Group

ISBN 97881-7223-714-1

HarperCollins *Publishers*
1A Hamilton House, Connaught Place, New Delhi 110001, India
77-85 Fulham Palace Road, London W6 8JB, United Kingdom
Hazelton Lanes, 55 Avenue Road, Suite 2900, Toronto, Ontario M5R 3L2
and 1995 Markham Road, Scarborough, Ontario M1B 5M8, Canada
25 Ryde Road, Pymble, Sydney, NSW 2073, Australia
31 View Road, Glenfield, Auckland 10, New Zealand
10 East 53rd Street, New York NY 10022, USA

Typeset in 10.5/13.5 Palatino Linotypo
Nikita Overseas Pvt. Ltd.

Printed and bound at
MicroPrints India, New Delhi

To Shivani
who continues the jahajin tradition

CONTENTS

ACKNOWLEDGMENTS

At the heart of this story are all the old people from Central Trinidad who spoke Bhojpuri into my tape recorder back in the 1970s. And my grandmother, Margaret Ramesar, who helped me transcribe the tapes. The version of the Saranga story I translated and used in this book was told to me by Mrs Dhanpat Badri Singh.

Hugh Tinker's *A New System of Slavery* and Marianne Ramesar's *Survivors of Another Crossing* were my main reference books on Indian migration to Trinidad in the 1880s. Marianne Ramesar and Brinsley Samaroo also answered my emailed questions about the experiences of the migrants who arrived in Trinidad and worked on the estates in the 1880s. And Brinsley Samaroo answered my questions about the Canadian Mission in Trinidad.

Google.com was always just a click of a mouse away for the little details about ships and ocean currents that I needed to stop and check.

Ravindranath Maharaj (Raviji), Jerome Teelucksingh, George and Brenda Dixon, Clifford and Wendy Ramcharan, and my uncle Vernon Ramesar checked out details about Trinidad as I needed them.

Santosh Kumar Marwaha gave me the information I needed about the Garden Reach area in Calcutta, the journey down the Hooghly river to the Bay of Bengal, and details about the running of a steamship. Madan Mohan Lal reconstructed for me the details of the migrants' train journey from Faizabad to Calcutta. Rev. Ashok Singh of the Delhi Bible Fellowship helped me reconstruct the type of Hindi that would have been used in the Presbyterian liturgy in Trinidad in the 1880s. Tapan Bose and Dunu Roy told me about the crops grown in Basti in the 1880s; that wheat and wheat flour were introduced into the area much after my migrants had left. Vijay Pande filled me in on the obscure Bhojpuri terms in my transcripts, from his knowledge of Indian Bhojpuri.

The National Science Foundation, Washington DC, funded one of my research trips to Trinidad to record Bhojpuri. The American Institute for Indian Studies gave me a grant to travel to India and look at the sources of Trinidad Bhojpuri.

Tejeshwar Singh, Ashok Srinivasan and Imrana Qadeer read the manuscript and gave valuable suggestions. V.K. Karthika, my editor at HarperCollins, took time out of her maternity leave to read the manuscript. Shivmeet Deol of HarperCollins walked the last mile with me, coaxing me to keep polishing away the raw edges of narrative, both English and Bhojpuri.

My husband Dinesh was the one who first voiced the thought that this story should be a book, and he was there for me as a safety net while I wrote about turbulent times. My cousins Celia Gibbings and Vernon Ramesar stretched warm arms across two great oceans and kept my head above water for the journey. And my daughter Shivani stayed close by me as I wrote, and helped me find my way to the end of the story.

The bowsprit, the arrow, the longing, the lunging heart —
the flight to a target whose aim we'll never know

– Derek Walcott, *The Schooner* Flight

♦

Step from the road to the sea to the sky

– Red Hot Chili Peppers, *Snow (Hey-Oh)*

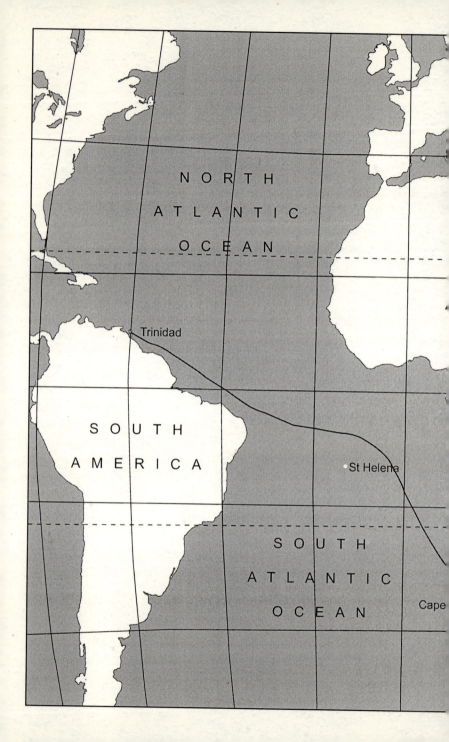

BEFORE THE DARK

WHEN THE SUN HAS SET AND THE DAY IS OVER, THERE comes a short spell of magical light: bright as day, but without the heat and glare and shadow. The struggles of the day have lost their sting, but the night still seems far away. And for a time it feels as if this extended moment could go on forever.

Time to go.

I turned and picked up the big cassette recorder and a few blank audiocassettes. My heels made a brisk rap on the wooden floor as I passed through the upstairs living room to reach the steps leading down to the dining room.

My father had turned the car for me, and it waited under the shed just outside the dining room. The bonnet was up: Kojo, our old family retainer, was filling the radiator. I put the tape recorder and the blank cassettes on the backseat and slid into the driver's seat. Satisfied, Kojo closed the bonnet.

I eased the car past the two bends in the driveway and waited at the gate, revving up the engine to shake off the confining feel of the large house behind me. Then I roared out, up the road, left at Isaac Junction, past all the houses in Macbean Village, and off towards the cane lands.

Just before St Mary's Junction, I pulled over to the side and stopped. A figure in faded blue jeans peeled off from the gas station sign ahead.

Fyzie.

I slid across to the other seat. Fyzie came straight to the driver-side door, opened it, bent down to smile a high-energy smile, and jumped in to take the wheel.

Then we took a left towards the sea, heading towards Orange Valley, where the fishermen bring in the early morning catch, and drove towards the remnants of the sunset. Beside a small wooden house on stilts, we stopped.

Sitting below the house in a jute-sack hammock strung between the stilts was a very old woman: Deeda.

She had asked for a few days to think out the story, to make sure there were no lapses of memory. She wanted to make sure that all the details fit as they should.

Two old women in orhnis and an old man had come to hear the tale. Old people, at sunset...

Someone switched on a light and Deeda's bleak look seemed to soften. In the artificial light she suddenly looked younger. Something of her old magic was back.

She reached for the microphone in my hand. '*Hum pakri?*' Should I hold it?

'*Na, hum pakrab.*' No, I'll hold it.

I had already pressed play-record, and the tape recorded that exchange as her introduction. I looked back at Deeda and she began the story.

'*Ego baanar rahal an ego banariya, du-jana.*' There were once two monkeys, a male and a female.

'Ta duno jana baithal rahal ego daar par, aa tarey rahal...reeba. Nadiya. Pani.' They were both seated on a branch and below them was...a river. Water.

'Ta banariya bolela banarwa se, ki "Dekh, aisan ghari, aisan sammat aail ba ki jaun i jal me kood jaai, ta maanus ke janam paai."' So the female told the male: 'Look, at this moment the stars are right, whoever jumps into that water will be transformed into a human.'

'Ta banarwa boley: "Tu kood, na! Hum kahey ke kudi?" Ta banariya, ohi jal me, kood gail.' So the male said: 'You jump, then! Why should I?' So the female, she jumped into the water.

When she jumps, she is transformed into a human. But what can the poor girl do, no home, no door? Where will she go? Well, at that moment, a prince who has come hunting in that forest passes by, and when he sees her he falls in love.

The girl says: 'Prince, I am naked.' So he takes off the pagri from his head and throws it to her, and she wraps it around herself.

Now where could she go? She had no mother or father. So the prince sat her behind him on his horse and rode away with her.

And while they were going she spoke up: 'Prince, I won't go with you to your palace now. For twelve years I will remain here, unmarried. Then, after twelve years, I will come to your palace.' And he agrees.

Before he leaves, he builds a cottage for her, and leaves maids and servants to look after her. Then he goes away.

Now the girl begins to search all over for her monkey. And one day in the distance she hears sounds of a kalandar, with his troupe of dancing monkeys, and she asks her servant to call the kalandar to her.

In the kalandar's troupe is her monkey. He is the one without any hair, it all fell off when she left him. So she points to that monkey and says to the kalandar:

'Make that monkey dance.'

The kalandar tries to get him to dance, but he is too new, how can he dance? So the kalandar hits him with his stick. Then she says again:

'Make that monkey dance!'

The kalandar tries again, and when the monkey doesn't dance he hits him again, and the monkey flinches and grimaces at the blows. Then the girl comes and stands looking down at the monkey, and sings:

> Tumhe ta laagey lakari, re, pyaarey,
> Humein laagey kareja-kheenchey hunkari.

> Blows are falling on you, my love,
> My heart is tight with pain.

And the monkey replies, singing:

> Arey, humein ta laagey lakari, re, rani,
> Aa tum karo mahaley-beechey bhoga ji!

> Yes, blows are falling on me, queen,
> And you are living well in a palace!

So the girl says to the kalandar: 'Give me that monkey, sell him to me.'

And the kalandar says: 'No, I won't. I earn my living from these monkeys.'

The girl's face turns red with anger, and she says, again: 'Give me that monkey!'

So the kalandar says: 'I can't give you that one, he is new. He doesn't know how to dance.'

So the girl says: 'If you don't give me that monkey, I will get the prince to pass an order and have him snatched away from you!'

So he gives her the monkey. Sells him to her.

Now the girl keeps the monkey with her as her pet. One day, she goes to have a bath, and tells her servant to keep a watch on her monkey. So the servant puts a leash around the monkey's neck, and goes away. Then, when he is alone, the monkey makes a noose out of the leash and hangs himself.

When the girl comes out of her bath and sees her monkey dead, she orders the servants to bring her a load of sandalwood from the prince's palace for the cremation. Then when the pyre is burning, she jumps into the flames, and they burn together.

And they are reborn. This time the monkey comes back as a boy, and is called Sada Birij. And the girl is born again in a merchant's home, and her name becomes Saranga—

I flipped the pause button and turned to look at Ajie, my grandmother. She had dozed off with her chin resting on her chest while I was writing the last bit. I looked down again at my yellow notepad, covered with transcription in double-spaced Devanagari, and translations of individual words jotted between the lines in English. It was easy enough to follow Bhojpuri when face to face with people like Deeda, when the excitement and eye contact passed on their intent, if not always their meaning. But back home late at night, sitting at the old drop-leaf table in the upstairs living room with only a tape to go by, I would be lost without Ajie.

I shook Ajie gently, and she opened her eyes and got up to head for her bed, with its mosquito net already down and tucked in for the night. I turned off the light above the living-room table and took the tape recorder back through my room into my study.

I pulled my Sanskrit dictionary off the shelf above

my desk. Saranga. I found the word 'saaranga', with a short final *a*, adjective. It was a title of Lord Shiva. The feminine form, with the long *aa* at the end, would have to be a title for Parvati, his wife. The most independent of all the goddesses. Shiva and Parvati were more allies in battle than lovers.

Then I sat a while and thought about Saranga's mysterious prince, and how easily he had agreed to give her the twelve years she had asked for. He must have known as soon as he set eyes on her that she was not a creature of his world. But even so, he had granted her an enormous window of time to shake off the past and move forward to take her place by his side.

A CARGO OF WOMEN

I PARKED THE CAR UNDER A TALL TREE IN THE SCHOOL OF Education yard, on the northern fringe of the University of the West Indies campus in St Augustine. Rosa had summoned all of us for her seminar, and we had come to create a cordon of women academics around her. Elsewhere in the yard other little cars were taking the shady spots too.

The last time she had ventured onto this topic, things had not gone well. Her talk then had been punctuated by indignant outbursts from a small group of Indian men in the audience. This time our presence was intended to keep the discussion on a more academic plane. We filed into the room early and captured the best places around the table.

Rosa walked into the hangar-like shed that served as a seminar room, eyes shielded behind gleaming glasses. She patted her crisp afro into place and waited for the room to fill up. The chairperson introduced her as one of our leading feminists, and then she looked down at her notes and began her talk.

She took her time getting into the topic, starting with a summary of the early years of the migration from India.

This first wave of migration had not produced a viable Indian community in Trinidad, she said. The migrants then had been selected in an ad hoc manner, and had mostly been down-and-outs from Calcutta and the surrounding hinterland, and 'hill coolies', aboriginal tribals from the Chhota Nagpur plateau. Their death rate had been very high, both on the ships and on the plantations. And being almost all men, they had left no children in Trinidad.

But this changed in the 1860s, she said. Driven by famine, large numbers of farmers from the United Provinces and Bihar, in north India, were coming forward as migrants, putting aside their age old reluctance to cross the kala pani, the black water of the Bay of Bengal, which meant losing caste. With these farmers were other peasant groups from the region, suddenly made landless because of new land tenure laws brought in by the British colonial government, or rendered unemployed because of cheap imports from Britain, then in the thick of the Industrial Revolution. But what turned this balanced mix of peasant migrants into a self-perpetuating community was women.

A pause. Someone coughed. Rosa looked up a second, and then launched into a flurry of statistics about the sex-ratio of the migrants on various ships during this period. Then she came to the point.

'Roughly thirty per cent of the migrants on every ship were female. Some of these were women coming with their husbands, of course, and children. But most of the men were not travelling with wives. According to the records, most of these women were adults travelling alone.'

Alone! Here was the big point at issue: the notion that Indian women might, in fact, be no different from other Trinidadian women in having shown signs of independence. Indian women no different from Afro-Caribbean women! What a blow to the ideal of the great Indian family, where every Indian male must be yoked to the only other creature on this planet subordinate enough to stand behind him and shore up his self-esteem through famine, indentureship and poverty: an Indian woman. Were Indian women always as headstrong as we now looked to be? Were Indian marriages, after all, no better than any other male-female bondings?

Not a sound from the back.

The chairperson leaned towards her microphone and scanned the front row for signs of life. One of my aunts, a historian, was sitting there wringing her hands nervously, searching for the least provocative words to make her point, conscious that her accent would mark her as a Jamaican. Then she raised her hand:

'If you look at how the migrant ships were designed—I have a sketch here—look, this whole front area above the cargo hold was for single men. Right behind was a smaller section for married couples. Now right at the back,' she lifted the sketch and pointed, 'right at the back is a section for single women.' She put down the sketch, and added: 'What they aimed for was a forty-sixty female-male ratio, but they settled for thirty per cent women migrants.'

The chairperson intervened here to forestall any outburst from the back: 'I didn't think there would be that many adult Indian women still single.'

Another hand went up in front, this time a young feminist: 'No, no, they wouldn't have been single as such. There would have been widows, yes, and children. But a lot of married women must have showed up too, you know, as migrants. Nowadays you even find married women leaving their husbands and escaping with political refugees. It may just be the easiest way to make a clean break from a bad marriage.'

A rumble of sound from a back corner this time. Rosa shot me a look, and I remembered that I wasn't there just as a passenger. I tested the mike first, and found the right distance so that my voice would carry. 'Actually, I'm doing some interviews with old people who came on the boats—'

'Interviews in English?' a voice came at me from the back. Someone seeing me for the first time would probably not take me for an Indian. Besides, who in Trinidad our age, and educated to boot, could speak the old people's language any more?

'...in Bhojpuri. I first started looking at Bhojpuri a couple of years ago, when I was doing my undergrad thesis here. Now I'm collecting data on Bhojpuri for my PhD dissertation. I found the best way to get people to talk was to ask them to tell stories, you know, folktales or things out of their own lives, long ago. Old people like to talk about long ago.'

I paused to get my bearings. Stay close to linguistics, girl, this feminist stuff isn't your scene, you'll screw it up!

'I don't really care what they say, so long as they keep on talking,' I continued. 'I just want long samples of natural speech to analyze. You can't get rich complicated sentences just by asking for them. These old people don't have a concept of literal translation. But complex structures have a high probability of showing up in discourse if the speaker is focusing on something else. Like events, and getting the story right.'

'Yes?' A prompt from Rosa. The migration, remember?

'Okay, so the easiest thing to ask about is an adventure. And the biggest adventure in their lives seems to have been the boat trip from India, and the friends they made for life on the journey. Well, most of the people I interview seem to be women, almost all over ninety. Very few of the men seem to make it that far.' I paused. I could see Deeda's face in my mind's eye.

'One old lady I just interviewed is more than a hundred years old. She says a hundred and ten! She told me a lot, about the barracks in Trinidad, the boat trip, her village in India, and how she got to be recruited. The way she talked it seemed to be mostly women all around her. She came as a single woman, but she was married, and she had a child with her.'

'I want to hear that tape,' Rosa broke in. 'But how would I follow it?'

'Not to worry! I'll translate it for you.'

We walked out together to the car, Rosa and I, after the seminar. I checked the tape recorder on the backseat. The tape with *Rani Saranga ke Kheesa*, the story of Rani Saranga, was still in it. I looked in the bag next to the tape recorder and found the tapes with Deeda's earlier narrative next to the microphone. I took them out and waved them for Rosa to see.

Rosa took a ride home with me. I parked and brought out the tape recorder and Deeda's earlier tapes. I had already transcribed them with Ajie's help, so I was ready to do a slick professional job with the interpretation. Rosa shifted a vase from her coffee table and I put the tape recorder there, and changed the cassette. Then we both leaned forward to listen to Deeda.

I pressed play, and soon Deeda's voice came on: *'Batiyaai, bahin?'* And my own response: *'Haan, haan, tohaar kaa naam ba?'*

Should I talk, sister? Yes, yes, what is your name?

'Parbati, humaar naam ba. Pension meelela ohi se. Parbati.'

Parbati, that's my name. That's the name I get my pension with. Parbati.

'Par doosar aise bolawe ke ba Deeda. Ohi naam sagro jaala, family *me, sagro. Kirwal,* Indian, *sab, sab puchela, kirauniyan jaala pani ke hiaan, sab puchela: "Eh Deeda, tu hiyen ba?"'*

But I have another name they call me by, Deeda. That name goes with me everywhere, in my family, everywhere. Creoles, Indians, everyone, they all ask, Creole women go to fill water at the standpipe and ask: 'Deeda, you're here too?'

Then my own voice: *'Tu muluk ke ba?'* Are you from India?

Deeda again: *'Humni sab ke muluk se li aanal. Pakar-pakar ke* fool-am *karal. Haan, kunwaari hum rahli – na sacchey kunwaari rahli, hum biyaah kar ke ayli. Aa humaar aadmi mulkey me ba. Hum akeley ayli okey chhor ke.'*

They brought all of us from India. They caught us one by one and told us a lot of lies. Yes, I came as a single woman – I wasn't really single, I was married before I came. And my husband is still in India. I came alone and left him behind.

Then the voice of her next-door neighbour: *'Bhaagi aawal, bhaagi aawal!'* She ran away, she ran away and came here!

I let the tape run as Deeda's neighbour urged her to go back to the start, from when she was in her village. Deeda had nodded at this, and then her voice came again.

'Haan, bhaiya, humaar janam bhail ba muluk me, Basti jeela.'

Yes, bhaiya, I was born in India, district Basti.

'Humaar baap kahaar me doli dhowat rahal, baabhan-
chhatri ke. Doli. Ohi me ghus ke baithaylen, tab du aadmi ehar,
du aadmi ohar, ohi me jaai. Humaar baap rahal rauniyar kahaar,
aa maai rahal dhodiya.'

My father was by caste a kahaar, and he would wash the
palanquins that the brahmins and kshatriyas travelled in.
Palanquins. He would seat them inside, and then with two men
lifting this side and two men lifting that side, they would go. My
father was a rauniyar kahaar, and my mother was a dhodiya
kahaar.

When I was seven years old, my father had me married.
Then, when I was twelve, I went to live with my mother-in-law.
The year after that, I had a son, Kalloo. Then my husband went
out with other men from the village as a migrant worker, to a
place near Allahabad. The next year they went again. And the
year after that. After that I was alone with my mother-in-law
and the child.

When Kalloo was going on four years, a drought came. Last
year's rice crop was bad, and now no rain for this year's crop
to grow, and no money to buy food to eat. We should have planted
bajra, millet, but again we hadn't, so we had to depend on the
rice. I was the one cooking every day, and I could see the rice
getting less and less. I kept thinking, what will happen to this
child if I starve?

Some people had already gone from our village, said the
village was no kind of place to stay now, best to get out of there.
Kaa karey ke hoi, bhaiya? What to do? My mother-in-law was
ready to go too. She had wanted me to come with her and bring
the child, but I had said no, I wanted to wait for Kalloo's father
to come. Then a few days after my mother-in-law went to stay
with her brother, I started to get worried. I had to find work, but

what work was there in the village? So I took the last few handfuls of parched rice my mother-in-law had kept aside, and some sattwa powder, from roasted channa, and tied them in two bundles. Then I picked up an extra sari, and walked with the child to the town of Faizabad.

And that was where I met the arkatiniya, the lady who was recruiting people to go with her as migrants.

She met me on the street, just as I reached, and told me they were looking for labourers to go to a place called 'Chini-dad', a land of 'chini', sugar. In Chini-dad there were big estates where they made sugar. They wanted labourers to work in the sugarcane fields. She told me they were especially looking for women to go, and she promised me an extra advance if I signed up. Only one year there, she said, and then they bring you back. Plenty of money.

Kaa batiyaai, bahin? What could I say? I told her I wanted some time to think. So she sent me and my child to sit with a group of people who were thinking about signing up, said she would come back and ask me again after some time.

In the group there was a family, a husband and a wife, with four small sons. The wife was expecting another child. Her name was Ramdaye. They were from Basti jeela, just like us, and the same caste as us, kahaars. We made up our minds to stay together. If they went, we would go. We would sign up and travel as one group.

Then the arkatiniya came back with two brothers who looked like pundits, and a few other men, two ahirs, cowherds, and a lot of other men, mostly kurmis, farmers. One of the men, Ojir Mian, had broken his foot and was walking with a stick. There was a woman too, a nauniya, from the barber caste. She had had a fight with her mother-in-law and had walked out of the house. One of the ahirs was a tall, dark, skinny man named

Sirju, and he was carrying a dholak, a drum, with him in a bag.

The arkatiniya told all of us to come with her: a doctor had to see us before we could sign up. But first we should eat. All of us were looking too skinny, she said. We mightn't get to go if they thought we were sick.

So we went to the depot in Faizabad to wait for the doctor to come and check us. On the way to the depot I was behind Sirju, and I saw him pick up a whole hand of bananas from a stall without taking his eyes off the road, and stuff it inside his dholak bag.

That night when all of us were sleeping we heard a whole set of screeching and commotion, and then Sirju's voice shouting: 'Chor! Chor!' Thief! Thief!

We got up fast, somebody lit a lamp, and in front of us Sirju was sitting up trying to make out what was sitting at the other end of his bedding eating one of the bananas from his bag. Then he saw it was a monkey.

'Badmaas!' Rascal! Sirju snarled and dived at the monkey to take back his bananas, and the monkey leaned forward and bared all its teeth at Sirju.

'Hut jaa hiaan se!' Get out of here!

So the monkey picked up the bag with the dholak and all the bananas and jumped off the bedding, and climbed up on a beam, and sat and watched Sirju, and kept on eating the banana.

Sirju sat and scratched his head. Then he turned and saw Kalloo hiding behind me and called out to him: 'Eh, boy! Should we let him keep the bananas?'

And Kalloo growled back: 'No!'

So Sirju looked up at the monkey and said: 'You heard the child?'

The monkey continued eating, and Sirju stood up and smiled. Cool and calm he shinnied up the pole, talking to the monkey in *a soft voice, like it was his friend. He got up on the rafters and started to move towards the bag. All the time he kept looking the monkey in its eyes, joking with it, telling it to give the boy back his bananas.*

And the monkey kept watching Sirju and shifting backwards out of his reach.

And then all of a sudden the monkey did a funny thing. It stopped shifting and grinned back at Sirju, and left the bag with the dholak and the bananas on the rafters, and turned and jumped out the window.

And Sirju reached out his long arm and caught the bag before it fell.

After that Sirju got a new name: Langoor Mamoo. Uncle Langoor. If he could climb like that, and talk to a monkey and get back his bananas to boot, then he and the monkey had to be family.

The doctor came a few days after that, and he checked all of us quickly, and asked us a few things. Then he said it was okay, we could go, he didn't see any trouble with us. He checked Ojir Mian's foot, and said it would take some time to get better, that was all. Then he asked the arkatiniya if she had told us everything about the girmit we would have to sign. She said yes.

I kept that word in my mind—girmit—so I could ask her afterwards what it was.

When I asked her she told us that that was a paper we would have to sign to go as migrants to Chini-dad. We would have to go in front of the magistrate and he would ask us if we understood what we would be signing up to do in Chini-dad and if we agreed to keep our side of the bargain.

What bargain? I asked.

Only what I already told you about, she said. Working in the sugarcane fields, things like that. How long you have to stay there. How they have to pay you for your work there. And how you get your passage back when your time is finished.

You said one year? I asked her.

That is all, she told me.

So I said it was all right, we would sign the girmit.

So the next day all of us went in front of the magistrate. There they wrote down your name, father's name, any children going with you, if you were man or woman, your caste, what work you did, your village, district, all of that on the girmit, and underneath you had to make a mark to say you agreed to everything. Then you were ready to go to the main depot, in Calcutta.

We had to go by train. So we went the next day after lunch to wait at Faizabad station for the Howrah passenger train to come from Lucknow. They made us squat in a line and wait. The train was only going to stop for half an hour, so we had to be fast.

The arkatiniya asked me if I wanted to give her my silver beras, the bracelets I had bought with my advance on the way to the station, for safekeeping. She said somebody might steal them on the train. See? She was keeping things safe for a few other people too.

I had seen some women giving her their jewellery, but that didn't sound right. So I said: 'Na, humhoon raakhab'. No, I'll keep them myself.

When the train came all of us from Basti took up one end of the bogey. The train was going to take a day to reach Calcutta. As soon as it started Kalloo said he wanted to go up and sit next to Langoor Mamoo on the higher bunk. And then after Sirju took him from me I looked up and saw him push his hand inside his bag and bring out a banana and give it to the child to eat.

We were okay all the way to Banaras. Some of the men were even cracking jokes and teasing each other, and the children were asking them things, and climbing up and down like monkeys. We reached Banaras station by evening, and Sirju saw a man frying phulauries on the platform, dropping handfuls of ground dal paste into hot oil, and he made him come to the window. The man took two big leaves and made up a set each for Sirju and Kalloo with chutney.

But at night! We had to sleep sitting up in the same place, no space to move. The train didn't go fast, and we stopped at all the stations on the way to Calcutta. Early in the morning the train stopped in the wilderness between Gaya and Dhanbad. They told us to stay on the train, so we sat in the bogey and waited like they told us. But Sirju managed to slip out the door and go and see what was happening. They had taken off the engine, he said. They were going to put another one.

While we waited for the engine the sky got darker and darker with rain clouds gathering, and the whole train started to get quiet. Most of the migrants by now were tired of travelling; they were just staring, not talking, and their eyes were looking wide and stupid, like they were in a trance, like there was nothing in front of them, only space. And all this time the sky was getting blacker.

It was the monsoon we had been waiting for.

And then when they put the new engine and we were close to Dhanbad, lightning started to flash and thunder rolled, and it started to rain, rain like the sky up there was mocking us, throwing down all the rain that would have kept us in our villages, now that we had given up and become girmitiyas. Sirju gave me a signal and I scrambled up with my belongings to sit next to him and Kalloo on the top bunk.

Down below water was coming in through the windows, everything was getting wet. Everybody's clothes, everybody's food, and they had to come and show us how to close the shutters to keep out the rain. But I kept Kalloo in my lap and wrapped the end of my sari around him and held him tight, and we stayed up on top.

It rained like that the whole day. And it was still raining when we reached Howrah station in Calcutta and the train stopped.

Then they came inside and told us to pick up our belongings and come out of the train and make a line, in the rain itself, and they made us march across the Howrah bridge. Lucky thing it was still daytime, they told us. They used to stop traffic on the bridge at night, and unhook it in the middle so barges and steamers could pass.

Then we had to walk in a line next to the river, past the ghaats, while rain kept pelting down. People were standing there and watching us, how we were walking like we didn't know where we were going, just one foot in front of the other, like we were blind. And somebody shouted: look at the jeeta janazza, the walking dead!

We walked and walked in the rain, with the river next to us all the way, and after we passed the Khidarpur docks we got to Garden Reach depot, and the sheds we had to stay in. All of us went in fast and squatted under the shelters and they gave us hot tea, and we dried ourselves and looked out at the rain.

We stayed in the depot under those sheds for a whole month, waiting for more migrants to come. Our boat hadn't reached yet, and we couldn't leave from Calcutta until the middle of the monsoon, when the level of the river was higher, they said. We had to wait.

The day after we reached the depot it was bright and sunny, so they told us they had a place in the yard where we could bathe. Then they gave all of us new clothes, a sari for every woman, and a dhoti-kurta for the men, and everybody got a *shawl they could use as a blanket. So we went and bathed. When it was lunchtime again they made us squat in two lines outside the sheds, and everybody got a big metal thariya, in which they put some boiled rice, some dal, and some curry potatoes for all of us. That was when I realized I hadn't seen hot food since the depot in Faizabad!*

Then one night another group of migrants came to join us. At the head of the line was a big tall man with a fair face and a pink pagri, two big boys behind him, and a pretty little girl, fair like her father. I told Kalloo to go and make friends with them, and to bring the girl back so I could talk to her. So he went.

He came back with the girl, and I asked her what her name was. Janaki, she said. And what about your mother, I asked. Well, she was dead a long time now, it was just the four of them. I asked her where they were from. Aligarh.

Aligarh! So far! What were they doing in Calcutta, with a set of purabiya migrants from Basti and Faizabad?

Well, her father had had some trouble with the police, she said, so they wanted to go far from Aligarh. He had been in a fight, and somebody might have died, she wasn't sure.

I looked at the pretty girl with the big light eyes and the slim little hands, and she pulled the end of her sari more tightly over her head to cover her hair, and pulled her feet away further under the skirt of her sari. But still she looked straight at me, straight into my eyes, not shy, waiting for another question. I had a lot of questions, but I didn't know how to start.

When I didn't say anything for some time, Janaki asked me my name, and I told her, Parbati. She thought for a minute. What should I call you? she asked. Well, you could call me Didi, I said, big sister. No, she said. Too common. I know, I'll call you Deeda!

And that is the name I have to this day.

At first I thought Janaki was a child, but she told me no, she just looked small. She was really going on twelve years, and she was on her father's girmit as a single woman. She was going to stay in the single women's section with us on the boat. She shifted her belongings and came to stay next to me and Kalloo in the depot, as she couldn't stay with her father and her brothers. She only went back to them when it was time to eat.

And when she got her new sari and was to go and bathe, she asked me to come with her. She wanted to wash her hair, and didn't think she could manage by herself.

Then I saw her hair. She had the longest thickest plait in the whole world! So I helped her to oil and comb it, and then I helped her wash her hair.

Janaki was not like us: she did not speak like the rest of us, like a purabiya. She spoke the Hindi of Aligarh, Khari Boli, but she could understand us, and we could understand her. Even in the rain she kept her sari long, with the bottom reaching the ground, almost dragging as she walked. Everyone was surprised that she never even let her feet show. And she kept the pallu of her sari over her head, tight, so that you couldn't see her hair at all. What you could see were two big light eyes, just like cats' eyes, a straight pretty nose, and her slim little hands.

That was enough for us. Only a woman from a good family would cover up like that. And all of us made up our minds that Janaki must be the best looking woman we had ever seen.

In the next group of migrants there was another woman, also named Janaki. She was a widow from Faizabad, with three sons. The youngest one was still a baby. She was a sonaarin, from the caste of goldsmiths, and she had been thrown out by her in-laws after her husband died, so that she couldn't try to take the property.

Two women named Janaki? That would cause too much confusion. So we decided that the younger Janaki should get another name, just like me. And since she was the best looking woman we had ever seen, Kalloo had the idea of calling her Sunnariya, the beautiful one. And that is the name that stayed with her—

I paused the tape here to take a break. Rosa went into the kitchen to make us some tea, and I followed her there.

'Sunnariya was my great-great grandmother,' I said. 'Ajie's ajie.' Well, not Sunnariya. In our family history we always referred to her as Sundaree. That was the 'correct' way to say her name in Hindi. I had first heard the name Sunnariya from Deeda.

'Ajie's father used to talk about her,' I continued. 'She was his mother. He used to say that she was very beautiful, but then he never told me what she actually looked like. I always wondered if Ajie had taken after her.'

We brought our tea back into the living room and sat cradling the warm mugs in our hands. Neither one of us felt like talking. The spell of Deeda's story was still upon us, and the world of St Augustine and the faraway traffic sounds from the Eastern Main Road were unreal and unwelcome. But my translation speed was flagging, and I needed to unwind a few minutes before returning to Deeda and Sunnariya at the depot in Calcutta.

I went and sat out on the porch. Rosa's ferns and potted plants kept me company. In the sky was the same timeless light as when I would go with Fyzie to record Deeda. I emptied my mind and stared at the sky, and for a while I had the eerie feeling that I had slipped through a gap and become Deeda. I actually remembered walking into Garden Reach depot and squatting under the thatched roofs that evening and looking out at the rain.

I turned and saw Rosa looking at me. She was ready to continue. I came back to the tape recorder, sat, and released the pause button.

'Haan, bhaiya, aisanhu saaban ke mahina beet gail, a tab ohi jahajwa aai gail.'

Yes, bhaiya, the month of Saavan passed like that, and then the boat came.

Then everything started to happen all at once. It was monsoon, and the river was full of water, deeper. It was the best time to leave, they said. Now every day they would bring more things to carry on the boat.

Heaps of coal. Barrels of grease for the boat engines.

Big, big barrels of water. All the things we would be eating: rice, dal, white flour and dried saltfish. All in barrels, so that rats couldn't get at them. Potatoes, onions, pumpkins. Dried peas in jute sacks.

Sugar and salt and masalas in jute sacks.

Big, big pots to cook food for all the migrants, pots the size of barrels.

Jute that they were carrying to sell in Trinidad.

Buffaloes, goats. Fodder for the animals.

Medicines.

And new people had come, people who would go with us on the boat: bandhaaris, who would be the cooks, and masaalchis, cooks' assistants, bhangis to keep the boat clean. And laskars: stokers to shovel the coal for the boat engines and greasers to keep the engines covered with grease.

As our boat was a steamer we had to have Indian laskars. It was only Indian stokers who could tolerate the heat inside the boiler room, where they would be burning coal to make the steam.

Same thing with the greasers: the boat engines would be hot. Our laskars were Muslims from East Bengal, and all from the same family. But they could speak some Hindi and understood us.

All of us had to line up again so that the doctor could check us. In the line in front of us the two pundit brothers were together. One of them, Sahatoo Maharaj, had a fever. The doctor told him to go and wait in the clinic as he wanted to check him again. But all of us from Basti were good, no problems. And Sunnariya and her father and brothers also passed. Then the doctor gave Sahatoo Maharaj some medicine and sent him back to wait with us.

The next few days we heard that they were fixing up the jetty at Khidarpur docks, putting up rails on the side, changing one or two cross-beams under it, fixing the covering on top. Then they brought the boat up to the jetty, and loaded all the supplies and the animals, and all the people who were going to be working on the boat. We would go on last.

Out of all of us women in the group, Sunnariya was the only one who didn't feel frightened to be going so far, and on a big ugly iron boat like that. She said her father had told her it was okay, plenty better to be in a new place and to forget about this one. The way she said that, her eyes looking so sure, shining like cats' eyes, we didn't say anything back. Kaa jaani? What did we know? Maybe she was right.

I thought about Kalloo's father. When he used to go away, he didn't go so far, and he came back every year for a month. What were we doing leaving him like this? Was he back in the village now? Had he realized where we had gone?

Stop! If I went on thinking like this I wouldn't be able to manage.

The day before we had to leave they gave us a feast. Better eat good, they told us, you're not going to see food like this again for a good long while. They cooked all the vegetables they knew we liked, as they said they didn't know if we would find them later on in Trinidad. They even killed a goat and cooked it for us.

After the feast Sirju and two or three other ahirs brought out dholaks to beat, two other men brought out tassas, and Sahatoo Maharaj and his brother brought out bansuris, bamboo flutes. Some of us sang songs.

Then everybody said: Okay, Deeda, now you have to tell a story! So I said okay, put all the children in front, I will tell a story. That was the day before we left the depot.

The day we were to leave, Sahatoo Maharaj got a fever again, but he didn't want to tell anybody, didn't want to make any trouble. So his brother decided to go to the clinic to see if he could get some more medicine to take with them on the boat. Meanwhile they told us to make a line again. And we picked up our belongings and started moving towards Khidarpur docks.

They saw Sahatoo Maharaj still under the shed, and sent somebody to grab hold of him and make him come on the boat. He tried to push them off, and talked to them roughly, and it looked like they were going to have a fight. But Sahatoo Maharaj wasn't strong enough for that, he was still sick. Then somebody came from the clinic and told him something, and pointed to the boat, and he got up by himself and picked up his belongings and quickly came to the end of the line.

We went and lined up by the jetty. More than five hundred of us standing in that line to go. Sunnariya's father, Mukoon Singh, was heading the line, taller than all the rest of us. The pink pagri on his head was high up, like a banner for us to follow. Just behind him were his two boys, and then Sunnariya. Then all of us started to walk behind Mukoon Singh. Now the water in the river was far, far down below us. Sunnariya's father

*walked across the jetty to the boat without looking back. Then
the rest of us went across, in a line, over the jetty, and went down
the ladder onto the deck. We were really going!*

*Then the laskars told us the tide in the river was rising. It
was time to go. So all of us went to watch as they tied one big
thick tug line to the back of our boat, and then they tied the other
end of the rope to a small tugboat down in the river below. The
tugboat started belching smoke, and next thing we knew we were
getting dragged behind it away from the docks and the other
ships, and down the river.*

*Then all of a sudden when we were far from the docks and
in the middle of the river, there was a big shuddering roar that
came from deep inside our boat, and the deck below us started
to shake. Smoke started to belch out of the big chimney. Then
they came and tied another tug line to the front end of the boat,
and the two tugs started to move in a circle, turning our boat
around so that the front end would point downriver. Now the
laskars loosened the lines and threw them down for the men in
the tugboats to catch, and the little boats started to head back
to the docks. We stayed there for a little while, just watching
them go, and hearing the sound going away too.*

Then suddenly: 'Bhaiya rahi gail! Jahaj roko!'

*Sahatoo Maharaj's voice: 'My brother is not here! Stop the
boat!'*

Everyone froze and stared at him.

*Then Sahatoo Maharaj grabbed one of the laskars, shouting
at him to make them turn around and go back, and when the
laskar didn't do anything, Sahatoo Maharaj ran towards the
engine room, below the big chimney in the middle of the boat, and
begged them to take us back. And when they didn't listen, he
spun around and headed for the railing, and started to climb it,*

ready to jump off the boat.

Then all of us pulled him back and made him sit down on the deck. Sirju told him he would go and bring his brother for him, said he was sure he had seen him go below. Someone else also said he had seen his brother somewhere. So Sahatoo Maharaj sat on the deck and waited, staring at the water, while some of us went to look for his brother.

But in the end nobody could find him, and we had looked everywhere. Then the doctor came on the deck and when he saw the condition Sahatoo Maharaj was in, he made us take him to the clinic, just down the deck. We got him to lie down and the doctor gave him something to make him sleep.

Slowly, slowly we moved through the city of Calcutta. The boat made only one stop, at Diamond Harbour. No diseases, the doctor told the port officers who had come on board, and no problems. Nobody to take off the boat.

Then we started again, and we went and went and now it was only swamp, jungle and the river in front of us. For a long time a big grey fish with a long beak swam next to the boat, looking at us with one eye like it wanted to guide the boat down the river.

'Shushuk,' Kalloo said, that was the name the river people had for it, a dolphin.

The laskars said that one boat full of migrants had made a mistake in this swamp and had sunk before even leaving the country. It was the shallow water we had to worry about, not the deep water. The sandbars at the bottom of the river kept shifting from day to day. Every boat going on this stretch of river had to take on a special pilot who knew how the sand was shifting each day and where the deep water was.

Langoor Mamoo said then that he didn't see how sand could

be so dangerous. But the laskars told him that when a boat got stuck, after a time with the tide tugging at it both ways, the sand would shift, and the boat might find itself on sharp rocks below. Then the hull would crack in the middle, and the boat would go down.

It took us four whole days to go down the river, as we were going against the tide. Easier to manage the boat that way, the laskars said. The doctor made us stay on the deck most of the time. He didn't want us to stay too much in the quarters below. But people still went below, keeping quiet, moving about like they were in a trance.

They sent out Sahatoo Maharaj from the clinic, and he mostly sat on the deck, talking to himself, where was his brother, and things like that. We didn't bother him. We didn't know what to say, but we were all feeling bad for him. We didn't feel like raising our voices near him, even the children kept quiet. The only sounds around us those two days were of Sahatoo Maharaj sitting on the deck and talking softly to himself about his brother, shouts from the laskars changing shifts, and all the time the chug-chug of the boat engine, taking our boat down through the mangrove swamp.

The river kept getting wider and wider, and the muddy green colour was turning to a greenish blue. The laskars told us that we were reaching the end of the river. Sandheads was the name of the place, they said.

And then the land on both sides ended, and in front of us was only the sea.

A small boat came up next to us in the water, and the man from Khidarpur docks who had been steering our boat down the river climbed down a ladder and got off our boat with his helpers. Now we were by ourselves.

So this was the kala pani, the black water that was supposed to change you forever. Turn you into an outcaste. Water all the way to the end of the world! Now our boat started to pick up speed, and head out straight towards the dark water of the open sea.

And at that moment it suddenly came to me, as clear as the sky, that I was never going back, that I would live and die across the kala pani.

Kalloo came and sat down next to me on the deck and I put my arm around his shoulders and held him close. I turned my head back to get one last look at the coastline we were leaving behind us.

And then I turned to face forward and sat looking at the sea stretching out forever and ever in front of us, and I stifled the panic rising inside me, and tried to think—

AT SEA LEVEL

I WAS RIDING ON A MOTORCYCLE FOR THE FIRST TIME IN my life, going pillion behind Fyzie. My father had sent the car to the workshop to get a few dents knocked out, so for the time being I was stuck at home, grounded. And I was going stir crazy.

It was Fyzie's idea that we should take his bike. I wasn't so sure. It was one thing for me to get battered and bruised, but the tape recorder? I wasn't going to risk taking the tape recorder on the bike.

And then Fyzie asked if we really had to go and 'do taping'. Couldn't we just lime? Lime! Just hang around the place, idling. My parents would have a fit. Liming was not something you went out to do if you were on the academic fast-track. So by just going forth to do nothing in particular I was taking my first steps into a brave new world.

There is something different about going on a motorbike. All the places you whiz by obliviously in a car, winking out between origin and destination, suddenly leap into sharp and living focus. All the people who existed only as props on the landscape come forward, with lives and concerns of their own, engaging you, not intimidated by you. All of a sudden the same empty place is full of people. I had spent almost all my life in Trinidad, but that evening it was like I was really seeing it and living in it for the first time.

We parked the bike and walked through the market. We got two Carib beers and strode around drinking straight from the bottles. Then Fyzie headed for a dalpuri stall and before I knew what he was doing, he bought two dalpuris and handed me one. I bit into the paper thin roti, bursting with split pea stuffing, and lapped up the spicy, juicy curry shrimps wrapped inside it, and shrugged off obsessive thoughts of eating light that belonged in another world of idleness.

When I came down from the University of Michigan to do my doctoral research on Bhojpuri in Trinidad, my father knew that I could get badly stuck if I tried to plan and do all my interviews alone. He had seen me in action before, when I was collecting data for my undergraduate thesis on Bhojpuri. He had to step in and help me out, and take me himself to meet our old butcher, Chirag Ali, who had come on the boat from India with Deeda and two of Ajie's grandparents.

This time Dad gave me a few days to shake off the feel of Ann Arbor and catch up with the family, and then he asked me to come and see him in his workshop, where he made gold jewellery.

Nine o'clock the next morning he was waiting for me outside the workshop with one of his craftsmen, Fyzie.

'Right,' he said. 'Fyzie will take you every day after work. He know the whole of Caroni, and every body there know him too. And he accustomed to the car. Now you will finish fast.'

And we walked out together to stand on the pavement and wait with his other workmen for the doubles man, who came on his bicycle every day at this time to sell doubles, which they always had for breakfast together. I followed them all back to the workshop and we sat there amid all the chemicals and the goldsmithing tools and gobbled up the little fried rotis made up into sandwiches with spicy channa as filling.

In the market, Fyzie had gone off with one of his friends who was having some problems with his motorbike. So I stood there alone, taking in the feel of Chaguanas market in the late afternoon, trying to relate to a new sense of belonging in this place. Then I felt someone behind me touch my elbow softly, and I looked around, and down. A little old woman with a white cotton orhni over her head was standing there looking up at me full of excitement, smiling toothlessly.

'*Tukey chinhli!*' she said. I recognized you!

Deeda's neighbour. Rampyari was her name, I remembered, age eighty-five, born in Gorakhpur. She had come on a boat with her mother as a child. All of Chaguanas market around us vanished, and we stood together in a timeless little cocoon of Bhojpuri, crazily happy to have met like this.

Deeda had been asking if I would come again, she told me. She wanted to see me before I finished and went back. Was I really going to India?

I told her I wasn't sure, but I would know soon.

Okay, she said, don't go without seeing Deeda first. And then she turned and left, going around the corner and vanishing from sight behind the stalls. But the cocoon stayed, it came and wrapped itself around me like a shimmering ball.

Deeda...

It was Dad who had brought her into my life. He had taken me to meet her when I was doing my under-graduate thesis, and all the way back home he had kept exulting about what a dignified old woman she was. From the way they had talked I could sense that she had a special relationship with our family that went back very very far. Meeting her that time was like being given a precious glimpse into our past that was hidden from us now.

So when Fyzie and I were driving through Orange Valley one evening, a picture of Deeda as she had looked then, sitting on the hammock below her house, flashed before my mind's eye. And I had looked up and there was the house on stilts, and there was Deeda, sitting on the same hammock, looking perfectly at peace with the world, and I had told Fyzie to stop. We had parked the car and walked into the yard, and she had recognized me at once and smiled, pointing to a chair next to the hammock.

And she had leaned forward and said: You have come this time to hear about Sunnariya!

Sunnariya...Sundaree! Of course! Dad had said on the way home that Deeda and Sundaree had come on the same boat. And I had wanted to go back and ask her about Sundaree then. But I didn't go. I knew I wouldn't have been able to follow all she was saying. I could have taped it, why hadn't I thought of it then?

Yes, Deeda had continued. Your great-great grandmother. She was my friend. We came on the same boat from India, and we stayed in the same room in the barracks at Esperanza.

'*Tu jaanat rahley!*' I burst out. You knew her!

Deeda's eyes twinkled.

Tell me about her! I begged. I don't even know what she looked like!

I will tell you, she said, but not today. I want a little time to think, so that I remember everything. Come back in two days, but not so late. Come early, and I will tell you about Sunnariya.

And then her voice faded out, and as I turned to go the cocoon vanished and Chaguanas market reappeared around me, and Fyzie was back.

'One of the boys in the workshop having a fête together wit' some of his friends,' he said. 'Yuh want to go?'

A fête! The other local thing besides liming that had been a strict no-no for me all my life. The way my parents talked you would think that liming and fêting were two of the most degenerate things in the world. So what else could I say on a night like this?

'Let's go!'

We limed around Chaguanas until it was a good time to go, and then we were back on the bike, passing through cane lands. In the distance one of the fields was burning, flames leaping high into the night sky. Cane fields were burnt, they said, to clear out all the snakes and scorpions from the fields so it would be safe for the cane cutters to go in and harvest. It wasn't good for the cane, but it was a necessary evil. The cane would then have to be cut within three days and taken to the factory for processing, or it would start to rot. In the air above us we could see the long flakes of black soot drifting towards Chaguanas to rest on all the clotheslines, on people's clean floors, and on the knees of crawling infants.

Camboulay, they called it in French Creole, *cannes brûlées*. Burning cane fields, the sign that Carnival was approaching.

Fyzie and I strode into the fête brave and bold, and across the room Bobby's jaw dropped when he saw who Fyzie had brought as his date for the evening. Then he came across and escorted us in nervously, and brought me to meet his friends.

'Diz mih boss-man daughter,' Fyzie announced, and the ice was broken.

Bobby's fête was not just any old party, it was a Carnival fête. Better keep on looking cool, girl, I thought, before they realize that you never go in a fête up to now. Loud music was booming around us, in the beginning pop music and then, as things hotted up, calypsos, all the hits from this year's crop.

Fyzie kept me next to him all the time. 'Yuh don't know who could be drunk,' he said, 'so doan dance with anybody you doan know. Me an' Bobby and mih pardners is okay. If a fight do break out, yuh wouldn' know what to do.'

'No,' I agreed.

'Okay, first thing, doan run. Just stay in one place. At leas' you know what happening in front of you. If you rush outside you might find yuhself in a bigger set of trouble,' he said.

A calypso started to play, this year's road march for sure, and people hit the dance floor with a whoop, and

Bobby came around pulling all the rest of us onto the floor to dance. Time for break-away.

A brass band was playing the tune, and then going for a second pass on the tune with some variations. Then suddenly no more melody, no more bass notes.

Weightlessness! Now only drums, loud and hypnotic, on and on and on. People were not dancing now. This was the eye of the storm. They were jumping up in the air in sync with the drums, arms out to keep their balance. No one could get off the dance floor now. You had to stay the course.

Leaping, leaping, higher and higher, everybody around you in the same, same madness, and then when you thought your legs couldn't take it any more, when you were sweating, when you thought you were going to die for sure, when your breath was coming rough, and in gasps—

Then the bass notes came on again, and the rest of the band, and the tune reappeared with a bright triumphal sound. People whooped and came back down to earth, and started drifting off the floor smiling, massaging their aching legs.

Bobby came and announced that food was ready, to come and eat.

'I am enjoying this lime!' Fyzie said.

I was stunned. Enjoying? I had thought he was only doing his work, like my father told him to do. Looking after me. I thought that I was stopping him from having the real fun, running after endless chicks, as he would put it. I looked at him, but he was looking ahead at something across the room, distracted.

We went back to Couva on the bike, and I got off outside the tall silvery gates to our yard. Kojo was sitting in front of the house on a wicker chair, dozing with a flashlight in his lap. He woke up and shone it at me, and peered through the gate to make sure it was me. Then he rounded up our two German Shepherds, herded them back into their enclosure behind the house, and came again with a bunch of keys to open the gate. I slid through the gap as the gate opened and hurried up the driveway, and stepped down into the house through the dining-room door.

My father was sitting at the far end of the dining-room table waiting for me, and he gave me a hurt look, as if I had deliberately stayed out late to make him sick with worry. I flashed him a bright vacant smile, riding high on the night's adrenaline. Then I walked straight past him and up the stairs to my room.

Easy! Why hadn't I tried that before? Tonight I could feel the cage door swinging open and a stronger bolder me stepping onto the threshold.

On impulse I walked on into my study. The tape recorder was on my desk, and the tape of the story of Rani Saranga was lying next to it. I had been planning to do more transcription with Ajie that evening, but had gone out instead. Now it was too late to trouble Ajie, she would be fast asleep. I reached out tentatively, pressed eject, and the cassette chamber sprang open, and I inserted the cassette of *Rani Saranga ke Kheesa*. Then I pressed play, and Deeda's voice filled the room.

Well, why not? I thought. Why not another first tonight?

I paused the cassette and got my yellow notepad out of the drawer, sharpened my pencil to a point, and decided to have a go at transcribing the next part of the story by myself:

'Sunley? Tab u janam bhail saukaal ke gharey, tab bhail Saranga. Aa u janam lel Jagdeep hiaan, ta u bhail Sada Birij.'

Did you hear? Then she was born in a merchant's house, and she became Saranga. And he was reborn in the house of someone named Jagdeep, so he became Sada Birij.

They were sent to school to study, both of them. And they studied and studied, but what could they learn? They were not made for learning. She would write something, and then give it to him, then he would write something, and give it to her to read, so after a while the teacher said: 'No, what I need is a divider between them. In the classroom. So that she can't see him, and he can't see her. So that they can't talk to each other. Then they might study.'

So he called a carpenter to make the partition. But Saranga convinced the carpenter to leave a gap, so that somehow, through that gap, the two of them could manage to speak, and send messages.

The school had a garden. The children had to take turns to go there and water the plants. All the children had to take their turn, and one day Saranga and Sada Birij had their turn together. They went, but do you think they watered any plants? They went into the garden, cut some leaves and made a nest, and both fell asleep there.

After they had been out a long while the teacher told the other children: 'Go and take a look, those children I sent, where are they?' So they went and looked, and they came and said: 'They are both asleep.'

So the teacher went to look. When he saw them asleep together he sent for their parents. Both sets of parents came and he said:

'Look, both these children of yours have learned all they have to learn here. Now you take them both home and arrange marriages for them.' So they said all right.

They took them to their separate homes and got ready to fix their marriages. Saranga's parents sent for the pundit and the nau, the matchmaker, and told them to take a tika and find a boy who would be good for her.

So they went, and in the town of Dhara Nagari, far away, they found a bridegroom. They put the tika on his forehead so that the match was fixed, and came back to plan the wedding. And they got ready to make the announcement.

Then Saranga's father called Sada Birij's father and said: 'Look, get your son out of here for a while.'

So they sent him off to another town and told him to collect taxes, and not to come back until he had collected all the money that had to come in. That way the wedding would be over by the time he came back.

They sent another boy with him, and both the boys got talking as they went. Sada Birij noticed that his companion's eyes were full of tears. So he asked him: 'Why are you crying? Why do you have tears in your eyes?'

The other boy said: 'What can I do? If I had stayed at home, all this time I would have been seeing the dancing, I would have been eating fried rotis.'

Then Sada Birij asked: 'Who is getting married?'

Then his companion said: 'Don't you know? Today is Saranga's wedding day!'

Sada Birij said: 'Saranga's wedding day?'

'Yes.'

Then Sada Birij went as fast as he could, and collected all the taxes and money he had to collect, and brought it back and gave it to his father. Then he got on a horse and rode off to find Saranga —

'PLENTY BETTER NOW'

THE LINGUISTICS DEPARTMENT AT THE UNIVERSITY OF the West Indies had been looking for someone to be the next speaker in their series of seminars on languages of the Caribbean. Someone working on Bhojpuri this time. And I just happened to be there.

This series had started as a way of getting postgraduate students to share their early results with their colleagues in the department, and to shake them out of the shells they must be building around themselves as they went about getting their data. The seminar wasn't supposed to be anything fancy; just a look at the language itself, its basic grammar, a few of its basic words.

The earlier seminars in this series had all been about Creole languages from the different islands, as well as from Guyana. English Creoles, French Creoles, Papiamento from Curaçao and a Dutch Creole from Guyana. Now everyone thought it was time to look at other Caribbean languages besides the Creoles. So my task would be to demystify the alien sounds still heard around the sugar estates for my colleagues at UWI.

The venue was the same seminar room in the School of Education where Rosa had had her seminar. And besides the linguists some of the same audience was expected: the social scientists, and a grave looking contingent of gentlemen from the Hindu Maha Sabha.

One of my old lecturers, whom we used to call Sollo, was sitting sprawled across the seminar table, and he lifted his head slightly and introduced me. In world-weary tones he reminded the others that I had done my first degree in linguistics at UWI, and that I was now doing my doctorate on Trinidad Bhojpuri at Ann Arbor, Michigan. Then he lifted an eyebrow at me as a signal to start.

'Okay, first of all,' I said, 'the language is Bhojpuri, as Sollo just said, not Hindi. Bhojpuri is a totally different language from Hindi and is grammatically closer to eastern languages like Bengali.' I paused and waited for this to sink in.

'Bhojpuri shares a lot of word stock with Hindi,' I said, 'because Hindi is its neighbour directly to the west in India, and because the Hindi belt has ruled over the Bhojpuri region for centuries. But Bhojpuri is not a dialect of Hindi, and it certainly isn't "broken" Hindi.'

There were some important differences between Trinidad Bhojpuri and Bhojpuri in India, I said. The language was less fragmented in Trinidad than in India, more of a unified lingua franca for the community. I wasn't sure how and when that had happened, but the language seemed to have come together in the migration to Trinidad.

'So in that sense it really is a Caribbean language.' I said.

How Trinidad Bhojpuri had come together I didn't know as yet, I said. Had some exotic sort of fusion taken place? Creolists were always fantasizing about things like that, but when everybody understood each other from the start I didn't think there was any need for such drastic hybridization. Had one of the Indian dialects simply taken over and displaced the others? More likely. Or was a lot of the variety still actually there, though we were not inclined to see it as a sign of disunity, but as 'richness', as stylistic options?

I paused. 'Sometimes we can only see what we are looking for. In Trinidad we think of Bhojpuri as one language, in India they think of it as a chain of dialects. And that colours how we see the data.'

One good lead I had about convergence was that the dialect in Trinidad was a lot like the Bhojpuri spoken in places around Basti a century ago. There was evidence from the nineteenth-century Linguistic Survey of India to support this. The time of peak migration from places like Basti had coincided with a sudden surge in the number of women migrating, and a spurt in the number of young children on the estates. Children on the estates were generally left for most of the day with one older woman, called a khelauni, when they were below the age of six, and even a bit later, when they were at the age of stabilizing their first language.

Once a lingua franca variety had emerged, later migrants would have simply adopted it, or at any rate their children would have. The dialects brought by the original migrants from India would have vanished. We had seen the same thing happen with Creoles and their African parent languages.

So I was inclined to go with the view that the blossoming of Bhojpuri into a lingua franca in Trinidad had a lot to do with women coming away from India as migrants, and the community childrearing that was practised on the estates.

I went on to give an outline of the grammar, writing up verb forms, pronoun forms and noun suffixes on a blackboard behind me, reading off the words with a flourish. Then I wrote up the different forms of the verb 'to be', present, past and future: *'baati, baatey, ba; rahli, rahley, rahal; hob, hoibey, hoi'*. Plural forms, compound tenses, optatives and subjunctives. And compound verbs, similar in meaning to Russian perfectives. I also gave a few honorific verb forms one didn't hear much any more.

Sollo had some comments afterwards about the striking differences in the way the past tense was handled in Hindi and Bhojpuri. In Hindi, transitive verbs in the past tense agreed with their logical objects in number and gender. In Bhojpuri the verb always agreed with the subject, as it did in Bengali, or English. Bhojpuri really was radically different from Hindi. When you got away from the words to the grammar, it was obvious.

Sollo had spent time learning Hindi when he was a student abroad, though he wasn't Indian himself. Simply out of curiosity. I was glad to get a few technical questions from him that made me think. And I was even more thrilled to be able to answer questions about Bhojpuri for a change, and not just ask them.

But most of the questions from the rest of the audience were not based on my lecture at all. The biggest concern was what was happening to the language.

'What you mean, happening?'

'Well, is it getting creolized?'

'Creolized?'

'You know, changing.'

'It isn't changing,' I said, 'the big change that brought it together was long ago.'

'No, a lot of young people speak it, and they don't do all of that, all those things you talking about. In fact, the way they talk, it don't look like it have a grammar!'

Shouts from the linguists at this heresy: how could a language not have a grammar?

But I had caught their drift. And they were right.

'What you are talking about is something called language death. These young people are actually making mistakes, because they don't have native speaker competence in the language. They are making mistakes like any foreigner would make. The language is like a foreign language to them, though in other ways they are still Indian.'

Language death! Foreign language! Now the shit hit the fan.

'So you think this language should die?'

'Look,' I said, belligerently, 'I am the only person in this room who really know how to talk this language. Why you looking at me? Look at your own self first: *you* know this language at all?'

'Forget that! It have plenty people speaking this language. How you could say it dying?'

'Look, maan,' I said, 'when you say a language dying, you don't mean it don't have nobody at all who know to talk it. What you mean is that all the people who talk it, they old. It don't have chil'ren picking it up these days. It not passing *on*. The chil'ren talking somet'ing else now.'

'So what *you* t'ink? *You* want this language to die? We shouldn't do anyt'ing to stop it?'

Not too long back I would have been asking the same rhetorical questions. But it was Deeda who had set me right.

One day in front of her house I had seen a rusted half-drum on a stand, with a handle to turn and husk rice. So I asked her, nostalgically, if she didn't think that food had tasted better long ago, with masala freshly ground on a seel-lorha at home, instead of the curry powder we now got in the supermarket.

She gave me a sceptical look and told me that she didn't care at all. All that good food I was talking about, for her it was just a lot of hard work, and she was tired of that. Any amount of curry powder was better than always being poor, and tired. No, she said, things were plenty better now.

Something had exploded inside my head when she said that, and the mist cleared. I'd been such an idiot! All my middle-class angst and nostalgia suddenly seemed like an affectation, and insensitive to boot. Would this also be true of the language? All the people who spoke it were poor, and they hadn't been to school. Could that have something to do with why it was getting lost?

My mind scrolled back to when I was a child, hearing Ajie and her father, whom I called Nana, because he was my father's nana, joking together in what sounded like Hindi. I would be utterly frustrated at not being able to follow what they were saying. I would butt in with the Bhojpuri phrases that I knew, only to find them laughing at me indulgently. Look at that, they would say, a child trying to speak the language!

Then Nana would fondly tell me to go and study my French, Spanish and Latin, and to forget about this language.

I could tell that he was touched that I wanted to learn the language, because he eventually did show me his old primers that taught the Devanagari and Kaithi scripts, and I spent days on end learning how to write the alphabet in Kaithi. And he had then tried to steer me towards 'grammatical' Hindi, which he seemed to have mixed up in his mind with the Aligarh dialect his mother had spoken. But he had worked hard and sacrificed all his life so that we could move forward, not backward. And Bhojpuri, as far as he was concerned, was a thing of the past, a tie to the estate.

So I smiled as enigmatically as I could in the seminar room, and looked up to face my inquisitor.

'It isn't up to us, you know. It is the poor people who still speak the language who will decide if they want to pass it on or not. You and I are out of the game. They will decide, and you and I will only talk about it.'

And on that note I bent to pick up my notes, inclined my head at Sollo and took his leave.

ON THE HIGH SEAS

Rosa CAME TO MEET ME AFTER THE SEMINAR, AND WE
stopped to pick up doubles from the doubles man on the
old railway line outside the School of Education before
heading back to her place for more of Deeda's story. We
sat at her table and fortified ourselves before venturing
out with Deeda and her shipmates onto the Indian Ocean.

This time the cassette was cued and ready. I pressed
play and released the pause:

'Haan, bhaiya, humaar jahaj ke naam rahal Godavari.
Steamer *rahal, ba paal bhi lagaawat rahal.'*

Yes, bhaiya, the name of our boat was the Godavari. *It
was a steamer, but they could put up sails too.*

Godavari was the name of a river in India.

*As soon as we were a good way into the sea, they shut off
the engines, and the laskars climbed up the poles and tied cloth
sails to catch the breeze. Said it was better to use the wind while
it was there, then we wouldn't waste so much coal. And after
that the boat really flowed through the sea like a river, with just
the sound of water around us splashing.*

*They had different quarters on the boat for moglasiyas, single
people, and married couples. The single men's quarters were in*

*the front of the boat, under the main deck, the married couples'
quarters were behind that, and the single women's quarters were
in the back, below both the poop deck and the main deck.*

*Most of the moglasiyas were not really bachelors. They were
men and even women who had left their families in the village,
as people from the eastern districts had been doing since the
Moghul days, to go out alone as migrants.*

*And some of the married couples were not really married.
They had only had a sagaai, an engagement ceremony, in the
depot, not a saadi-biyaah, a real wedding. But that was good
enough. They could stay in the married quarters.*

*When they first took us down to the single women's quarters
I was glad to see the same kind of bunks we had seen on the
train to Calcutta. I remembered how Kalloo and I had been safe
from the rain on the top bunk.*

*So before anybody could say what they wanted, I said I
wanted to go on top, that I didn't care if I had to climb. I knew
that we would be safer up there while we slept. Then I scrambled
up and put down our belongings, and sat there with Kalloo,
watching the others below.*

*Sunnariya said she didn't want to climb, that she didn't do
things like that. But the other women told her that the lower
bunks and the floor were for older people, that as she was the
youngest single woman in the quarters she had to go up.*

*Then she looked up and saw the two of us, me and Kalloo,
sitting there, peaceful. Nobody was interfering with us at all. We
were really by ourselves.*

*So she decided that the best thing was to take a top bunk
next to ours. Everybody was satisfied with that, and she came
up her ladder and sat down on her bunk.*

*The other Janaki, the sonaarin, sent her two older sons to
stay in the single men's quarters, as both of them were more*

than ten years of age. And she kept the baby, Ramlal, with her. After that everybody called her Ramlal ke maai, Ramlal's mother.

They didn't like us to stay below too much. You could only get to stay below all the time if you were sick. Otherwise they wanted us to come up on the deck. We had to walk about on the deck the whole day, and sometimes they even made the men run. And that was okay. After some days we got accustomed to the way the boat would pitch and toss, and people stopped feeling sick and staying below.

Every morning they would wake us up early and make us roll up our bedding, and then the bhangis would come and wash down all the floors, on the top deck and in the quarters, and once a week we all had to bathe. The doctor sometimes came in the morning to see that the deck was really clean, as he said he didn't want people getting sick.

They fed us twice a day, dal and rice, once in the morning, when the sun was up and bright, and once again in the evening, just before sunset. In the evening we would also get rotis with our food. They would make us squat in a line on the deck and wait, and then they brought out the food and put it into thariyas for all of us. Sometimes they used to put imli, tamarind, or khataai, dried mango, in the dal, and give us raw onions and dried salt-fish with the food. This was another thing they did to keep us from getting sick on the boat.

And then at night they would send us back to the quarters and close down the hatches. The women had to sleep the whole night with the lamps on, so that none of the sailors could come in the dark and try to interfere with us. That was a rule.

They were worried about the animals too. We were carrying six buffaloes to use for pulling carts, and twenty goats. We were going to use the milk for putting in tea. The animals were supposed to walk on the deck just like us, so that they wouldn't get sick without fresh air and exercise down below in the hold.

Sirju said that he knew how to mind buffaloes, and that he would bring them up from the hold and make them walk on the deck. And another man, Chirag Ali, said he would mind the goats, together with his younger brother. And Kalloo used to go with them, so I didn't have to worry about him. Sometimes he would bring back lumps of gur for me, brown molasses that Langoor Mamoo had got for him from the kitchen. And he would bring pieces of dried mango pickle for Ramdaye, since she was expecting a baby.

So for a time it was like that. Kalloo used to go with Sirju and Chirag Ali and his brother, and I used to walk about the boat by myself, to see what was what.

One day I went up by the front of the boat, and I saw a white man with a beard turning a big wheel and steering the boat, keeping his eyes on the sea. After that I used to go there sometimes by myself and stand outside the wheelhouse and watch that man holding the big wheel, with his arms out in front of him, and I used to think about how the whole boat and all of us were in that man's hands.

And sometimes I would stay back on the deck at night, after everybody had finished eating, before they closed down the hatches, and look at the sea. Some nights, when everybody else had gone, and the deck was quiet, I would hear Sahatoo Maharaj playing his bansuri, alone. I would sit there and listen, without making any noise or moving, so that he would think he was really by himself.

Then one of the men in the men's quarters got fever.

The doctor came and took him to the clinic fast, said he didn't want other people to get sick. Next day his fever was worse, and his face had broken out in red spots.

And the day after that, four more men from the men's quarters got fever and had to go to the clinic.

Every day the doctor would go to the men's quarters to check everybody, and take away whoever looked even a little bit sick. Everybody else had to stay outside in the fresh air. The women in our quarters were not to mix with the men since there was no sickness in the women's quarters. The doctor didn't want the fever to spread where it hadn't reached.

Then the first man died. Measles.

There was nowhere to run, we were all on the same boat. The most we could do in the women's quarters was stay away from the men and hope for the best. I kept Kalloo with me after that and didn't let him go with his Langoor Mamoo to walk the buffaloes. And I kept a watch on the women in our quarters, so that nobody could hide if they were sick.

A few days later another man died, and the others in the clinic were still sick.

All of this we only heard. We were kept separate from the men and didn't see any of this. We knew they must be disposing of the bodies. We had heard they were throwing them into the sea.

And then, in our quarters, two women got measles. The nauniya who had been recruited with me, and Sunnariya.

Then I didn't care what the doctor said about staying away and leaving the sick in the clinic. I knew I wasn't going to leave Sunnariya for strangers to look after. I left Kalloo with Ramdaye and went with Sunnariya to the clinic.

There I found out that the red spots in measles didn't only appear on your skin outside, they came all inside your stomach too. Sunnariya was running fever and everything she ate was passing through her like she had cholera. I sat with her night and day, wiping her face with a wet cloth to bring down the fever, and giving her nibwa-pani, lime-water with sugar and salt. I didn't give myself a chance to sleep until I saw that she was sleeping.

Three days like that I managed, and then one morning her fever was gone. She was still weak, and not able to get up, so they told her she would have to stay an extra day.

And then, on that day itself, the other Janaki, Ramlal ke mai, came to the clinic with Ramlal.

By that time I knew how to look after someone with measles, so I stayed back to help her with Ramlal. He was not keeping in any food at all, so I told her to forget about that, and to just keep giving him her own milk, the whole day. To keep on nursing him.

She kept him in her lap all the time, feeding him, while I wiped his face and neck to cool him. But it was no use. The fever didn't go down, no matter what we did. And he was getting weaker.

It wasn't like it was with Sunnariya. It was worse.

The doctor left everything and came to help us. He tried all the medicines he had. He even put Ramlal in a basin of water to make him cool off. But nothing was bringing the fever down. It was out of control.

And then, after a few hours, Ramlal died.

The worst thing in the world is when a child dies—

'Ajie! Ajie!' A child's voice. Then a pause.

'Ajie! Di dawg jus' come an' t'ief a whole half-a-roti, an' he gawn!'

Another pause. ' 'i gaan?' Deeda's voice.

'Yeah, he gawn!'

Another pause. 'Arright, den let-he gaan!'

The tape ran on emptily for a bit now, and I reached out and pressed pause, as I had done when I was with Deeda. Like Deeda I was beset by memories.

I had heard about Ramlal from Nana, but I hadn't known until Deeda told me that the sonaarin's name had also been Janaki. I knew that she had had three sons when she left India. Two were accounted for, they had each left a long line of progeny in Trinidad.

What about Ramlal, I would ask. Who are his descendants? We knew some Ramlals in San Fernando.

Nana was sure that that Ramlal couldn't have had any descendants in Trinidad. His trail had simply gone cold. No Ramlals we knew had come from him.

I think he died on the boat, he mused. He must have only been a baby.

I got up and called my father to tell him that I would be late that night. I told him that I was translating a tape for Rosa. I didn't want a repeat of that other night when he had sat up and waited for me looking so personally distraught by my lateness.

Then, with a clear conscience, and lots of time ahead, I turned my mind back to Deeda's tape.

A whole half-a-roti! Trinidadian rotis are spectacularly bigger than the thin brown chapattis that exist in India. In Trinidad rotis are huge and at least an inch thick. A single sada roti can feed a woman and two small children. One roti is just a big mug full of white flour, baking powder, salt and water, kneaded into dough. Nothing else: sada, plain. The dough would be made early in the day and left to 'swell' for a few hours, and then made into big sada rotis some time before the meal on a big thick griddle, where they would puff up and split open like pita bread. The rotis would then be cut into halves, and all wrapped together in a towel to keep warm.

And that is where Deeda's dog had found the half-a-roti, wrapped in the towel.

All flour in Trinidad is imported, and rotis in Trinidad have always been made from white flour. Phoolaawa, they call it, a bilingual pun, as phool means flower in Bhojpuri. The Hindi word atta, which means whole-wheat flour, simply doesn't exist in Trinidad Bhojpuri. There isn't even a memory of the word, because our ancestors had never seen brown flour in India, unless they were from further west, as Sunnariya had been. Wheat was not yet being grown in the eastern districts the migrants came from, and the sale of wheat from the north-west to the eastern parts of India had not yet started.

The first wheat flour to come to Calcutta in the nineteenth century was white flour, and it had come by ship from Europe. So the first time the migrants saw wheat flour would have been in the depots, the same white flour that was gaining popularity in Calcutta. And out of this experience grew the tradition of making large translucent stuffed dalpuris, and thick white layered parathas, common to the entire purabiya diaspora but unknown in the purabiya heartland. And huge sada rotis.

That last bit on the tape Rosa could easily have followed without me. It had been in Creole. The child had spoken just like any other Trinidadian child, while Deeda had spoken a variety of Creole that had survived only with the jahaji Indians, the ones who had come on the boats.

We sat a moment with mugs of tea. I needed the tea to warm my throat. I had been talking non-stop, translating.

'That is some old lady!' remarked Rosa.

There was something about Deeda, I thought. I just couldn't find the word. 'She can read my mind!' I said. 'She always knows what I'm thinking. And I feel as though I've known her forever.'

Rosa smiled. 'You know, I get the same feeling. Like I can guess what she's going to do next. Funny! She reminds me of someone.' And she shook her head to dispel the thought.

Then I turned back to the tape recorder and released the pause:

'Haan, bhaiya, ohi khesariya ke mahamaari me kul sab chaudah aadmi bilaasi bhail, chauda aadmi.'

Yes, bhaiya, in that outbreak of measles altogether fourteen people passed away, fourteen.

And half of them were children.

Sunnariya got better, and soon she was just as she was before. The only thing she kept from those days was a mark on the side of her nose, where she had scratched one of the spots. It wasn't enough to spoil her looks, but it was enough to remind us of how close she had come to dying, and of the other people on the boat who had not had the same good luck as her.

When Janaki the sonaarin came back to the women's quarters, we all felt bad for her, but we didn't know what to say. Then Chirag Ali's wife, Jaitoon, started coming to the women's quarters during the day, and she and Janaki got very close. Jaitoon had seen her own baby die, before she and her husband had become migrants. So she was the only person who had an idea what to say, the only person Janaki could turn to in those bad days.

The measles went away, but the whole boat felt like we were travelling with a curse, like all the light had gone out from our lives. People were quiet, like they had lost hope, like getting on this boat was the worst thing they had ever done.

And then the boat slowed down and stopped. The wind died, and we just sat in the sea, water all around us, going nowhere.

By now everybody was tense, quick to take offence, and ready to fight about any small thing. And all the goras, the white sailors, were watching us carefully, waiting to flog people if they caused any disturbance on the boat. Something was heading up to happen.

And then one day a fight broke out in the men's quarters. Two men were quarrelling over some sookha tambaaku, dry chewing tobacco, and suddenly one of them pulled out a knife.

Three other men tried to grab the man with the knife, and two other men tried to grab for the tambaaku, and soon everyone in the quarters was in the fight. We were on the deck right above, and we could hear all the commotion below.

Then Mukoon Singh went down the hatchway to the quarters and told his two sons to close down the hatch behind him and to stay back on the deck. He didn't want any noise coming out of the quarters.

The first thing he did was to go and stand in the middle of all the noise, and everybody backed off. Then he put out his hand for the knife. And he took the knife and tucked it into his own waistband. And then, in his clear Khari Boli, he told everyone to listen to him, to listen good.

When everybody was watching him and listening, he told them that he had been watching how things were going for some time, getting out of control. But from now on in the quarters everybody would have to answer to him. This was his quarters, and he wasn't going to stand for any nonsense. And for sure he wasn't going to see anybody giving the goras an excuse to come in and try to rough up his men. Because if they came and tried to flog anybody from his quarters, he would make sure their blood flowed, he was not afraid of any goras.

He paused and stared at the men to make sure his words had sunk in.

Then he looked at the two men one by one. He had already killed a man who gave him trouble, he said, before he came on this boat. And he could do it again. So smarten up, he said. We are going to settle this thing right now!

He made each of the men tell his side of the story, and in the end he made up his mind. Then he asked the other men in the quarters if they agreed with him about who should keep the tambaaku, and everything settled down.

As he turned to go, Mukoon Singh stopped and took another look at the man who had pulled out the knife. You made a big mistake, friend, he said. You pulled out a knife when you were not ready to use it. A knife is not for show. When you take out a knife you have to use it before they know what you are going to do.

And he took out the knife and rapped on the hatch with the knife handle, and it opened and he went back out on the deck.

That night on the deck everybody stayed back after we had eaten. Sirju and his friends brought out their dholaks, Chirag Ali and his brother brought their tassas, and Sirju sat in the front of the group with Kalloo.

Then Sirju closed his eyes. Everybody waited, hushed. He stretched out his arm as though it could reach all the way back to Faizabad and find the song.

And then his voice rang out:

> Arey, beeraha ta gaawa, ta gaawaha gareriya,
> Beeraha ta soona, ta soonaha gareriya!

Beeraha! The lament of the gareriya, the shepherd, migrating to look for work, leaving his family behind. People from our region had been migrating like this for hundreds of years. I had always thought my husband was the migrant, going far away and leaving me behind. But now I was the one crossing a whole ocean and leaving him behind. I felt hot tears in my eyes, to think of him, and of where we were now listening to a beeraha.

Then Sirju started to play the dholak, he played and he played, faster and faster, until you couldn't see his fingers at all.

Then the other ahirs together with Kalloo took up the beat, and started to play the dholaks, and Chirag Ali and his brother took up their sticks and started to beat the tassas. Faster and faster, keeping up with Sirju, burning out all the bad energy from the boat, turning it into power, until...

We were floating. Only Kalloo was playing, all by himself, and the other men were just clapping out the time for him. All of us held our breath. He played the song all by himself. Then he played it again, a bit different this time. Then I could hear him counting below his breath with the beat: one, two, three, four, five, six, seven, eight!

And the whole group started to play again with him. Stronger and stronger. Louder and louder. And then, when we felt like the sound around us was growing into a heartbeat strong enough to bring a dead boat back to life...

Mukoon Singh got up and started to dance. As he turned towards me I caught a glimpse of his face. He was dancing for himself, and for the whole world. He didn't look at anyone, he looked at all of us and right through us. His eyes were shining bright gold like the inside of a furnace.

One by one the men got up and fell in line with him. Even Ojir Mian put down his stick, stood up on his two legs, and joined in the dance.

All this time we, the women, kept sitting to one side, only watching. We understood that this was not our night to sing and dance. We stayed quiet, and tried to feel a new current starting. And we hoped that something good would be around the corner for us migrants now.

Next morning, after many days without any wind to move the boat, we got up on the deck and saw the laskars going down in a line to the boiler room. And in a little while we heard the shuddering roar from below, and saw smoke coming out of the smokestack again, and felt the deck throbbing and alive under our feet.

Then the boat began to pull forward, slowly, and move through the water, away from that place, like it was trying to shake off a bad dream.

The next day I let Kalloo go out again with his Langoor Mamoo to walk the buffaloes on the deck. When he came back he told me about a man in their quarters, Ramsukh, who was carrying different kinds of mango seeds to plant when we reached. He had been keeping the seeds since the summer, seeds from all the varieties that they had in his village. He said he didn't want to go to a new place khaali haath, empty-handed.

When I told the other women in our quarters about Ramsukh and his mango seeds, one of the women came and told me quietly that she was carrying something too. She showed me: in a little cloth bag she was carrying some damp soil from muluk, and growing in that soil was a root of hardee, turmeric. The masala that turns food yellow, and keeps wounds from getting infected. She was keeping it alive so she could plant it when we reached.

By now Ramdaye was heavy and waiting for her child to be born. She did not like to climb out to the deck, so I started spending time with her below in the quarters. She already had four boys, I said. What did she want this time?

A boy again, said Ramdaye. That is what everybody says. What do you think?

We already have too many boys, I told her. What we need now is some girls. I am going to have a hard time finding a girl for my Kalloo!

Well, we will see, she said. Plenty of time for that! He is still small!

So we went on like that, without wind, the engines pulling the boat, heading down to the Cape. Not too long now, they said, until we reached the Cape. Not to worry: the worst part of the journey was over.

There was nothing to do except sit down on the deck and wait. And look out at the sky and the ocean. Then one day when I was standing in the back of the boat, watching the wake the boat was making in the water behind us, I looked up and saw that the sky behind us was turning black, black like when we were on the train to Calcutta.

The laskars saw it too. Soon there were shouts from the goras, and the laskars were running up the masts and the rigging, bringing down the sails that were still up, and keeping them down in the hold, below the quarters, and carrying down the barrels of fresh water, carrying down everything to keep in the hold. The boat was going to need weight down at the bottom, they said.

The cooks put out the kitchen fires and brought down their pots and utensils and supplies to the hold. They would not be giving out hot food this evening. Instead, they gave out a ration of ship's biscuits with salt and raw onions to everyone in the quarters.

Then the laskars started calling everybody and telling us to go below into the quarters. We were going to have heavy seas.

And then I felt Sunnariya next to me, touching my elbow softly. Come, she said. Come into the quarters. Bipti the chamain, the midwife, was calling me. Ramdaye was in labour and it wasn't going right. Bipti didn't think she could manage this one by herself. Come!

Sunnariya and I went down into the quarters and the laskars closed the hatch behind us with battens from the outside.

Bipti was waiting for me and she took me to where Ramdaye was lying down. Ramdaye looked weak, but she didn't look to be in any pain.

So what was the problem? I asked.

Well, Ramdaye's labour had started in the night, and it had been going okay, but then her peeras, her pains, had stopped. She was somewhere in the middle. What could we do?

I remembered the time when Kalloo was born. My mother-in-law had not allowed me to lie down at all. She had made me get up and walk for as long as I could manage. Walk, she had said. The child will come faster.

So I reached out and put both my hands under Ramdaye's arms, and told her to get up. We were going to walk.

Trust me, I told her. I know what to do.

Ramdaye got up slowly, heavily, and she held my hand, and we started to walk.

We reached the back end of the quarters, next to the stern, and then the first big wave hit the side of the boat. Ramdaye moaned and sank down to a crouch, and I went down with her and held her two hands tight, and told her to hold on, we would pass through this thing together.

We got up again, and leaned against a bunk. Now the boat was pitching and tossing. I held both of Ramdaye's hands tight and thought of that man outside, in the wheelhouse, holding the wheel and managing the waves.

It's okay, I said, it's okay.

Then the next wave hit. This time the boat rolled with the force, and then it came to rest upright again. The ballast down in the hold was keeping the boat from capsizing. Ramdaye took a deep breath and looked at me again. By now we were both squatting sideways against the bunk. I held her hands and braced for the next one.

The next wave hit the deck with a roar. I looked out the porthole and all I could see was green. We were inside the wave!

Then I felt a stream of cold salty water wash over me. Both of us were wet. The hatch above us had sprung a leak. We were taking in water!

The boat engines were still throbbing, and now I could feel the boat beginning to turn so that the waves would be lined up behind us.

Then the engine began to race. They were firing more coal to the boiler to outrun the waves! I told Ramdaye to take a deep breath and brace herself. This was the big one!

Then the next wave hit, and the boat seemed to lift up and the water outside the porthole was white and full of froth. This time the boat did not pitch or toss. We were travelling with the wave.

Ramdaye's face was tight with the effort now, she was holding her breath. Then she let out her breath as the boat came to a rest.

Sunnariya brought me some cold sweet tea for Ramdaye. Drink this, I told her, it will give you strength.

The engines raced again and another wave hit, and the boat lifted up again. I looked out the porthole and I could see ocean spray. We were near the top of the wave, and I felt again that feeling I remembered of being carried up high above the pain, just barely able to sense all the churning going on below.

Things were moving now. Ramdaye would hold her breath as each wave lifted the boat up, up, up, and took us a long, long distance before leaving us resting on top, smiling, safe.

Ramdaye lay back now, tired. I propped her up so that she could see too.

Not long now, I said. Brace for a last big one.

And then, the last big wave and the long, long ride and the storm was over.

The last few waves were smaller, tamer. The boat engines slowed down, and the light outside the porthole was silvery bright.

The little girl's head came first, and I reached in and freed her shoulder and she came out easily.

Sunnariya brought her shawl for me, and I wrapped up the little girl and held her in my arms, and she started to cry, very softly, like the rain outside the porthole. I handed her to Ramdaye with a smile.

'Lo, Ramdaye, humaar patoh aai gail!'

Look, Ramdaye, you have given me my daughter-in-law!

Above our heads there were sounds of the laskars removing the battens and opening the hatches, getting ready to bail out water from our quarters, and asking us if we were okay. We could see the men already on the deck behind them.

Sunnariya looked up the hatchway and told them that Ramdaye had just had a baby girl.

Ramdaye and I were the last to leave the quarters and go up. By the time we reached the deck the sun was already peeping out from behind a cloud, and the rain was going off into the distance, just drizzling onto the sea.

Sahatoo Maharaj was waiting for us on top, waiting to see the baby. He had already consulted his books and was ready to give her the right name. The name had to start with 'Bh'.

We stood there and waited. Then Sahatoo Maharaj smiled his first smile since we had left Garden Reach depot in Calcutta, a whole lifetime ago.

Bhagmaniya, he said. That would be her name, Bhagmaniya. The one who brings good luck. She had brought the boat safely through the storm. And she would keep us safe for the rest of the journey.

I handed Bhagmaniya to her mother and wandered off towards the front of the boat alone.

The man was there in the wheelhouse, holding the wheel and guiding the ship. I stood there quietly and watched him, and thought about how he had stood there all through the storm with the wheel in his hands, turning the boat to make it ride the waves and run with the storm.

And then he turned and saw me standing there. His eyes had the same silvery light as the sky after the storm. And just like that he smiled at me, smiled with all the energy that he had gathered from the storm.

And that energy travelled across the deck to reach me where I stood, and I felt the corners of my mouth twitch, and then I was smiling back at him with the storm light in my eyes too.

Then I turned and walked back to be with the others, to see about Ramdaye and the baby. And as I walked on the wet deck I heard one of the laskars say that now the bad spell was truly over.

In another few days we would be rounding the Cape of Good Hope—

OUT OF MY DEPTH

I WOKE UP THAT SUNDAY MORNING WITH MY MOTOR running fast. I could hear my pulse racing, and I surged out of bed ahead of the sun.

Ajie was already making tea for everyone, and I took a mug and went into the downstairs living room to see who might be there. Just one uncle, my father's youngest brother. Up early and reclining in Dad's Morris chair with a newspaper, sipping his tea.

I sat down on a wicker chair opposite him to have my tea, but I found that I was just too restless to stay put. I was raring to go. I gulped my tea and leapt up from my seat and sprang back up the stairs to stare out the back window and think, think, think.

And after some time I heard footsteps behind me. Dylan, my uncle's older son, was awake. Dylan was in his last year of high school. I had first met him when he was three, and his father had just come back with his family from Wales. He had stood there in the living room downstairs, looking like a bewildered little druid, and I had instinctively pulled him over to sit with me in the same Morris chair his father was now sitting in. And that bond had remained, and grown.

'Want to go to Maracas today?' he asked with a yawn and a stretch.

Maracas Beach! That was it. I could instantly see two metres of glassy green wave looming up behind me, and knew that what I needed right now to tilt against was something as big and invincible as that. We could take his younger brother with us and pick up another cousin, Brian, from his school in Port of Spain where he used to go on weekends to feed the rats in the biology lab. And Fyzie.

So we picked up Fyzie and headed for Port of Spain. Brian got into the car, and Fyzie made a wisecrack about boys who looked after rats versus boys who looked at chicks. Then we were off, driving past Maraval, up on the North Coast Road, high in the mountains, with forest up on our right and the sea far down below us on the left. Then we descended towards Maracas and turned off towards the beach, and parked the car under some coconut trees, facing the water.

My cousins were in no mood to go into the water.

Too wet, they said.

Okay, so come and sit on the beach.

Too much sand, they said.

So they put on a tape, rolled up the windows, and filled the car with pop music. But I went out to change.

I strode out into the water alone and passed the minor splashes, looking for a good wave to bodysurf.

The first wave was no good, barely any ride there.

The next wave picked me up and smashed me to the seafloor. I made sure my swimsuit was still on me, and got up.

And then I saw Fyzie get out of the car, strip off his tee shirt and stride towards the water, jeans and all, and walk straight up to me. Then we went out together to find the big one.

Soon, cresting right in front of us, that green glassy wall with the backlight shining through it! I climbed the face in a few strokes, and with one last burst of energy thrust my head forward and out of the wave. I tucked my arms under me as a rudder, and whooped as I took that long, long ride to the shore.

I stood up, and Fyzie was next to me. He had caught the wave too.

Then one by one my cousins began deserting the car and straying into the water. Fyzie gave me a sign that we should go out further this time.

Whoa! This was Maracas, remember? You know about undertows? Sharks? I was brave, but there was a limit.

All my life I had gone to the beach only with my parents. My father would sit on the beach staring at me in the water, nervous as a cat, because he couldn't swim. My parents had also fed me a whole lot of superstition about how children were especially prone to drowning, or to being carried off by sharks, if they were waiting for the results of an exam. Well, I had been taking exams all my life, and I was always waiting for some result or the other. And the only result I saw here was that I never got to go too far from the shore!

And then I looked at Fyzie again and thought, why not?

So I turned with Fyzie and dived through the next big wave, past it, and swam out with him beyond the breaker line.

Up ahead of us a lifeguard was rowing a small boat, keeping a lookout for sharks. Fyzie waved out to him, and he stretched out his oar to us, and we climbed in and sat down with him.

My cousins were staring at us from the shallows.

Fyzie, it seemed, had once sailed a pirogue with two friends, mostly on runs between Trinidad and Venezuela. Just one of those things he had taken up on impulse, knowing nothing about the sea before that. So he and the lifeguard went on for a while like a pair of old salts.

I turned to stare at the horizon, all the sailor talk now just a vague backdrop in my ears. In the distance I could see an oil tanker making its way westwards, on its way to Chaguaramas, to continue south to hook up at the oil refinery at Pointe-à-Pierre, where I was born.

Fyzie suddenly noticed that I was miles away and lost interest in the sailor talk.

Enough of this lime! Fyzie got up and jumped off the boat into the water and turned to look at me.

'Come! Time to go!'

I stood up in the boat and took a clean shallow dive back into the water. Then we swam back towards the shore and came in on a breaker.

Back on the beach we went off with my cousins to get some fried shark with hops bread and green bandhaniya chutney, made from wild coriander grass. Shadow benny, they called it, *chardon béni.*

'Where dey get dis shark, you t'ink?' Brian wondered.

'Go an' aks di life guard,' Fyzie replied. 'It have enough-a-dem here.'

An equal relationship, I thought. If the sharks caught us, they ate us, and if we caught them, we ate them.

On the drive back we dropped Brian off first and headed back towards Couva.

As I reached the open road past the Caroni River I let the car find its own pace. The engine purred and the car hugged the road tight, and I could feel my own motor beginning to hum, and then to purr, and then to race.

Now I could hear a buzz inside my head and my pulse was beating in my ears again, and then the car was speeding, overtaking everything in sight. I turned off the highway at Chaguanas. I wanted to feel some curves in the road. Now the back wheels were leaning into the curves, no brakes, like a downhill slalom.

Fyzie sat in the passenger seat next to me with a broad grin, in his element. My cousins in the back were thrilled.

We dropped Fyzie off, and Dylan replaced him in the front passenger seat. Then we drove on down to Couva. It was still daylight, and the dogs were properly locked up. Dylan's brother got out and opened the gate and we drove into the yard.

Then I went up the back steps and stood again at the back window—my window of time, I called it. And all of a sudden I felt I could see the dinosaurs as they must have looked millions of years ago, walking on the lawns of the 'dead house', the mortuary attached to the hospital, across the back street, behind our yard. I was only a tiny blip in the life of planet Earth. I needed this sense of perspective to think.

The French had an expression for it: *un coup de foudre*. An attack of madness. A swarming mêlée of manic energy seeking a focus. First there came the madness. Then came the search for a suitable human being to pin it all on. And then, when you had a victim designated to receive all this wild energy, you said you were in love.

I was looking for that focus.

The point is that I was stuck, badly stuck. And I needed impulse power to free myself and find the open waters again. If I didn't, the next big move in my life would trap me for good. Life was going to turn very serious. Colourless. Hostile. Full of impossible commitments to keep. Or something. I didn't want to focus on what I was afraid of.

My whole life had been heading up only towards going abroad: going abroad to study, going abroad to make my mark, going abroad to make a life. The living world around me in Trinidad, the world I was only now getting to know, was something ephemeral. Trinidad was just a nursery for this exotic plant.

I was stalling. I didn't want to go. But the energy of that big house around me, with everybody nervous and wary of the world outside the gates, was oppressive. I wanted to break out of it all. Break out and do what, I could not say. But I had simply had enough of the constant constraint, and of the diligent preparation for a mythical future world that maybe wasn't there at all.

I was wondering if there could possibly be a reason to opt out of this.

Now I found myself back home from Michigan in a timeless moment just at the start of the Carnival season. No fixed schedules. Everything was possible! Bobby could wear his Carnival costume in Chaguanas and captain his own ship for a day. And I could be just another Trinidadian girl, without a life sentence ahead.

Just a small window of time to dream. Or it could even be forever…

And so the game started, the game of cat and mouse. Fyzie could sense my mood, but he could do no more than drop hints, guarded hints that he was there, that there were endless chicks who liked him. Look at me. Give me a chance.

And I filed all this away, but kept scanning the horizon, to see if anyone else might come into view. Not Fyzie! He was not something I could handle. Let him stay with his endless chicks. No, I thought, what I really wanted was someone I could present as a valid excuse to give it all up and turn my back on the big unsparing world beyond the Caribbean Sea. Someone who cared about this thing called happiness.

So the tension between us became a sort of seasoning, a bit of background spice that livened up our hunting expeditions into the heart of Caroni.

And a lot of little old ladies in long skirts and orhnis, and a lot of little old men, would meet us in the evenings around sunset, and open up to us, and be energized by us.

And they would tell us that they had seen it all too, and had acted on impulse too, and had also gone out beyond their depth. In fact, they would tell us, they had actually gone out much, much further beyond the breaker line than we could ever hope to do, and they had done it all long before we were even born.

STREAMS

A GOOD NIGHT'S SLEEP WAS THE ONLY ANTIDOTE TO high-flying euphoria. I shut my eyes that Sunday night with a will, and brought on the dull grogginess that would allow me to drift away on a saner current. Not too much saner, I hoped. I wanted just enough dullness to let me preserve a sense of focus. Next day I would be back in academia.

And I woke up next morning to find that the storm had abated. The sound inside my head had quietened down from the noise of wind shrieking in the rigging to just a good background buzz. I would have the power to run, even to accelerate. But I wasn't overheating.

Rosa and I were to meet for lunch at the Senior Common Room of the University of the West Indies, where the faculty got together and drank Carib beer, played billiards and told themselves that they had the best dalpuris in the country. The SCR also had a beautiful sunny back garden to sit in and let the world go by.

As I passed the Caroni river I realized I didn't have to race my engines. I was moving northwards in a slipstream, thoughts were coming and linking up in my mind strangely and ingeniously. If I kept my mind free I could sit back and just watch them come in to roost.

And then I turned into the SCR yard, came down to earth, and parked.

Rosa was waiting for me out back holding a Carib.

'For you too?' she asked, redundantly.

So we sat in the sun on our wicker chairs holding our icy cold bottles of Carib. I allowed the sound in my head to fade up and capture the crystal clear light and the intense colour of the flowers.

'What plans?' Rosa asked.

'Well, back to Michigan, to finish up,' I said. 'I have to turn this thing into a dissertation.'

'You know what I mean,' she said. 'After.'

A long pause. I collected my thoughts back from all over the garden. 'After! You know, all these years I never really thought about it! I just figured I would find a university job abroad. But now that I almost finish my work I feel like is only now I getting to know this place. I really don't want to go back.'

'What happen?' she smiled. 'Changing your mind now?'

'I don't know. Every time I start to think about staying here I catch myself, and I get the feeling like I running away from something, like I taking the easy way out.' I could feel myself sliding back down to earth as I talked, all the early morning lightness fading fast.

Her eyes narrowed. 'I don't think we talking about work now, right?'

'No,' I said. 'Not work. Just me. I feel like everywhere I turn I am trapped! One side my parents expecting big things from me.' I broke off, took a breath. 'The only time in my life I was ever able to just be happy was these last few months in Trinidad.'

Should I go on? Rosa had never seen this side of me.

'And the other side?' Rosa prompted.

'All my life I just assumed the man I would end up with was somebody I met over there,' I gestured northwards, 'someone ahead of me in every way, stronger than me, older than me, somebody I couldn't push around, someone I could show off like a prize.' Like Saranga's mysterious prince.

'Girl, that is an old-old story!' she laughed. 'Women famous for that! And then we complain that these men taking advantage of us. That is what you heading up to tell me?'

'Yes! What would happen if we didn't buy into all of that? Didn't look for someone,' I gestured again, 'up there? Any chance it could work?'

'Well, it's a good thought. I don't see anything wrong in reversing things.'

Reverse things! What if I did?

So I played out this new scenario in my head, giddy at finding myself back on the open road. What would my parents say if I told them I wanted to settle in Trinidad? They might fuss at first, but if I ended up looking peaceful and busy and doing some absorbing work, they would probably be able to live with that.

So what was stopping me?

I had begun this time in Trinidad as a desperately needed stay in port, to make repairs and recharge my reserves. But in truth, I was still in thrall to a much older indenture. I was the one who was not ready to give up the sea.

What about Fyzie? I began to wonder now how much of my interest in Fyzie had to do with this secret impulse to keep sailing. As much as my father liked him, my liking him too was putting their relationship under severe strain. It was as if I was deliberately heading into a storm, as if I had gone out of my way to find someone impossible.

And Fyzie had surprised me. I hadn't expected to be anything but another of his 'endless chicks'. I hadn't expected him to turn serious. Now I was responsible for him too.

What was I up to? I wanted Rosa to help me sort this out. I turned my mind to the bug in my brain that was keeping me on the move. 'I get this hollow feeling giving up mid-way. Sitting on the beach, that's what my great-grandfather used to call it. Just watching other ships pass me by. It's like it's burned into my brain cells to keep doing something, heading somewhere. Up. And if I change tack now, is like I letting down generations of people before me who crossed the sea like lemmings to make something out of themselves. I have to think about them first.'

I got a sudden vision of the glow on Dad's face when I got my BA results at UWI. My results had meant much more to him than to me. And I had known then that I was making up for all the things that hadn't happened in his life.

Rosa shook her head. 'Girl, you don't owe your whole life to people who dead and gone. You only have one chance to live, remember that. Start to think about yourself.'

I nodded, unconvinced.

'You don't believe me,' she smiled. 'Okay, for me is easier. I already decide to settle here. The rest is a smaller problem. But you have a lot of other demons to fight. You know what I think?' she said.

'What?'

'Leave this thing till Carnival over. For now just go with the flow. Some of what bothering you is the Carnival madness. Right now you are in costume playing a different role, getting a chance to be someone freer and stronger than you think you are. Maybe you need that for a while. Don't try to decide about where to settle now, or you might make a choice that doesn't fit the bigger picture. When Las' Lap over on Carnival Tuesday night you will start to see your life in a fresh light.'

I was back to that window of time.

And with that we got up to go and get our dalpuris.

Half an hour later we withdrew from the SCR like foam drifting back out after a wave. Far, far out beyond the breaker line we floated, to Rosa's flat, to tune in to Deeda.

Insert tape. Press play. And Deeda's voice again:

'Ta ohi toophaan ke baad paal lagaai ke aage gaylin. Bole Cape Town me ruk jaai humni, koela bharey ke.'

Then after that storm we put up the sails and went on. They said we would stop in Cape Town, to fill up with coal.

So we sailed around the Cape, around the end of Africa, and made our stop at Table Bay.

We stopped there for two days, because the laskars had to bunker all the coal onto the ship, enough to last until Trinidad, shovelling it into the openings on the side of the ship that sent it down near the engine room. And besides the coal and fresh water and medicines and other things we needed, they also took on some fresh goat meat and some pumpkins to cook, the biggest pumpkins I ever saw in my whole life.

So the second part of the journey started well.

After the storm something had happened to all of us. It had all started when Sahatoo Maharaj had stood on the deck and smiled. We stopped looking back. I think we had finally crossed the kala pani, in our minds, changed from being the people we were before. The sad notes of the beeraha we had sung as we crossed that other ocean had brightened into a new song, a song with no dark corners, and no storms. Now we were looking at everybody else on the boat with us as our family, apan palwaar. And we started calling each other something new: jahaji bhai and jahaji bahin, ship-brother and ship-sister, and speaking of each other as jahajis, shipmates. People who had travelled across two big oceans on the same ship had seen too much together to be anything but family.

I can't say there were no fights on this part of the journey. Men are not like that. They will fight. But I can say that any trouble in the men's quarters never reached the ears of the goras. Mukoon Singh and his two sons, Heera Singh and Houri Singh, kept control. The men had to go to them with their quarrels, and Mukoon Singh would sit with a moonsie, a man from the caste of court scribes, and he would decide what they should do, and the moonsie would write it down. And after he wrote it down it was pakka, final.

The goras seemed to realize that the men's quarters were out of bounds for them. The laskars sometimes went down into the men's quarters, and passed on news about what was happening up front, and the bhangis came every day and washed down the quarters, and spread disinfectant every week.

But besides the doctor, no gora ever went into the men's quarters.

We started off from Table Bay with a good tailwind, heading up for Trinidad. We didn't have to use the engines. We had wind in the sails, and we were moving in a strong current.

The boat slipped forward on the water following the needle of the compass, the laskars said. North by north-west. And as we sailed, we pointed our faces to the north too and started talking in a different way. The storm had loosened up something in almost all of us. We stopped talking about all that happened before. It was as if we had left the people we used to be behind us, around the Cape.

When we left Table Bay we found that with the supplies we had also taken on a cat. When the cooks heard about the cat they were glad, because they said that was what we had needed all this time to control the rats that were always troubling the stores. So they let the cat go wherever it wanted, never tried to stop it, and it hunted for rats all through the boat. The laskars said that the cat would bring the migrants good luck.

But all the migrants stayed away from the cat, because they said it looked like it was wild. I heard that it had once had a cat-fit and attacked one of the goras who had gone too close to the women's latrine and had tried to pet the cat. Could be that that was why the goras also kept their distance from the cat.

But to me the cat did not look wild at all. I never saw it do anything bad. Most days it would just climb up and sit in the sun on the poop deck, above the women's quarters, and go to sleep with one eye open. And sometimes when I was alone on the deck it would come down and sit not too far from me and purr loudly, and keep me company.

One evening, instead of giving us dal and rice and rotis, the cooks made something they said the goras liked to eat on long journeys. They boiled up dried saltfish and onions and ship's biscuits into a soup—

I paused the tape here again, as I had done when I first transcribed it.

I could feel the cold Labrador Current collide with the warm Gulf Stream. The ocean was alive.

My mind drifted back first to those nights sitting on the upstairs porch of our house in Couva, where Nana had a rocking chair. He and I would sit together on it, with me on the armrest holding my little globe with the map of the world.

Nana would turn the globe backwards and trace with his finger the route his mother's ship had taken, around the Cape of Good Hope, and then north-west diagonally across the Atlantic on its route to Trinidad.

His finger would pause on Cape Town. That was where they had stopped. Cape Town had been the coaling station for ships on the route from India to the Caribbean. Running a steamship meant needing to refuel en route. It meant a stop in Cape Town.

We would go back together some day, he would say, him and me, and visit India. We would retrace the journey, stopping at Cape Town, and going on to Calcutta. Then we would go inland to Faizabad, where his father had come from. See? And Aligarh. We could even take in China on our trip, it wasn't too far from India.

How would we talk to people, I would ask frantically. I was always obsessed with not understanding the old ones around me speaking Bhojpuri and Hindi. And our next-door neighbours were Chinese, from Guangzhou, so I couldn't understand their language at all.

And he would smile indulgently. Not to worry, he knew Hindi.

And China?

We would use interpreters.

That word stuck in my head forever: interpreter. There was such a thing as people who knew languages so well that they could tell you everything that everybody was saying! I had grown up frustrated at hearing every day a language I was deliberately not allowed to understand. How did others surmount this and actually learn?

Much later I pieced together the details of the route. Since the *Godavari* was carrying live cargo, human labourers, and there was no danger of this cargo rotting on the high seas, they didn't have to rush. They could save on coal, and coaling stops, and use the sails whenever there was wind. All steamers in those days had a provision for putting up sails as an emergency measure in case of engine breakdown.

So the *Godavari* would have caught the receding monsoon winds that blow through the month of September, and they would have borne her south-west across the Indian Ocean towards Africa. There would have been a lull at the equator, as she reached the doldrums, at which point she would have had to use engine power to connect with the southbound East African Coastal Current, and then the Agulhas Current, the second fastest ocean current in the world after the Gulf Stream, and it would have borne her south through the stormy Mozambique Channel between the island of Madagascar and Africa, known for its gale force winds and monster waves a hundred feet high. The waves that battered the *Godavari* in the storm would have been significantly milder than those boat-breakers.

Then she would have rounded the Cape of Good Hope, and gone into port at Table Bay, Cape Town.

She would then have proceeded north on the cold Benguela Current from Cape Town, sailing quite a way out to sea to catch the Atlantic South-East Trade Winds. She would then have sailed past St Helena, an island half way between the Mid-Atlantic ridge and Africa, and continued north-west, riding the winds across the Atlantic towards Fortaleza, on the bulge of Brazil. Heading north she would have transited the doldrums at the equator on engine power, and then caught the northbound Guiana Current, and used the North-East Trade Winds to reach Trinidad.

Then that scene cleared, and I was in the kitchen downstairs, back at home in Couva. My mother was making Christmas cakes. Probably a bit nostalgic at the thought of yet another Christmas without snow.

And I would hear her telling me about something called hard tack that they would eat when she was a child in Newfoundland. Hard tack was the other name for ship's biscuits.

Bis-cuit: French for twice-baked. They were baked twice to dry them out so that they would last through a long journey. Sometimes they were baked four times.

What she would do, she said, was grip one in her hand and then strike the palm of her hand against the corner of a table, and the hard tack would splinter, and she would put a piece into her mouth, and over time it would soften, until she could chew it.

When you cooked the hard tack with dried Newfoundland codfish you got Fish and Brewis, or Fish and Bruise, as she called it, the traditional food of Newfoundland.

And that was what the cooks on the *Godavari* had cooked that night for Deeda and the other jahajis!

Newfoundland was the other stream in my story: two grandparents who had separately sailed across the north Atlantic from Scotland and Ireland to arrive in Montreal, where they had met and married, and then moved on to Newfoundland.

All the salted codfish the migrants had been eating throughout their journey had been fished in Grand Banks, off Newfoundland. The cold Labrador Current collided there with the warm Gulf Stream and spawned the most abundant fishing grounds in the world.

We were all connected!

I shook my head to clear the bright noise inside and turned back to the tape recorder:

'Tab roj-roj, ohi pagla samundar me jaat-jaat-jaat-jaat, humni sab thak gailin.'

Then day after day, just going on and on and on and on in that crazy ocean, we got tired.

Tired! The boat was quiet, so quiet. Just splash-splash and the wind in the rigging. No engines were running now. We had hardly needed to use the engines this trip. The wind and the current were carrying us easily, and there was nothing to do. Only wait, and wait, and wait.

Three months is a long time to do nothing. Some of the migrants were getting a dull stupid look in their eyes again.

Sometimes little girls would take pieces of coal and draw boxes on the deck and play peesay, standing on one foot and kicking the lumps of coal from box to box: 'Peesay, peesay, peesay, taa!' Grind spices, grind spices, grind spices, rest!

And sometimes a few of the men would throw lines into the sea and catch fish.

Saltwater fish—we were catching it ourselves! Now we had really crossed the kala pani. In Basti we used to catch fish from a pond in the village, or from the river. And in Garden Reach they used to cook fish for us sometimes, but only river fish. In Calcutta they had said that a Hindu was not allowed to eat sea fish.

Once a laskar showed us a whale far away, blowing water into the air. The goras liked to eat that fish, they said. They had special boats to go and catch it. They said its meat tasted exactly like beef.

But they didn't say that about the saltwater fish we were eating.

One day Ramdaye came up on the deck and I heard her singing to the baby:

> *Jaise roj-roj aawela tu, teir suni ke,*
> *Aaiyo, re, nidiya nidar ban se!*
> *Kaa hoi sonawa, ho, kaa hoi chandiya?*
> *Humra ke chaahi, Maiya, tohri-hi godiya!*

> *As you come every day when you hear my call,*
> *From the forest of sleep, come to me, a nap!*
> *What good is gold, oh, what good is silver?*
> *All I want, Maiya, is only your lap!*

And look at all of us in a boat going half-way around the world!

In the beginning I used to roam about the boat seeing what was what. I didn't do that now. I was just waiting for this journey to finish. Kalloo didn't need me so much, he was almost always with his Langoor Mamoo.

So I would just spend most of my time up on the deck with Sunnariya, not saying too much, just hoping we would be together in Trinidad. In Trinidad I would find fresh water again, I knew, and my stories would come to life again. My stories needed shadow as well as light, sweetness as well as salt. And earth to sink roots in.

Ramsukh, the man with the mango seeds, was always there too. He would always be talking to the laskars, asking about the new place we were going to. He wanted to be the first one to see it when we reached.

The cat was also getting restless, sitting up on top of the poop deck, looking west, twitching its tail from time to time. Then one morning we woke up and found that it had climbed the rigging and made a place for itself on the rim of the crow's-nest. For two days it sat there, its face turned to the west, listening to something we couldn't hear, not moving.

And then we could hear it too.

One morning when we came up on deck the sea was as usual, but the sound of the waves coming from the west was louder, a different sound, something like a distant roar.

And in some time the laskars showed us a line of white waves rising far to the west. We were close to land.

Everybody came up on the deck to get their first glimpse of Trinidad—

The breaker line! Deeda and the other jahajis were looking at the breaker line from the other side!

The *Godavari* would have sighted land on the east coast of Trinidad, probably north of Galeota Point, the south-east corner of Trinidad, near Mayaro. No hills there, the first sign of land the jahajis detected would have been the white lines of surf rising in the distance. Land would still have been hidden from view because of the earth's curvature. But someone sitting high up in the crow's-nest would have seen it first.

By then the jahajis would have been in the same desperate mood as Columbus and his crew on their third voyage, when they found Trinidad, fearing by now that they would never see land again. But unlike Columbus they would not have tried to make landfall then and there on the beach. Their journey was not over yet.

The *Godavari* would have continued sailing north on the trade winds, circling the island, heading towards Galera Point, at the end of Toco. From there she would have turned west, riding the trades through the gap between Trinidad and the island of Tobago, sailing past Blanchisseuse and Maracas Bay, heading towards Chaguaramas. From there she would have turned south, away from the Atlantic and into the sweeter calmer waters of the Gulf of Paria.

And then she would start her last lap: down the islands, through a gap between the five islands of the Bocas, the Dragon's Mouth, off Chaguaramas, the stepping stones to South America, a mere 14 km away. And she would stop and drop anchor in the deep waters a distance away from a tiny island just west of Port of Spain, in the Caribbean Sea. Nelson Island. Nelson Island was the Immigrant depot, set up to relieve pressure on the actual harbour in Port of Spain.

So the *Godavari* never actually reached Port of Spain harbour.

'*Nelson Island depot! Pahunch gaylin sab! Tab bole line banaao, ek line me jaybey.*'

Nelson Island depot! We were there! Then they told us to make a line, that we would get off the boat in a line.

We had already taken up all our belongings from below. We were waiting on the deck in a line. I can't remember who was heading the line, but Kalloo and I were standing together with Sunnariya and her father and two brothers, not too far from the front.

A small steamer was coming to take all of us from the Godavari.

Mukoon Singh had taken off his pink pagri and had kept it with his belongings. That was the first time I got to see his hair. It was thick and brown, like Sunnariya's hair.

I asked Sunnariya why he had done that, taken off his pagri.

Sunnariya told me that the laskars had given him the idea. They had said that at the depot when they checked us they were going to divide the migrants into three groups: healthy migrants, who could land straight away, migrants who needed to stay in the depot hospital, and migrants who looked like 'misfits', like they might be dangerous. They didn't want the kind who would talk back to them. They would be rounding up the 'misfits' to send them back.

Mukoon Singh did not want to stand out. That was why he was not going first. He was already taller than the others. Without his pink pagri he didn't think he would attract so much attention.

So we were going to keep together, the six of us, together with the moonsie, Mukoon Singh's friend, near the head of the line, and hope they would send us together to the same estate.

I lifted Kalloo on my hip and carried him as we walked off the gangplank to the steamer. I was thinking about Sahatoo Maharaj losing his brother. I turned to look and saw him in the line behind us, still on the deck of the Godavari. And I saw Ramdaye and the baby and her husband and the other boys.

Janaki the sonaarin and her two boys. Langoor Mamoo, Chirag Ali and Jaitoon, Bipti the chamain. Ramsukh.

Everybody with that same dull dead look, a look that said, 'Don't pay us any mind, we are just coolie migrants.'

Nelson Island. We got off the steamer.

'Boung-coolie reach! Gi a bag! U na jaane mej par baithey!'

The bound coolies are here! Give us the jute bags! They don't know how to sit on chairs!

Then they came and took away all our belongings. Dhuaan me daale ke, they said. To fumigate. We were going to get them back. They just had to make sure we were not bringing any diseases to Trinidad.

Then the doctors came to check us, one by one. And whoever was looking weak, they kept to one side, and the rest of us they cleared. Then we had to wait for two weeks on Nelson Island for the people to come from the estates and decide which of us they would take.

In those two weeks we stayed together all the time, Sunnariya and Kalloo and I, together with her father and brothers and whosoever of our friends wanted to go to the same estate as us. Langoor Mamoo. The moonsie. Janaki the sonaarin and her two boys. Chirag Ali and his brother and Jaitoon. Ramsukh, the man with the mango seeds. And while the estate people were watching us and deciding who to choose, all of us felt like we were watching them too, and making up our minds about them.

The first estate people to reach Nelson Island were from Esperanza Estate, and they didn't want to waste time. When they saw that we were already a group they decided to take all of us and a few more, forty in all. Then they told us we would leave for Esperanza by the first sloop.

It was a smaller boat, with only two sails, and it took us down the west coast to the estate. Ours was the first stop, Goodrich

Bay, with a long, long jetty reaching out far into the sea. They tied the sloop to the jetty and we got off and started walking with our belongings towards the shore, where mule carts were waiting to carry us to Esperanza Estate. The journey across two big oceans was over.

I was twenty years of age less three. Seventeen. Now a new part of my life was going to start—

BLACKOUT

Estate land ahead, Spring Estate. We parked the car on the side of the road and got out, intent on sweet plunder.

We waded straight into the cane fields, no machetes, no knives, determined to make off with a few stalks of cane. We were going to uproot a few good ones, take them away, and then park the car somewhere more peaceful and peel them with our teeth, and chew them.

'Yuh mean dey doan arrest yuh for dis?' I asked. '"Praedial larceny", somet'ing like dat. T'ree months in jail?' I had learned all these exquisite terms from my mother.

Fyzie just laughed. 'Doan make joke! I doin' dis my whole life!'

But this was the first time I was pulling out cane that actually belonged to a sugar estate. It was one thing to cut from your own patch of juicy 'eating' cane in your back yard. But this was tough industrial cane growing on Spring Estate near Couva.

The real thrill, then, was in the barefaced daylight robbery. And stripping the cane with just our teeth.

When I told Dylan in the house at Couva about this planned raid, he responded with his acid teenage wit. You can take the coolie out of the cane field, he had said, but you can't take the cane field out of the coolie. In other words, thanks, but no thanks, count me out.

It was funny how, on the one hand, we lionized our ancestors who had worked in the cane fields, yet on the other hand we kept our own evolved selves light years away from the sugar estates. Our hearts bled for the poor aging cane cutters, the last repository of 'our' culture. But to go near the life of the estates was to place your feet too close to the quicksand.

We had come a long way. We were not going to be dragged back down.

But I was too far away from it to be in any danger. Besides, I was curious.

So we made off with our cane and parked under a patch of bamboo by a river, and the car radio gave us a fevered background of carnival music for our feast.

It was actually easy to strip the cane with our teeth. And even more fun sinking both jaws into a joint of peeled cane and letting the juice run sticky down our arms. Then we went and washed up in the river.

In our minds we were still setting out every day to meet old jahajis and record interviews with them. But more and more often, we just didn't get around to it. We simply limed. We just hung around together, feeling the tension like a pulse beat in the veins. Looking straight at each other now, staring, daring, waiting to see who would blink first, playing pirate, waiting for the big one.

We were moving in a current, dropping hints at each other, taunts. Smooth and flowing motion, he would say. Going for a blackout, I would retort. And the pressure was building.

Tonight we were too keyed-up to keep to ourselves. So we sailed to Bobby's house and rode a wave of high voltage pop music the last fifty yards into his bedroom.

'Wha' goin on, maan?'

Bobby paused to make up his mind if we were all right.

'Wha' yuh have? Put on somet'ing good, maan!'

Bobby looked through his tapes and the music score resumed, moving with us, dancing with us, sometimes ahead of our mood, sometimes lagging behind. We sat on the edge of our chairs distractedly sipping the rum and Cokes Bobby had brought us. Looking for something to do to burn up the chaos in our heads.

Then Fyzie leapt to his feet. 'Let's go to St Mary's Junction.'

Bobby took a rain check. He had to go and help make the float for his Carnival band. They were doing the bow of a sailing ship, and he was to be the captain holding the big wheel.

So Fyzie and I drifted away by ourselves. Headed for that tiny junction which would have to be worth the singleminded zeal we were showing in getting there.

As we made our approach we saw the light from a flambeau beckoning. Just a burning rag stuffed into a bottle of kerosene. A flambeau meant an oyster stall. We looked at each other guardedly and then I walked straight up to it and started ordering for both of us. Fyzie lifted his eyebrows and suddenly got a dazed look, like this wasn't really happening. I was waiting for him to blink.

The oyster man shucked the raw oysters for us and put them into two glasses, and put in a few good shakes of the sauce, full of vinegar, tomato and bandhaniya.

'Extra pepper?'

'Of course!'

The oyster man gave us a sly look. We took the glasses and sipped. I felt the slippery raw oysters slide down my throat and braced for the burn from the Congo pepper. Then we moved on.

'Pardner, it have a pusher here?' Fyzie's voice.

Pusher? I thought. Then Fyzie was going off with someone, and they both vanished around a corner. I was left to myself. Nobody came and disturbed me. It was just me, the flickering flambeau, and the darkening sky. The window of time was wide open.

We vanished to some secret place. I don't remember where it was, or how we got there. A steel band was practising somewhere in the distance or maybe it was the radio.

And then I was in a current, sailing through the gap. Just go with the flow, girl, it's just Carnival madness madness madness...

Faster now, a roaring sound in the distance, the breaker line, don't make landfall yet...

I opened my eyes and two eyes stared back, black as coal. Eyes beginning to glaze and go out of focus. Flickering flambeau shadows on the ceiling...

I sailed past the bay, riding the winds...not yet, not yet...we going for the big one, don't stop...

Now just the drums, loud and hypnotic, you have to stay the course, stay...

Underneath me a monster wave was building, a deep rumble was starting, now it was swelling, cresting...

I held my breath coming in for the last lap, just a few more strokes, a burst of speed, I was being pulled up, high above the trough, catch it and ride it!

Then the wave was upon me, lifting me, white foam out the porthole, black spots exploding in front of my eyes, one more second to go, the bass notes were coming on...Now!

I convulsed on the high note as the wave shot through me and slammed me to the ocean floor. In the blackness of the depths I rolled with the surge and struggled with all my limbs to fight the undertow and make my way to the top, my lungs bursting for air.

Darkness. A gap in time. I struggled and opened my eyes and it was night.

Fyzie was staring down at me.

'Yuh had me frighten', girl,' he said. 'Yuh whole face was blue! I thought you was really gone.'

But the anchor holding me down now was too heavy. I couldn't utter the words inside my head. I couldn't move. I could barely stay afloat. I took a deep shuddering breath. Air at last!

And then I didn't even want to reply. I just wanted to drift back out. I turned my head away weakly and closed my eyes again.

HAI, SARANGA!

WHEN I WOKE UP NEXT MORNING IT WAS BRIGHT daylight. I found myself in my bed at home in Couva, with a dull headache at the back of my neck, and absolutely no memory of how I had got home the night before. I looked through the mosquito net and saw that Ajie had left a mug of tea for me, covered with a saucer to keep it warm.

I sat up cautiously, picked up the warm tea and tried to remember.

All I could recall right away was the dream. The same dream of black spots exploding, of trying to hold it off, then of fighting an undertow at the bottom of the ocean. Of flailing with all my limbs desperately to reach the top to get air, and of opening my eyes to find that time had passed. Oh, no!

The phone rang shrilly in the upstairs living room. I got up and answered it.

'Are you all right, girl?' A Scots accent. My friend Sheila, who lived close by in Balmain.

'A slight headache in the back of my head. But why are you asking me?'

'You were here last night, girl! Don't you remember?'

I thought and thought, and drew a blank. 'No. Really, what happened? How did I get back home?'

Fyzie, it seems, had panicked to find me crashed out. And the only doctor I ever mentioned and seemed to know well enough to drop in on at night was Sheila's husband. So he had taken me there, and Sheila had ingeniously tried to revive me with hot strong coffee, fed to me from her son's baby bottle. Did I remember?

I thought again. No.

Then she and her husband had driven me home. Her husband had tried to concoct a story, en route, about having had to give me a sedative.

Then I vaguely remembered the last bit. Of opening the back door of an unfamiliar car and getting out blindly, with a will, and walking up the steps to reach my bed and crash out again.

'Don't worry, your car's here, safe and sound. So why don't you come over in the afternoon and pick it up. We'll have some scones. Four thirty?'

That gave the first shape to my day. I went back to bed, still not quite right. I felt that old familiar sensation of gravity having grown, of having to expend extra effort to shift my hand two inches to the left on the bed, forget lifting it. The morning was going to be a total washout.

Ajie came back from the shop at lunchtime, and came upstairs to check on me. Her face was preoccupied. Blackouts always had that effect on the family. They seemed to trigger memories, and then a curtain fell. They never talked about who else had had these blackouts too.

'You should stay home tonight,' she said. 'Too much of late nights going to wear you down. And we didn't finish writing the story.'

So I sat in Nana's old rocking chair on the upstairs balcony after lunch, put my feet up on the railing, and looked at the afternoon sky, while the normal people worked away in their offices, or wherever. I would have to wait till after school hours for my uncle to come and give me a lift to Sheila's house, and for Sheila to be back from school herself, to recover my car.

Dylan was made to tag along on this expedition for safety. Ajie was worried about my driving alone after a day spent mostly lying down, and had told him to go with me. I don't know what heroics he would have been able to do, but he didn't mind coming. For the scones, he said.

As we walked in through Sheila's kitchen door I could hear her at the piano in the corner of her dining room, past the patio, practising a song she would teach in school:

'Speed, bonnie boat, like a bird on the wing,'
Onward the sailors' cry,
Carry the lad that was born to be king
Over the seas to Skye.

She looked up as she saw me and smiled, and got up from the piano.

Sheila had been the only force in my life tugging me back to look at the Celtic side of me. My mother was Canadian, but she had never brought me up to think of myself as being Canadian like her. When she had married my father, as a college student, she had faced ugly prejudice from some of her Canadian professors. And she was determined that my brother and I would not have to face that too. So all my life I had learned to block out that side of me, and doggedly demand acceptance in an Indian fold that the face in my mirror did not match. 'Don't play white.'

So we sat in her patio, looking out at her back garden, and the cane fields of Balmain moving in the wind beyond her fence, as we had the scones. Sheila poured the tea while Dylan admired the fine china teapot.

I gave him a look that reminded him to vanish while I tried to explain last night's mess to Sheila. So he strolled off to check out her music collection. And I got ready to face the music teacher.

Where should I start?

'I'm sorry about last night,' I began cautiously.

'No-no,' she said, 'but what happened? We just couldn't wake you up!'

I hesitated, looked away. Sheila would probably write me off if I went into details about last night, I thought.

'No, don't tell me!' Sheila had sensed quicksand. 'I don't want to know!'

And I breathed again.

'But who was that chap?'

I decided to take that one sideways. 'Someone who works with my father. He's helping me find old people to interview for my dissertation. About the language.'

'Hmm.' She shot me back a sideways glance. I could see her filing away all the unasked questions about the previous night. Some other time, not now. Then she returned to the issue at hand. 'The language?'

'Bhojpuri. That's what most Indians here spoke, once upon a time. I have to work out its grammar, and the only way to do that is get lots of stuff on tape, long narrative. Then I'll work back from that and figure out the rules.'

'And are you finding enough people to talk to? I didn't think there were that many any more. It's dying, isn't it? Like Gaelic in Scotland.'

'It's exactly the same situation. Just like with the highland clearances: the language beginning to vanish after the people got transplanted. In fact, I had to read up about Scottish Gaelic before starting this project.' I paused for breath. 'But there are some old people in Trinidad, even some of the original jahajis, the ones who came on the boats. I've found an old woman who says she is a hundred and ten, and her story checks out. She *is* that old!'

'So what do you talk about?'

'Well, her own life, of course, and now she's just told me a folk story that has me fascinated, about a girl-monkey who jumps into a river in order to become human, and leaves her mate behind. And then she keeps looking back for him, finding him and trying to pull him along with her.' Then an idea struck me.

'It's real proto-Hindi cinema! They keep pausing in the story and breaking into song. In the song bits, people can talk to animals and vice-versa. The songs in this story are the way to express inner dialogue, just like in Hindi films, things you think but can't say. A sort of magic space.'

'Is it the same tune all the time?' The music teacher's perspective.

'Yes,' I said, and made a mental list of the notes in the song: *do, re, mi, fa, so,* the first five notes of the scale. 'A simple pentatonic scale. Bright primary colours with leaf green.' Deeda had talked about a song with no dark corners and no storms. 'But that's not what really strikes you about the song bits.'

'What, then?'

'It's the language. Here is where translation gets really tough. I feel like I'm back in school doing a Latin "unseen"! Old case endings on the words, at times. The language in the song bits is much older, and not Bhojpuri, mostly. And it's really stripped down. You have to guess a bit: it isn't always clear who is the one speaking. Or you have to wait for the clues in the prose line after the song. I think it's mostly a medieval language called Braj.'

'Well, in many cultures songs are in an older language. People remember songs better than they remember ordinary language. They don't have to think as they go.'

'Yes, but there's something else. The language of the songs is a language known for a stream of radical proto-feminist poetry back in the medieval era. A whole lot of women were writing, and travelling around as singers, forcing a space for themselves within the existing tradition. Bhakti. One translation of bhakti is yin, as opposed to yang.'

'And does that have something to do with the story?' Sheila asked.

Dylan slipped back into his chair on the patio now and quickly tuned into our discussion.

'Yes. In this story it's the woman who is always ahead,' I said, expansively. 'And she actually leaves a mate behind in order to get ahead. That isn't typical. What you're supposed to get in a Bhojpuri folktale is undying loyalty and submissiveness.'

I paused again. No, that wasn't quite right. Saranga wasn't just a tough-as-nails go-getter. 'But still, you do have her looking back all the time and hoping it could work out with her monkey-mate. Even though she is now in the big league and all set to marry a prince.'

'So you think her looking back is just a bit of a compromise? So the story doesn't end up encouraging all Indian women to dump their men?'

'I thought of that but what if it's something more than that? Isn't that sort of vacillation normal? A bit of fear of the big world out there, you know, even after you've taken the plunge? A regret at the loss of the Garden of Eden?'

'Or it could just be good old-fashioned guilt,' said Sheila.

Guilt, I wondered.

'Don't you know that women are always feeling guilty about doing better than their men?' Sheila went on. 'Building them up to be something more than what they are?'

Dylan looked down and smiled.

'It's this thing called commitment,' she concluded.

'I...I hadn't thought of that.' I conceded. 'But I think you're right about the storyteller trying to play down the controversial overtones. There is a lot of confusion in the story up ahead. I remember the girl struggling to keep her relationship with the monkey going, but not fighting too hard against moving on.'

'Something not quite sorted out there.'

'Right,' I said, 'I think the storyteller is actually tussling with the story itself. The story seems to be alive and kicking, and radical, and it wants to pull her forward.

And the storyteller is fighting to take it back onto the conventional route.'

'And who's going to win?' she asked. 'The story or the storyteller? Does she go with the prince in the end, or the monkey?'

Now Dylan leaned into the wind. 'The monkey sounds like a creep! Reminds me of somebody I know!' A sharp edge of irritation in his voice and a meaningful stare in my direction.

'It's just a story, man!' I retorted.

Sheila gave me a long speculative look.

'Any chance of an Indian fairy tale going against the genre? You know, teaming an upwardly mobile girl-monkey with a good guy from a different species?' Dylan asked, with a cheeky show of teeth.

Sheila caught the drift. 'Right, Dylan!' she beamed. 'A happy ending. Now all we need is a prince...'

'Well, don't get your hopes up,' I said, 'I still have a long way to go.'

Sheila walked us out to the car at the magic hour right after sunset, and I did a reversal on my usual course. For a change I pointed my nose towards another lodestar, that other old woman in my life full of Bhojpuri and waiting for me, and headed back home.

Then at the witching hour, when all were snug in their beds, Ajie and I got into place. Now the only light on upstairs was the light hanging above the drop-leaf table in the living room. The tape recorder sat in front of us on the table, between us, like a high-tech crystal ball.

And Ajie got ready, with her vastly superior knowledge of the language, to relay to me the garbled bits, and to help me zero in on the words I couldn't quite understand.

'Ta u oisan phurti gail, paisa taseel-oseel ke aawal, aur okar baap ke del. Aa dei ke ab aapan ghora par answaar bhail. Aur aail, jab aail tab ohi Saranga ke doli ab jaat rahal nadiya.'

Then Sada Birij went as fast as he could, and collected all the taxes and money he had to collect, and brought it back and gave it to his father. Then he got on a horse and rode off to find Saranga. When he reached the wedding Saranga's palanquin was on its way to the river.

And Saranga said:

> *Arey suno agila kanhaara,*
> *Suno pichala kanhaara, re, pyaarey,*
> *Aa le-le ke ye sanwarawa,*
> *Aa chuwe na paawe anga ji.*

> Listen, front palanquin-bearer,
> Listen, rear palanquin-bearer,
> As you carry this passenger
> You must not touch any part of her.

Sada Birij heard her voice, and he nearly fainted in despair. He kept sitting dead silent on his horse. And she went up and happily washed up and bathed, and then she turned and saw Sada Birij there in a swoon. As she got up inside the palanquin she continued her love song:

> *Arey, jinse morey laagi lagana, re, pyaarey,*
> *Unke mai raakho naa ta beechey ji.*
> *Unke mai raakho ghari-pahara pyaarey,*
> *Aa tumke mai raakhi, na, ta beechey ji.*

The man my marriage is arranged with
Is not the one I keep inside my heart.
The one I will keep in my thoughts forever
Is you, I will always remember you.

He got the horse moving, leaping. But since the wedding was
already in progress, his father locked him up in a room. And he
came and sat outside the door himself, and slept there. Now
Sada Birij couldn't get out. And Saranga's wedding was going
smoothly, the ceremony was on, everyone arrived and the
bridegroom went into the wedding tent. Without changing her
clothes Saranga went to meet Sada Birij and found him asleep.
She tried to wake him up and said:

Arey, kaise uthaawey dhaniya, babu laal rakhwaari?
How can this girl wake you, with your father on guard?

The sound reached Sada Birij's father's ears. Then he said:

Arey, utho, utho beta chhulaachana, pyaarey,
Aa raakho gori ke maan, ji.

Wake up, wake up, my lucky son,
And fulfill this fair girl's desires.

Wake up and fulfill this fair girl's desires, he said. One
wish, two wishes, whatever it takes. I'll pay for it. So Sada Birij
got up.

Then Saranga said to him: 'Look, tomorrow my palanquin
will take this very road, and you will sit and wait for me in the
Debi temple. As soon as I get there I will come inside to do a
Debi puja and when we meet there I'll tell you something.' And
she left.

But, bhaai, he went to his friends and asked for whatever
he could get that would get him high. Some say bhang, some say

ganja, some say opium. He had them all, bhaiya, and he went
to the rendezvous, but totally stoned. And when he got there he
fell asleep. When Saranga tried to wake him, why should he
wake up now? No. So when Saranga's palanquin passed that
way, she sang:

> Arey, suno agila kanhaara,
> Suno pichhala kanhaara, re, pyaarey,
> Aa Siew ke puja na hum jaao, ji.

> Listen front palanquin-bearer,
> Listen rear palanquin-bearer,
> I want to go and do a Shiv puja.

So the kahaars put her down there. And she went. Now she
tried and tried to wake him, he didn't get up. It was getting late,
and the kahaars called from outside:

> Arey, tumhe naagin daansey, re, pyaari,
> Akhiyaan daansey kaala janga, ji?
> Siew ke puja na ghari-pahara, gori,
> Aa tumke laagi bara deir, ji.

> Has the she-cobra bitten you, girl?
> Has the black snake stung your eyes?
> This is not the time to do a Shiv puja,
> It is getting very late for you.

At this point a little bird was sitting there, enjoying the whole
spectacle. And the bird said to himself: 'If I don't say something
now, her ijjat, her honour, will be lost.' So the bird said:

> Arey, anchara phaari ke,
> Kaagaj karo, re, pyaari,
> Aa naina kajarwa kaarhi ke,
> Aa likho harap dui-chaar, ji.

Tear off the end of your sari,
Make a piece of notepaper from it,
And take out the kohl from your eyes,
And quickly write down a few words.

Then what did she do? She tore off the end of her sari and made a paper, took out some kaajar from her eyes, wrote a note, and tied it to his wrist. And she left.

Then after some time he woke up, and he felt something, and when he caught hold of his wrist he found something had been tied there. When he opened the message and read it the poor fool said: 'Hai, Saranga, hai, Saranga!' Oh, Saranga, oh, Saranga! And he walked off.

Then when he had gone some way he met an old woman. And he asked the old woman:

Arey, ehi nagar morey gori gaye, re, pyaari?
Aa rowat-jaat ki khans, ji?

Did the fair woman I love come to this town?
Was she crying as she came, until her voice was hoarse?

And the old woman said:

Arey, ehi nagar tere gori gaye, re, pyaari,
Aa ghurti-rasti chintavata jaat he.

Through this town your fair girl has gone,
And all the way she was staring at the road,
Thinking hard.

Yes, she went this way, she said, but all the time she was looking around in all four directions.

Then the old woman called him: 'Come here.'

He went, and she peeled some sugarcane and gave it to him, and he sat down and chewed it all up hungrily.

And when he was done eating it, she said to him: 'Son, now take up the bits you've just chewed and chew them again.'

So he said: 'Old Mother, there's nothing left in them. Whatever juice there was has gone into my stomach. There's nothing left.'

So she said: 'Son, that is what Saranga has become. You've had the first juice. Now what is left of her has gone to her in-laws' home. So all the juice that you got, and the remains that went to her in-laws' home, now let it be. You just go back home.'

Why should he listen? Crying 'Hai, Saranga, hai, Saranga, I've lost you, oh Saranga, I've lost you!' he went on his way—

ESPERANZA

I TURNED THE CORNER AT ISAAC JUNCTION AND HEADED north from Couva, with mid-morning sunlight and the cool February breeze cheering me on. The car seemed to know the way by itself, so I gave it its head and let it run. My mind was busy with other things.

I was on my way to the university to meet Sollo. The day I had given my seminar I had mentioned to him that I wanted to try looking for a job at UWI, and I had phoned him and said that I wanted to come and see him about that.

But the truth was that I badly needed to get out of the house. The day before there had been a mighty showdown and the family had gone for my guts because of my relationship with 'all kind of dog and cat', as Ajie had put it. Ajie had heard a rumour, and they had got together to pin me down, to make me come clean. An uncle, an aunt, Ajie and Dad. While I had sat high up in the stratosphere, detached and invulnerable.

And then I had shrugged and said, 'So what if it's true?'

And things had exploded. Ajie had started to cry.

My brother had once told me that you could say anything at all to Ajie so long as you put your arm around her. But that isn't what I did this time. I just sat there, and watched her as she turned into a different person, someone I had never seen before. She began to shake, and then she was shouting at me, her eyes more alive than I had ever seen them, all the anger she had held back over a lifetime pouring out. She stared at me unseeingly, accusing me of everything my grandfather had ever done to hurt her, and in the end she just sat there sobbing, repeating herself, completely spent.

And in that moment I saw a beautiful woman who was now an old woman, past all the love that should have happened in her life. I had always thought she was content with being the eternal mother, an icon in the eyes of her children and grandchildren. Suddenly I saw all the heartbreak she had been holding back. We sat and faced each other across the table, the one who had lived only for others, and her alter ego, who was now living for herself.

Dad sat there looking trapped and resentful. Already torn between his mother and his daughter, he was the only one on the other side of the table who was really close to Fyzie. Fyzie had always brought out a playful streak in Dad, and Dad had always enjoyed teasing him about his girlfriends. Fyzie was also the one who sat with him every day, picking up the secrets of the goldsmith's craft.

Dad shot me a look, and I got up to go, leaving him to undo the damage. I had had a shock, and was frankly frightened by what I had seen. It was like a glimpse of my own self at my manic worst. I had slunk away back to my room.

I turned off the Churchill-Roosevelt Highway and drove into the parking lot at the other end of UWI, near the library. All of a sudden I felt transported back in time to my UWI days, into a world of sanity. I locked all the ghosts inside the car, and climbed the stairs to the top floor of the Arts Building to Sollo's office.

Sollo and I first went around the corner from his office and made ourselves some tea, reaching inside the fridge to get the tin of evaporated milk to top it up with. Then back to the good old days, Sollo behind his desk, and me on the other side. Shutters open, letting in the daylight.

'So I was wondering if there were any openings for someone to teach linguistics at St Augustine,' I ended, a bit lamely. I hadn't even taken the time to find out how UWI posts were advertised.

Sollo tried with all his might to do some magic. He had been my advisor for my undergraduate thesis, my first foray into Bhojpuri, and he did feel the linguistics department should have someone with a window open to the Bhojpuri scene in Trinidad. And he would have welcomed a Trinidadian, an old student, for the job. The department had been depending on academics sent by the Indian government, new migrants with their own adjustment problems. And they hadn't sent any linguists.

So Sollo played his ace.

'Well, I'm due for a sabbatical any time I want it. I can get you a year here if you're willing to take that. But after that I don't know. I'm thinking of moving on anyway.'

And with that grand gesture Sollo put me right in the dock. How badly did I want to be in Trinidad?

My first reaction was that it wasn't the same as a real appointment. But then I saw that that wasn't fair. If what

I wanted was a career in Trinidad and all that went with it, I should have jumped at Sollo's offer.

Sollo saw me hesitate. 'You're wondering why I'm so eager to move on.'

'No,' I mumbled. 'Not you. I was wondering about myself.'

'Well, you aren't the only person in this place programmed to go abroad,' he continued. 'All of us in Trinidad came from somewhere else.'

I remembered that Sollo was a sailor. 'It's the sea,' I said softly.

'The sea,' he mused. 'All that salt water behind us. It turns us into transients.'

And on that note we repaired to the Senior Common Room where I was to meet up again with Rosa. Sollo went off to play billiards, and I went off to get myself a bottle of Carib beer. Then I sat down in the garden and emptied my mind, and turned my gaze inward.

My thoughts drifted off to my first day as a student at UWI, moving blindly in a benighted group of new students looking around for a particular room. Paperwork, as we were signed up for different courses. The hugeness of the library building.

The SCR, out of bounds, unknown.

The shock of the change from a school environment to the vastness, so it seemed then, of a university campus. Large male lecturers in place of the female teachers we had had in school. The whole class being spoken to only in French by the lecturer, a foreigner.

But most of all I remembered the thought that kept recurring in my head that day: hold on to this moment, girl, tomorrow the fog will clear and the place will look so normal! You will never get another chance to see the place with these eyes, everything new and fresh. Remember all of this.

And then when I looked up I was back in the SCR and Rosa was sitting across the table from me.

Today we would travel back in time together to the day Deeda and her jahaji sisters and brothers first arrived at Esperanza Estate.

'Haan, bhaiya, humni sab ke bolal gol banaai ke baithbe, ta khaika meeli. Ta sab log uth ke gail. Ba hum chaari ohr taakat rahli.'

Yes, bhaiya, they told us all to go and sit in a circle, that they were going to feed us. So everyone got up and went. But I stayed back, looking all around me.

A big building with a tall, tall chimney. That was the moulin, the sugar mill, where they crushed the cane to take out the juice.

Some goras were standing about with red faces. Mules, buffaloes.

A line of barracks. Coolie lines, they were calling it.

And ganna, sugarcane, all around, fields starting to flower with cane arrows. In Trinidad they called it ketaari.

Indians and some kirwals, black Creoles. They had said there would be more than a hundred and twenty people working on the estate in crop time.

Then Sunnariya was calling me to come and sit down. One of the goras was trying to talk to us.

'Manzhé, bon djyé, ou pa vlé manzhé?'

They said he was one of the overseers. Manzhé?

'Manzhé,' he said again, and he lifted up one of the thariyas we were supposed to eat in.

Langoor Mamoo was the first to use his brain. Maanjey! Bartan maanjey! Wash the dishes! The gora wanted us to wash the thariyas first. And he picked up his thariya and went to one side to wash it from the barrel of water, dipping it out with the copper lota. Then some of the others went after him and started washing their thariyas and soon everybody had washed their thariya and come back to squat in a circle, watching the overseer. What now?

The overseer's red face got redder. 'Mwen dji manzhé!' And he brought his fingers to his mouth. We kept watching him. Then he whirled around, looking for someone: 'Ki koté i yé, Beharry?' he shouted to the whole yard.

Then an Indian by the name of Beharry, a longtimer on the estate, heard his name and came quickly from inside the moulin. Manzhé, he told us, was the French Creole word that meant 'eat'.

And so we ate our first food on Esperanza Estate.

I asked Beharry if all the goras talked like that in Trinidad.

On this estate mostly yes, he said. Most of the overseers' families had come from an island called Martinique, where there were sugar estates and people talked like this. Some time back in Trinidad they had kept the kirwals as gulaams, slaves, on these same estates, and they had used this Creole to talk to them. Sometimes they had trouble remembering that we were not their slaves, so I should be careful of the overseers. Especially that one in front of us. He had a habit of interfering with women.

When they took us to the barracks I was surprised to see that one of the barrack huts had a karailli vine, a bitter gourd vine, growing on one side of it, with a few karaillis that had turned yellow, ripe. I picked one and chewed on a sweet red seed inside. Yes, it was really karailli.

Karailli! Here in Trinidad! So we were not the first ones to think of bringing seeds from home. I decided that Kalloo and I would stay there, in the barrack hut with the karailli vine next *to it.*

Inside the barracks they had benches for us to sleep on, made of wood and covered with jute cloth. Like beds. They didn't want us sleeping on the floor. They were afraid the dampness wouldn't agree with us.

Sunnariya did not want to go and stay with her father and brothers. They were single men, she said, and she was an adult. So she decided to stay in the same barrack room as me and Kalloo.

This time Mukoon Singh did not ask her to come and eat with him in his quarters. He did something else: since we would all be buying food to cook from our own earnings now, he said he and the two boys would come and eat with us in our barracks, and help out with the expenses from their wages. Sunnariya and I would have to cook for the six of us. And we said all right.

It was a good thing we had reached in November. The work wasn't so heavy, mostly weeding. The cane was already arrowing, almost ready to cut. It was just a few more weeks till crop time. January, they said. We would be cutting the cane after the New Year.

So we had a chance to look about and get accustomed to the place.

They had taken three of the buffaloes we had brought on the Godavari, so Langoor Mamoo went and told Beharry that he knew how to look after buffaloes, that he had been minding these same buffaloes on the boat. So after that, he and Kalloo and some of the other children used to mind the buffaloes together, cutting grass to give them, and milking them.

It was a rule that small children could not go and work in the fields during crop time. They had to stay back. Their mothers had to leave them with the khelauni, the child-minder, and come and pick them up after their work shift.

So where was the khelauni, we asked.

Well, her time on Esperanza Estate had expired. And as it was a slack season, they hadn't bothered to take a new one yet. Children used to sit and watch their mothers and help out a little bit. Besides, they hardly had any small children on the estate. Who had been minding the children on the boat?

We stayed quiet. There hadn't been any work for us on the boat, so we hadn't needed a khelauni as such. I looked at Beharry as if to ask how he didn't know that, but he didn't look back. He was only translating what the overseer was saying.

Then I realized why he was not paying me any mind. So I stayed quiet, waited.

'Khelauni ta Janaki-didi rahalin, Faizabad-wali! Laykan ke ohi posat rahalen!'

Jaitoon's voice! The khelauni was Janaki-didi, from Faizabad. She is the one who used to look after the children.

Nobody said anything different. Many people quietly nodded. Janaki-didi had suddenly begun to look old, after little Ramlal had died on the boat, and she didn't look as though she could manage heavy estate work. Besides, she was a sonaarin, a goldsmith by caste. She had most probably never gone into a field in her whole life.

So Janaki the sonaarin was settled. Her two sons would work in the fields, and she would mind the small children during the day.

After some time, Heera Singh and Houri Singh didn't want to come to eat with Sunnariya and me. They preferred to take their food with the other single men. But every night Mukoon Singh came, and he would talk to Sunnariya, in their Khari Boli, and he would talk to Kalloo. And that was good. The child had been running wild on the boat with Langoor Mamoo, and picking up what all bad habits. Mukoon Singh would straighten him out.

And most nights he would go back after eating, and sit with the moonsie, and they would talk, and the moonsie would write down some of the things they were saying. He had kept a book for that. Sometimes some of the other men would come to him, just like on the boat, and he and the moonsie would help them decide what to do.

And then in the middle of December the season changed. The clouds were gone, and cool breezes started to blow. The cane was full of arrows, and everybody was beginning to feel a new current in the air. Crop time was coming.

They got all of us together and divided us up into groups and assigned the work. Our group had ten people: seven men, and the rest were Sunnariya and me and one old-timer, a manrajin named Acchamma. A manrajin was a woman who had sailed from Madras. The men would cut, and we would strip off the leaves from the cane, clean the cane and make it into bundles, all the same size. Then the men would carry the bundles to the edge of the field so that the carts could pick them up and take them for weighing.

All that work for the day was a 'task'. The sardaar, the team leader, showed each group their boundary marks: each group would have a whole acre of cane field to cut. We would line up and get our pay every fortnight when they set up the pay desk.

They asked us to make sure nobody was in the cane fields and see that the children were with us all the time for the next two or three days. And then, a few days into the New Year, one night the whole sky was on fire.

All of us came out to watch the first cane field burning, and to hear the crackling noise as the cane leaves caught fire and burned. The children were running around trying to catch the long pieces of soot flying in the air.

Next morning the cutting would have to start.

Then Beharry, the old-timer, made a small fire near the barracks and went and got some salt and karwa teil, mustard oil, from his barracks. Then one by one he made us rub the oil on our hands with the salt and hold our hands over the fire to bake on a tough skin. Tomorrow we would be holding cutlasses, or stripping off the leaves from the cane. If we didn't get our hands tough tonight, the cutlass would leave blisters tomorrow, and the cane leaves would cut up our skin.

Sunnariya and I went back to the barracks and cleaned some rice to boil next morning for the two of us and Mukoon Singh. Each one of us would take a calabash with rice and salt, and a big calabash full of water. First we would drink the water when we got thirsty, then after some time, we would eat the rice.

No days off till crop finish!

Four o'clock in the dark we would have to wake up. Better go to sleep early.

The men stayed at the fire, and Langoor Mamoo went and got his dholak. Chirag Ali and his brother brought their tassas. A few kirwals on the estate, who were married to manrajins, brought out bongo drums and kept them company. Beharry was going to teach them a new song.

As we closed our eyes that night we could hear the men outside still singing around the fire, with dholaks and tassas and bongos playing. We floated off like we used to at night on the boat, with the words of the song they were singing outside lapping like little waves against the barrack walls:

> *Chaar bajey uthey gulaambar,*
> *Ghar-ghar thokey waari,*
> *Utho, bhaiya, kaapi banaao,*
> *Kaam par ho taiyaari!*

> Four o'clock the overseer wakes,
> He knocks on every quarter,
> Wake up, bhaiya, go and make coffee,
> Time to work, get ready!

But that night I hardly slept at all. I kept waking up and wondering if it wasn't time to go already. So before the overseer came next morning I was already boiling the rice for Sunnariya, Mukoon Singh and myself. Then I woke Sunnariya and Kalloo, and we filled up the three calabashes and waited.

Four o'clock. Line up outside.

Sunnariya took Kalloo and left him with Janaki the sonaarin. Then all of us went to the field.

> Haath me le-le cutliss-kurukh,
> Kanhey me le khodaari

> Take cutlass and crook in your hand,
> On shoulder hoe is steady.

Sunnariya, Acchamma and I had to work together. In the beginning Sunnariya and I stripped the leaves off the cane they had cut, and Acchamma had to make the bundles. I watched how she did it, so fast. She said it was the fourth year she was doing this work in Esperanza. Next set.

Seven o'clock. The sun was rising. Stop and drink some water.

> Boli bhar ke pani le-le,
> Line par ho taiyaari!

> Fill your calabash with water,
> Line up and get ready!

Go back and strip cane. Make bundles. Move on.

Ten o'clock. They told us to stop for breakfast. The rice. Take a rest.

> *Aawal sardaar, sarkaar ke naukariya.*
> *The team leader came, the big boss's servant.*

The sardaar got up from the khatiya, the stringed cot where he was sitting with the overseer, and came at us with a sour face. Go back to work! Don't skylark! Like a steady refrain. Strip cane. Make bundles. Move on.

My hands were beginning to hurt. I had scratches on my palms. I looked at Sunnariya. She didn't look up. Now she was the one making the bundles. She didn't say anything, but I could see her hands had scratches too from stripping the cane. I hoped we could hold on until four o'clock.

Noon. The sun was right up overhead. We were sweating, and the soot from the burned cane was all over our faces. They said we could stop and drink water.

Some people said their water was finished. One of the old-timers came and said he had extra water, but we would have to pay for it.

Now the work was going slow. Hands were hurting. Now Sunnariya was back to stripping the cane with Acchamma, and I was making the bundles.

> *Ketaari maangey cheekan-chaakan,*
> *Booka maangey bhaari*

> *They want the canes clean and smooth,*
> *They want the bundles heavy*

Two o'clock. Sit down and think. Head spinning now! Drink some water. This is too much, too much. Try again. Get up and keep working.

> *Hold on till four o'clock.*
> *Don't even look up now.*

>> *Das foot ke laggi le ke, bhaiya,*
>> *Naap le task: taiyaari!*

>> *Pick up cane stalks ten feet long, boy,*
>> *Weigh the task! Get ready!*

Four o'clock. Finished the task. The sardaar came and told us to go home. They would take the bundles in a cart to go and weigh the cane bundle by bundle on the spring balance.

But the words of the song were still echoing inside my head.

> *Aawal sardar, sarkaar ke naukariya.*
> *The team leader came, the big boss's servant.*

Go back to work! Don't skylark! Strip cane. Make bundles. Move on.

I put my hands over my ears. Bas! Enough! Let me cool my brains!

The three of us walked back to the barracks and Sunnariya and I went and just lay down on our beds for a good while and looked at the ceiling. Hands hurting bad. Backs hurting.

We were too tired to get up and wash our hands, wash our faces. Too tired to make tea. Too tired to go and get Kalloo. Later.

Then Sunnariya said her father would be coming after his work. So I got up quickly and had a wash, combed my hair, put the pallu of my sari back over my head, and started to make some tea. Then I sent Sunnariya to go and get Kalloo—

I paused the tape here, then on second thought, I pressed stop. I was tired too. If that was just the first day, I needed some strength before I waded deeper into the Esperanza cane fields and found out how they managed after that.

Rosa went to the kitchen, and I followed her there. I think she was tired too. I had been stripping and cleaning the text for her all day, without a break, and she had been making the bundles.

The song Deeda was singing kept running in my mind like a rogue tape. If I had a jingle like that haunting me, taunting me all day in the hot sun, I think I would go stark staring mad.

'I want to meet this old lady,' I heard Rosa saying. 'I want to see her. I don't care if I can't talk to her.'

'I'll tell you everything she says,' I said uncertainly. 'But you will have to put up with the two of us talking in Bhojpuri.' I remembered how I had felt hearing Ajie and Nana speak over my head in Bhojpuri when I was a child. Deliberately excluded.

'All this time I've been hearing her speak in Bhojpuri on the tapes,' she said. 'You think I can't listen to her face to face? I know she wouldn't be doing it to cut me out.'

I turned to stare at Rosa, my eyes widening. She smiled.

Today I made the tea for both of us, and Rosa went and got the mugs, the milk and the sugar. I took my mug from Rosa and did something that wasn't like me at all. Normally I didn't take any sugar in my tea. But after all the hard work of the day, this evening I put three spoons of sugar into my tea and stirred.

Then I remembered that Mukoon Singh was going to come for his tea any minute now. I sat up straight and looked out the window, and waited.

MAGNETIC NORTH

I WAS SITTING ON MY FATHER'S MORRIS CHAIR SOLVING a crossword puzzle when the postman came. Then Kojo passed by and dropped a letter into my lap.

My address on it was given as Department of Linguistics, Frieze Building, University of Michigan, Ann Arbor. The department office had put a line in ink through the typed address and scrawled my Trinidad address to the left by hand. Please forward!

The sender's name was printed on the top left. The American Institute of Indian Studies.

My advisor in Michigan had encouraged me to apply to AIIS for a grant to go to India and look at Bhojpuri from that end. They had never given a grant to a non-American before, but he thought I ought to try my luck anyway. He had heard that they were thinking of changing that rule.

I tore open the letter.

When you don't really want something too desperately, when you don't care one way or the other how things pan out, that is when the wave of luck lifts you and carries you all the way to the shore. True enough:

they had never before given a travel grant to a non-American. I was going to be the first.

Just the airfare, Detroit–Delhi–Detroit, and the travel in India. The rest of the expenses I would have to manage myself. Not a problem.

I rushed to my manual typewriter and hammered out a letter of acceptance, and gave it to Kojo to post.

Trinidad was now on countdown.

I still remember my parents' faces when I gave them the news. Another academic coup for them to crow about! Pride!

An end to my worrying presence in Trinidad. I would be back in a larger playing field where they would not have to see late nights and 'all kind of dog and cat' in my life. Relief.

A looming realization that their days with me might be at an end, that this might be a one-way ticket north and onward. A sense of loss; they were staring at an old age stretching on and on before them without one of the two creatures who had maximally shaped their lives together.

This was my cue to reach out and mend fences with Ajie. I had been keeping some distance from her since the day she had let fly at me, but I couldn't let things hang indefinitely, or they would pass a point of no return. So I went with letter in hand and told her my big news.

As I told her I could feel her let out the breath she had been holding for the last few days. The guarded look in her eyes began to soften. I was back on track. India! The fantasy world we shared was glowing brightly again. I held her hands and looked into her eyes, willing her to smile. An old woman's face looked back at me. A light that had been there before was off.

Suddenly I remembered I also had a date with Deeda. I had promised to let her know if I would be going to India. I also wanted to know what she thought of me leaving Trinidad, as she had left India.

So I got ready to drive to Orange Valley that morning and look her up. My mind was aswarm with all the things that had been worrying me all this time in Trinidad. I was obsessed with the premonition that this trip to India was the start of my exit from Trinidad for good, that if I went to India now I would end up spending my life there, as Deeda had spent hers in Trinidad.

> *Kaa hoi sonawa, ho, kaa hoi chandiya?*
> *Humra ke chaahi, Maiya, tohri-hi godiya!*

What good is gold, oh, what good is silver?
All I want, Maiya, is only your lap!

It wasn't too late to change my mind. Deeda had been through this, too.

North by north-west I drove. North to St Mary's Junction, then west to Orange Valley, stopping at Deeda's house on stilts, a short distance from the sea.

Deeda was in her kitchen, cooking her lunch. Despite all her talk of liking modern conveniences, she still cooked on an old-fashioned chulha, an earthen fireplace.

A pot of dal was bubbling away on the chulha, surrounded by a few homegrown sour tomatoes, and a hunk of saltfish. I had never seen saltfish cooked like this before: simply roasted with the blackened tomatoes, to be pounded into the chokha, the grilled tomato chutney. I could smell the raw onions sliced for the chokha. And then when the tomatoes and saltfish were done I caught the sharper smell of mustard oil, garlic and pepper from the chhaunkh being fried to toss on top of them.

The north-facing window behind her head was open. I could see the mountains in the distance, and the sky behind her was an amazing cornflower blue. Like springtime.

And she was bubbling too.

So we sat at her little table with our plates of dal, rice and chokha, and I told her that I had just got news that I was going to India.

I think I must have been hoping that Deeda would put some brakes on me here, warn me that I should not close my options about coming back to Trinidad. That I shouldn't run away from home as she had done. But that is not what she did.

Instead Deeda got more excited than I had ever seen her before. She started telling me about her village in Basti, and about all the people in her life before, her parents, her mother-in-law, her husband, people who could not possibly be alive any more. Then she asked me if I knew where I would be going.

Not sure, I said. But somewhere around Basti. I had to check out the same places that the jahajis had come from, wherever I could arrange to go. And a place where they researched the languages of the area, where my advisor knew someone.

So for the rest of the time I sat and Deeda quizzed me on the details of my route to India. New York. Ann Arbor. Back to New York. Straight to Delhi. Onward by train to Lucknow. Then by car to the eastern districts of Uttar Pradesh.

She drank it all in and nodded. She had heard of most of these places and she remembered her train journey in India. Did they still have upper and lower bunks and ladders to climb, she wondered. Could you still lean out the window and buy things to eat from the station platform?

She asked me to come and see her again before I left Trinidad.

As I drove home from Deeda's house, the steel band on the car radio seemed to take on a faraway sound. Carnival fever was building, but it all seemed to be happening to somebody else.

I remembered what Rosa had said about seeing my life in a fresh light some time about now. The sun too was headed north, about to cross the equator. The migratory birds were also about to head back north.

The summons for me had come a few days early, that was all.

So when I went with Fyzie that evening I was conscious all the time that there was still some taping to be done. A few old people I was supposed to talk to. We didn't go to meet them that day, but the feeling was there, the feeling of countdown. Something had turned a corner and taken a new direction.

And it had to be on that very day that we stumbled into a rum shop in Chaguanas, known for its roast pork, and one of the men at the bar looked up from his glass, straight from Fyzie to me, and then back to Fyzie:

'Enjoy yuh Carnival, maan! But come Ash Wednesday, she gawn back to she husban' in America!'

Like I was just some white Miss-Tourist down from America for the Carnival, liming a hot Trini dude! I felt something snap.

'Yuh mudder ass!' I grabbed a chair and lunged at the man. He staggered to his feet. 'Who de fock—'

'Cool dong, sis, cool dong!' Fyzie grabbed me by the shoulders and pulled me backwards, held me tight.

'Ah go dig out he damn eye!'

'Put dong de chair!' Fyzie.

I smashed the chair down on a table. Wood splintered. A live current of anger surged through my hands.

'She maad, boy!' the man sputtered.

'An you siddong!' Fyzie. 'Come, sis, time to go.'

And Fyzie was behind me, steering me out to the car, opening the back door, pushing me inside and pressing my head down onto the seat. My pulse pounded in my ears.

The front door was opening and I heard Fyzie's voice again. 'Doan even lif yuh head till ah stop de car.'

I tried to sit up.

'Ah say keep yuh head dong!' Firmly. Gently.

The words of the man in the bar kept ringing in my head like an omen.

After that a sense of doom descended upon our relationship, the same kiss of death that makes a love affair impossibly sweet. We lived our days in a bright bubble where bad feelings had no place, and the two of us walked together in a daydream. Wondering if there was a way to keep the magic window of time open forever.

But as soon as I found myself alone the clock inside my head began ticking loudly again. Back to countdown. I had a journey to make, and that journey wasn't over.

And Fyzie was not going to give me a good clean fight that would clear the air and let me leave with an easy conscience. He was moving into the countdown phase as though I was being drawn away by an outside force, not by my own free will. And he was forgiving me even before I ran away.

I could have stopped myself, but I didn't. I was on a roll, doing something that had been scripted for me ever since I first knew myself. I was preparing to cross over to the big world. All my life I had imagined that when I got there I would find my way on my own. But now I knew that I wasn't alone.

There was someone very different from Fyzie waiting for me on the other shore.

A SMELL OF SUGAR

I REMEMBER THE AFTERNOON THEY BROUGHT MUKOON *Singh to our barracks. I had finished my work, and was home alone. Crop was over, and most of the cane fields were supposed to grow back from the ratoons, cane roots left in the soil. But we still had to replant some of the fields, and put manure.*

Heera Singh and Houri Singh carried Mukoon Singh in and laid him down on Sunnariya's bed. Mirgi bhail rahal, they said. He had had a seizure in the fields. He had opened his eyes afterwards and told the men not to take him to the hospital, but to his daughter's room in the barracks. He just needed to lie down.

He knew it would take him just a day to recover, and he didn't want to lose any time from work. If he stayed off work they would cut his pay, and he would have to borrow money to buy rations.

That was how problems had started for Ramsukh, the man who had brought the mango seeds. One day he had got fever, and he had stayed back from work. And they had cut his pay. Next day again he had missed work. And the day after that. And he was afraid to borrow money to pay for rations, didn't want to get into debt. So he had just gone back to work without eating, and then he had collapsed in the field, because he was too weak and hungry to work.

Then when he missed work again the next day the police came and took him to jail. They said he was a vagrant.

I didn't think Mukoon Singh was going to let them take him to jail so easily.

Then I heard Heera Singh's voice again. I didn't have to do anything, he said, just stay close by. If he needed water, just help him drink it. He wouldn't be able to get up by himself, not for some time. But he would mostly sleep. Could I manage until Sunnariya came back?

Of course! I said. Mukoon Singh was like my own family. Not to worry, I would look after him.

When they left I turned and took a look at him. His eyes were closed. I looked at his face for a good long while. He looked so much like Sunnariya! Then I thought he might feel better without his pagri. I went and touched it softly, carefully.

He mumbled something. He was not asleep. So I asked him if I should take off his pagri and keep it to one side. After a long gap he said, 'Haan.' Yes.

So I took it off and put it on the bed next to him, and went back to my work.

One of the buffaloes on the estate had had a calf and Langoor Mamoo had brought the first milk for us. The overseers didn't want the first milk, since it was bound to curdle when you boiled it. But we knew what to do with it.

So I was busy boiling down the buffalo's milk with sugar and ginger, watching it turn into big round curds with clear syrup all around. And outside the barracks, the whole estate smelt of the khandsaari sugar syrup boiling down in the vats inside the moulin.

It was like there was sugar in the air everywhere.

When the peynoose was ready I put out the fire and got up. Mukoon Singh must have heard me moving about, because he opened his eyes. He took a little while to remember where he was, and how he must have got to our barracks. I made a sign that he didn't have to explain anything, and then I asked him if he felt he could eat a little bit of the peynoose I had just made.

He smiled when he heard that, and said all right, but I would have to feed him with a spoon. Could I do that?

Of course! I put a little bit in a bowl and blew on it to cool it. It had just finished boiling, I said. It was still too hot to eat.

Then I sat down on the floor next to him and fed him slowly with a spoon —

When I was a child my father would sometimes get this same first milk, which he called collostrum milk, from a man he knew called Sirju, who had a herd of cows. He and Sirju had a relationship they could sort of take for granted. They didn't meet and do things together, but we had given him one of our German Shepherd pups to help him manage his cows. And he would send over collostrum milk from time to time, and Dad would boil it down in a huge pot and make peynoose for us.

Now I understood: Sirju's family and our family were jahajis. Our ancestors had come on the same boat from India. It was like being from the same caste, or better yet, the same gotra, clan. It cut across caste lines, and was a relationship you could take for granted.

Sunnariya came back later with Kalloo and saw her father lying there asleep. She stopped for a second, and then she realized what must have happened. She looked at me a moment to see if I was upset. Many people were wary of people with mirgi.

I told her that Heera Singh and Houri Singh had brought him earlier in the afternoon, and that they had said that he would

*not be able to get up for some time. We would have to keep him
for the night. We could look after him better than the men in his
barracks.*

*The smell of sugar was still in the air everywhere. Kalloo
looked around the room and found the pot of peynoose, now cool
enough to eat. I gave him his own bowl and sent him outside to
eat it.*

*Sunnariya told me she had stayed back to talk to Janaki the
sonaarin. Janaki's older son was sick, and after what had happened
to Ramlal on the boat she was worried. It was fever again.*

*Then I remembered that Mukoon Singh had said something
about the estate hospital. I decided to go and check on Janaki-didi
myself.*

*Janaki-didi was in her barracks with her two sons. She was
so worried that she couldn't think about what to do.*

*Okay, I said, first thing, don't keep this thing to yourself.
What if it is something that needs a doctor? We should go to the
estate hospital. And I called Heera Singh to help us take him there.*

*When we got there the doctor checked him. I heard him telling
the compounder that the boy was 'malade'. That was a word we
understood. We used it ourselves: it meant sick enough to justify
leave from work.*

*The compounder told us the doctor wanted to keep the boy
in the estate hospital that night. He could go home the next day
if he was better. But we should go back to the barracks, he would
manage.*

*Next day the boy was the same. The doctor decided he should
go to the hospital in Piti Bourg, San Fernando. I was to go and
get Beharry to go with us.*

*So they made passes for Janaki-didi, her two sons, Beharry
and me to go to Piti Bourg. Sunnariya would see about Kalloo
and fill in as the khelauni while Janaki-didi was out.*

I went to check on Mukoon Singh before I left. He had gone back to work in the fields. I told him he should stay in our barracks room while I was out. I wasn't happy about leaving him alone.

He smiled, and thought about it for a while. I was the first person he had met who didn't want to leave him alone, he said. It would take him some time to get accustomed to that. Then he waved at me, with his eyes shining like they had that night on the boat. I was going out of the estate.

Out of the estate!

As I got ready to go out of the gate I suddenly realized that this was really the first time I was going out of Esperanza Estate. I knew nothing else about Trinidad. We hadn't even got a glimpse of Trinidad when we first came to the estate. We could almost see the Esperanza cane fields when we got off the jetty at Goodrich Bay. I was still in India, in a way, still speaking the same language, but living in a different Indian village. I was just a migrant from Basti who had drifted a bit further away from home, living with other purabiya migrants.

The estate was big, but it was like a jail. If they caught me breaking bounds without a pass, the police would come and arrest me straight away, without any questions. I tied my pass carefully in a knot in one corner of my orhni and tied that edge around my waist, and draped the other end over my head. I was ready to go.

The five of us went to Savonetta Junction to catch the train to Piti Bourg. Savonetta Junction was just a whistle stop, so we had to be brisk.

We took the train to King's Wharf station in Piti Bourg and walked the rest of the way to the hospital. The hospital was the biggest building I had seen in my whole life. We went in there and waited for some time, and showed the papers from the estate doctor, and they admitted Janaki-didi's boy and put him in a bed. The doctor wasn't there as yet.

Then Beharry and I left the others and went out of the hospital. We didn't want to waste time just waiting there. Beharry wanted to see Piti Bourg. He said we could come back in a little while and find out what to do after the doctor had attended to the boy.

We walked out the gate and reached a wide street outside. First time outside Esperanza Estate! I checked to make sure I could feel my pass tied at my waist in the corner of my orhni.

We walked down Harris Promenade. We went the whole way down to Library Corner, trying not to stare too hard at all the people. Kirwals, mostly, black Creoles, and a few goras. Some Indians too, the men mostly dressed like goras, and the women wearing dresses with long skirts, and thin orhnis. Some of the women had on gold jewellery.

Then Beharry said he wanted to go further. He had heard that there was a school that had come up for Indian children from the estates in Piti Bourg. At first people used to call it the Coolie School, but now they were calling it Grant School. The school was on the corner of Carib Street and Coffee Street. We would see a big samaan tree in front of it. He had heard that they once used to hold classes under the tree.

We reached the place and saw a few big samaan trees on the corner, like dark green umbrellas, more than double the height of the building behind them, and twice as wide. That building must be the school, we thought. Slightly further on from the school and up a little hill was another building. People told us it was called Susamachar Church, and it was for Indians.

Good-news church?

We looked from outside for a little while, standing on the other side of Coffee Street. Beharry wanted to go closer and see the place, but I was not ready to cross the road. In Esperanza we had learned to stay far from the goras.

Some Indian people on the road told us that Canadian missionaries had built the church and the school.

Who were these missionaries? I asked.

White people, they told us, some kind of Christian. They wanted Indians to become Christian like them. They were riding horses and going all over the place from estate to estate and encouraging Indian people to become Christians. And they were building schools for the children.

We stood a while talking to them. On the roadside, in Piti Bourg! Like free people! Then Beharry gave me a signal: he was ready to go, he had seen the place. It was time to go back to the hospital to check if the doctor had come. But I kept wondering about these missionaries, and why they were concerned with us.

When we reached the hospital Janaki-didi told us the doctor had seen her son. We talked to one of the assistants. He told us not to worry, this was something they saw all the time with estate workers: dengué fever. The cane fields had a lot of mosquitoes, and this was what had caused the fever. They would have to keep the boy for a little time. Then they would send him back by himself when he was better. We should go back to the estate.

So the four of us went back to King's Wharf and took the train back, and reached Esperanza Estate the same day. To wait.

The smell of sugar was still thick in the air.

After a few weeks Janaki-didi's son came back, but he was still looking thin and weak. The fever was gone, but he was still malade. The doctor in the hospital had said that he shouldn't go back to work in the cane fields. They should look for some other kind of work that he could do.

So the compounder passed the word that Janaki-didi's family had been sonaars in India. And in a few days time a message came from the Boss of the estate that the boy should come and see him. His wife wanted somebody to make jewellery for her.

And that is how Janaki-didi's elder son started spending his days under the front steps of the big estate house with a hammer and some tools, beating silver to make jewellery for the Boss's wife.

And soon after that Janaki-didi opened up a little shop in the barracks area, to sell small things like matches, pins, salt and masalas. She kept the shop under a tree, and worked as a khelauni from there.

While Janaki-didi's boy was at Piti Bourg hospital he had met other Indians. Some of them were like him, patients sent from estates, and some were time-expired, free. And one of the things they talked about was the missionaries who were holding meetings in the estates and building schools for Indian children.

They were goras, yes, but they were not British, and not French Creole. They were from Canada, a different country. Besides, they could all speak Hindi, and only wanted to talk to us, he said, to the Indians in the barracks.

So one evening after work Janaki-didi's older son took Mukoon Singh with him to meet the missionaries, slipping out of Esperanza Estate without passes. And the first thing Mukoon Singh noticed about the missionaries was that they spoke the same Hindi as him. They didn't speak like the others in the barracks. He could talk to them easily.

Maybe it was the Hindi they spoke. Maybe it was a part of his bigger wish to put distance between himself and India. Maybe it was the chance to be seen as a serious part of a big group, doing something that used his book learning. Maybe it was just the good feeling of going out of the estate without permission, with nobody able to stop him.

But still he had always been the one to say that he was not afraid of goras. He had never liked them. He had always kept far from the overseers on the estate, and if he had to meet them he would look straight through them like they were not there at all. Why was he now interested in these missionaries?

Maybe it was his understanding that this was a new kind of current flowing, and he had to be a part of it. I never understood what he was thinking. But after a few weeks, Mukoon Singh came and told us that he and his family from now on were going to be Christians. Beharry too. And Janaki-didi and her family were also going to become Christians.

So one Sunday morning all of them got passes to leave the estate, and they went as a group to Dow Village, where a family of Indian Christians was using their house as a church for the time being. When Sunnariya came back she told me how they all got converted.

It was in Khari Boli, she said, like Baba and I speak. And a few parts were in English. We had to go and pledge in front of the missionary that we would be Christians from now on. And then all of us got Christian names. The men could keep their Indian name as a last name, and put the Christian name first.

You have a new name now? I asked her.

She waved the thought away, a flick of her wrist. Doesn't matter, she said. I am going to keep Sunnariya. And Janaki. And Baba is keeping Mukoon Singh.

And after that? What happened? I asked.

Oh, then they sprinkled water on all of us, and all of us got a piece of jawain ke roti, a piece of crisp roti with carom seeds in it, like parsad after a puja. And then all of us sang Christian bhajans together.

You have different bhajans?

Yes, one day I will take you to a prayer meeting, and you will hear, she said.

Go with her! I didn't look at her then, I looked out the window and decided to finish this talk. And after that? Anything else changed?

No-no, afterwards we just had a feast and came back to Esperanza.

I hadn't told her I wouldn't come, but I didn't want to go with them. I didn't see the reason to change myself. I never went and met these missionaries. I was not a part of the restlessness that had taken hold of Mukoon Singh, Beharry and Janaki-didi's son. They were talking about struggle, moving up, bettering themselves. I was happy with my life, as happy as I could be, seeing as I was still bound to an estate. But my time at Esperanza would not go on forever. And when I left the estate, in some time, I would be freer, and happier. I had Kalloo. I had Sunnariya. I had friends. And I was strong, and able to work. More than that, what did I want—

Why had we converted? That was something I tried and tried to get Nana to explain to me.

Where Mukoon Singh was concerned, he was vague. He thought he might have already been Christian in India, and that this was just a small denominational shift. Not dissimilar to the shift in dialect he would have been making to talk to the others in the barracks.

But it didn't make sense. How could someone like him have been Christian in nineteenth-century India? Why would a thakur have wanted to be Christian?

I asked Nana, then, why his father had become Christian. I was not too comfortable about the dissonance it created with other things Indian about us. We weren't white, after all, we were Indian. Why had we chosen to be different in this way?

Nana was imperturbable, and his reply always came pat: the caste system.

It was true that Nana was always very sarcastic to old brahmin men who tried to patronize him. He was always making fun of them, running circles around them in friendly arguments when they visited the shop.

But to me the caste system was something else. It was the little workshop behind our shop where the gold was smelted, milled, soldered, chiselled and electroplated gold-on-gold and the jewellery made. Where things they didn't even teach us in chemistry at school happened every day, things we discussed in the house using both the old Bhojpuri words as well as the modern scientific terms in English.

Every boy in our family, including my brother, had had to learn the basic trade. He had to be able, at least, to produce a number of taabeej, amulets, the first thing a boy was taught to make. The taabeej my brother had made were supposed to help cover the cost of his first year of medical school abroad.

We were still doing the caste trade we had done in India, I would say to Nana. So what was our problem with the caste system?

Nana would smile. He was in no hurry to win this argument. When you get older you will understand, he said.

And I did. Now I do. Nana's dream was to take his children into the middle class, and to take the next generation into the professions. Professions allied to goldsmithing at first: dentistry, chemistry, optics, metallurgy. Then later he had a bigger dream. The next generation would meet brahmins as equals on the brahmins' turf.

I had become a linguist. My brother was studying medicine in Scotland.

Nana had even sent his eldest son, Ajie's younger brother, to study medicine at the University of Edinburgh way back then. And he had returned and helped some of the others, including my father and his brothers and sisters, to go to Canada to university. But then he had died young.

So you could say Nana never shifted his sights far away from the Hindu fold.

It did cross my mind, now, that I was not the first in my line to get dragged into a northbound current. Mukoon Singh and Nana had both been there long before me. Both had sniffed the wind and decided that the way to the open waters lay due north. But there was also a strong countercurrent pulling them back to stay in place, a dogged pride that came from something very old. So they existed in a strange state of contradiction.

There was a fine line between an involuntary migrant and a focused immigrant. We were on the northern side of that line.

There was much that we were going to give up to get ahead, things that I, from my vantage point far to the north of that line, would not see the need to give up. In all my time in Ann Arbor I had never lost my Trinidadian accent. Ah, but I had always known my English was good. Imagine if it hadn't been. With my ears wide open to bright new sounds, would I have kept my old accent?

I was slowly beginning to appreciate how connected all my little struggles were with the larger struggle that enveloped my whole family.

BON BON

'NA-NA! HUM SAB NA MAANGI OHI KETAARI KHAAE! HUM sab maangila Bon Bon!'

No-no! We don't want to eat that cane! We want Bon Bon!

I could hear Sunnariya outside the barracks talking to Langoor Mamoo, laughing. She was talking like the other cane cutters talked now, the way people talked in Trinidad. She had been spending time with Janaki-didi and the children, and she had started talking the same way as the other children who spent more time together than with their families. She now only spoke Khari Boli in the evenings with her father.

Or when she was disturbed about something.

Bon Bon was a thick juicy kind of cane they had brought from Martinique. They didn't use it in the moulin to make sugar. Some of the overseers and the boss had their own patches of it behind their bungalows. Bon Bon cane was only for eating.

The only way to get this cane was to go and steal it from an overseer's yard. But why should that bother Langoor Mamoo? It would only make him more excited. All through, since the first day I had met him, he had been stealing things and giving them to the children. And sometimes even to us.

A whole year had passed since the first crop season. Now we were almost done with the second crop.

Most of us had stopped wearing saris. What we wore now were ghangris, long skirts, jhoolas, long blouses, and orhnis. We would tie one end of the orhni around our waists, and throw the other end over our heads. It didn't look too different from the saris we had had on before.

Some of the time-expired women who came in to work during the crop season used to go a step further: they would tie their orhnis only over their hair, and roll both ends around their juras, the buns they made in the back. They didn't cover their necks at all!

Some of the women had also started doing cutting work, and used to tie cutlasses at the waist to go into the fields, just like the men.

The moonsie had found a girl to marry, from the same caste, a Kayat, a scribe. She was on another estate, where her parents were indentured. A nau had made inquiries and found her, and they were going to get permission to have a sagaai. Then they would get married in three years' time.

Chirag Ali and Jaitoon were expecting a child.

Many people were also tying up without taking any help from the nau. Like Acchamma: she had run away from her husband in India, and found herself in Madras. Then when she reached Trinidad she got married again, because she said she didn't think she could manage by herself, without anyone at all. And she was not the only one.

And the men were happy for that. Most of them had come as moglasiyas, leaving their wives behind in India. They were thinking now that they didn't want to even consider making that trip back in the boat.

Some of the people in the barracks were also getting ready to do jarda, as they said in French Creole, to plant things for themselves in the cane rows between the new plants. Hardee, arooi or dasheen, and reheri ke dal, pigeon peas. Chowrai bhaaji,

with pink stems and green leaves, was growing like weeds
everywhere around the barracks, and we cooked it almost every
day like spinach. Dal, bhaat, bhaaji: that was our everyday
food, especially at lunch. Dal, boiled rice and chowrai bhaaji.

Mukoon Singh had started doing a lot of extra work for the
missionaries. They had been looking out for people like him, who
were from India and spoke the same Hindi as them. They wanted
leaders, they said, in every village, on every estate, who had
respect and could become catechists. They also wanted people
like him to be sitting with them at the pay desk every fortnight,
when they waited and took a share of what Christian Indians
were earning from cutting cane.

We never take money from the Church, he would say. We
help to pay for the Church.

But it didn't look so to me. All the schools, and the churches,
they were not coming out of this money. So why were they making
all these poor cane cutters give them money every fortnight? What
did they want with these people?

I never said this to Mukoon Singh. Now he was a part of
it too. Most evenings he would disappear after eating and go to
meetings outside the estate. And the evenings he didn't go out of
the estate he would sit with the moonsie. Together they would
pore over the books Mukoon Singh brought back from the
missionaries. The books were all in Khari Boli, which they both
spoke and understood, but were not too good at reading. Earlier
they both used a running-hand kind of writing in their notebooks,
without a line on top — Kaithi — something that Kayats had always
used to write down testimony in the law courts.

That would have to change. They would have to shift to the
Devanagari script that the brahmins used.

As for me, I was happy. Every evening the four of us,
Sunnariya, Mukoon Singh, Kalloo and I, would be together for

some time in our barracks, and I had started looking for ways to cook things I used to like back home.

But the best thing for me was the way Sunnariya was looking happy again, mixing with the children, talking the same language as them, and smiling. Mukoon Singh had said that she had begun to behave like an older woman after her mother had died, back in Aligarh. That was when she had started covering her head and hiding all her hair, and being strict about everything. Now I could see her easing up. Sunnariya was like a playful child again.

People must have been wondering about Mukoon Singh and me, how two people could meet every day and eat together and not think about taking it further. In fact, I myself was wondering. But Mukoon Singh hadn't definitely asked me as yet. He just kept looking at me as if he was waiting for something. He didn't want to push me.

I think he might have wanted to see if I was going to be a Christian too. If I would do it by myself. He wasn't going to pressure me. Other people, yes, he would pressure them. But he could see I had a different feeling about what was happening. Even if I never said anything.

So I wondered if he was waiting for me to convert.

I don't think he was worrying that I was not a thakur like him. He and I had passed beyond things like that.

He didn't seem to care about what other people thought. There was nobody on the estate brave enough to face Mukoon Singh and ask him a question about how he was living his life. And nobody was brave enough to think that I might be free, and in a position to consider any other man.

Better to take time and think, he used to say. We never could say what tests were waiting for us on the road ahead.

That day the work was over, and I had stayed back in the barracks to cook. Mukoon Singh had said that he would not be coming to eat that night, but I still had to make food for Sunnariya and Kalloo.

I didn't need Sunnariya to help me, so she went to meet Janaki-didi. This was a time when Janaki-didi was happy for a little bit of extra help, since many of the mothers didn't come to pick up their children right after work. They were too tired. Sunnariya used to make up stories with the children, and get them to try to guess what was going to happen next. She would start the story, and they would add to it after that.

Sunnariya had taken some of the children and gone to see if they could find Langoor Mamoo, to ask if he had managed to get the cane they wanted. She knew a place they could go with it, and she would show them how to peel it with their teeth.

So I was by myself, and things were very quiet. Too quiet, I thought. But then I realized that it could just be because Kalloo had not come back as yet. Anyhow, he was getting bigger, he would be staying out by himself more and more, I thought. And Sunnariya was with friends.

But it was getting a bit late. The sun would go down soon. Where was Kalloo? And where was Sunnariya?

Now I was starting to get worried.

I looked out the door. Kalloo was coming running, looking frightened.

He saw me and shouted: Come fast! Sunnariya is in trouble. One of the children she went with came back crying, and saying to send Deeda. Come fast!

I dropped everything and ran behind him. My heart was pounding. What kind of trouble? Sunnariya was not a child like that.

The cane near the barracks was still up. We ran through one of the cane traces where they had gone, towards a stand of bamboo, down towards the river. Then we turned and ran on the track next to the river.

And then from far away I saw Sunnariya walking up to us. Her orhni was off her head, her clothes were dirty, and her eyes had a bright crazy look.

I ran up to her and put my arms around her.

She pushed me away. No-no. The other children! Find the other children! They are lost!

What about you? I asked.

Don't waste time! she shouted. Go and get the children!

But Kalloo had already run off to find the two remaining children, and to get others to help. I myself wanted to take Sunnariya home. I tried to cover her head with the orhni, but she didn't pay me any mind. She was walking fast to get back to the barracks.

And then we went inside and she rushed to pick up a lota and started washing herself. Then she tore off her skirt and threw it aside. I ran and got my other skirt for her.

What happened? I asked. Tell me!

Where are the children? she started shouting at me. Go and find them!

Did something happen to you?

Yes!

What? Are you all right?

Find the children! They are in the cane fields!

My eyes fell on the skirt she had just thrown off. It was dirty. It had thorns in it, from a bush. I couldn't see anything else. Who had attacked her?

But she had told me to find the children. I went. At least I knew she was alive.

Back into the same cane fields. I don't know what told me I was safe there alone after what must have happened. But I was older, and older women don't interest men who attack young girls. So I ran. And I looked. And I looked.

And when I had given up and was coming back, Kalloo met me. The children had gone running to the wrong barracks, but the people there had taken them to Janaki-didi. They were crying. They had thought Sunnariya was dead.

Then I turned a corner and saw Sunnariya. She was coming back into the same cane fields to look for the children. The look in her eyes was something I will never forget. As if she didn't care any more. As if there was nothing worse that could happen to her now.

I caught hold of her and took her back to the barracks and closed the door.

She began to shake. But she didn't cry. I waited for her to tell me.

But I never found out what happened. Every time she told me it was a different story. The only thing they all had in common was the beginning:

One of the overseers, the same one who had tried to talk to us the first day, was drunk, and had come walking in the cane traces and found her sitting with the children eating the cane. He could see it was not cane from the fields, but from one of the overseers' yards. He called her a volè, a thief, and said that she would have to pay.

He had told her to come with him, and she had stared him in his face and refused to move.

Then he had grabbed her hand and tried to pull her. And one of the children had tried to hit him with a cane stalk.

Then he had hit the child, and Sunnariya had told her to run, run and get Deeda!

And they had all run!

The first time she told me the story, she said he had a knife. Next time he had thrown her into a thorn bush.

Another time she told me that when he was on top of her, holding her throat, and she was about to black out, she had made one last effort and focused her eyes over his shoulder and said: 'Deeda! Aa gayi!' Deeda, you're here!

And that he had jumped off her in fright, looking over his shoulder. And then she had run away.

Or that he was so drunk that he couldn't really do anything.

And then she put on a brave smile and said that she thought maybe he had changed his mind in the end, and hadn't wanted to do anything to her. That he had said so.

And my heart broke.

She was building back the walls around herself, saving whatever was left.

But I could not see any blood. It did not look as if the overseer had managed to rape her.

And I made her lie down, and I let her talk, all the stories she wanted to tell, I let her talk them all out of her mind until she was tired, and then she fell asleep. She fell asleep to dream about what had really happened, because she was tossing and turning, and mumbling in her sleep.

All I knew was that I had to stay there and watch over her sleep. Stay there so that she would know that she was not alone.

Stay there and wait for her father.

SACRIFICE

WHEN HE CAME BACK THAT NIGHT IT WAS ALMOST
midnight. He came straight to our barracks and called to me
from outside. I opened the door so that he could come in.

He had heard something from the men in the barracks,
something vague. About children crying. About Sunnariya coming
back with her orhni not properly covering her head, walking fast,
looking strange. About all of us running helter-skelter in the cane
traces. But nobody in the Esperanza barracks would dare to try
and molest Sunnariya.

So when he came in he was curious. But not alarmed.

I told him everything at one go, standing right there in the
doorway.

About the overseer, the same one as on our first day.

About how she had come back and washed herself over and
over again.

About how her mind had bent, so that she couldn't remember
straight.

About how he might have had a knife.

About how he might have tried to strangle her.

But the most important thing, I said in the end, was that she
was safe. The danger was over. And I couldn't see any blood.
She had not been raped, as far as I could make out.

As he listened, his eyes began to gleam.

And then suddenly he burst into tears, and for the first time in all our time together he stumbled forward and threw his arms around me, and he buried his head in my neck and sobbed.

At first he cried in relief, for all he might have lost, but had not. Sunnariya was there in the corner, fast asleep.

He cried in outrage, as a man who was now just a coolie, a proud man who was expected to sit by and let things like this happen to the women in his barracks, to his own daughter.

And I could sense that he was crying for everything he was about to lose, for the life we had both wanted together, which we could never have now.

Then he stepped back and wiped his eyes. He took a long look at Sunnariya sleeping there. And his eyes got a set faraway look. He slowly took off the pagri from his head and gently put it down next to Sunnariya.

I will take this back from you, he told the sleeping girl, when I bring back your honour.

He went to the door and picked up his cutlass, and checked the blade to see that it was sharp.

And then he quietly slipped out the door and into the night. Nobody stopped him.

The other cane cutters knew, the guards on the estate knew, everyone who was Indian knew that he would come like this in the middle of the night to take badla, revenge. So they had quietly slipped away, disappeared. They had given him all the space he needed to do what he had to do. The whole estate was as quiet as a grave.

He walked towards the overseer's bungalows. He knew the exact place: it was the bungalow at the edge of the group with a big patch of Bon Bon cane to one side. There was a light still shining in one room.

He went straight to that bungalow without even trying to hide. The door opened easily, and he walked inside.

The overseer was awake, and one of his Indian servants was with him, pouring him a drink. Mukoon Singh told the servant to tell the overseer who he was, and that he had come to make sure that the overseer would never again attack any woman as he had attacked Sunnariya. Then he told the servant to go, to leave the room and go back to the barracks.

Now Mukoon Singh and the overseer were alone.

The execution did not take long. Mukoon Singh walked straight back to the barracks with blood on the cutlass blade. He had left the overseer dead on the floor of his bungalow, his throat slit from ear to ear as if he were a goat for sacrifice. Just an animal, not a man at all.

Mukoon Singh opened the door to our barrack room and came back inside. He walked straight up to Sunnariya. He took some of the overseer's blood off the cutlass with his finger, and made a tika on her forehead. She woke up and opened her eyes, surprised.

But I could see that she understood. She knew her father. And she knew that the overseer was dead.

Then he looked at me. She cannot remain like this, single, he said. She needs a husband to protect her. I have let this wait too long.

And he reached into his waistband and took out all the money he had been saving from his wages. Here, he said. This is for her marriage. Go to Janaki-didi and fix her marriage with the older boy. He is a good boy, and he will be able to earn and look after her. And Janaki-didi will understand. She is our jahaji, and a Christian. She will not refuse us.

He stood and looked at me for a long time. His eyes were gleaming again, but this time he did not let the tears flow.

And then he reached out with one hand and touched my face. This is not the end, he said. Wait for me. I will come back for you.

And he picked up his pagri and turned and vanished into the night –

It is a scene I can so easily conjure from my childhood memories. I know this story well.

A February night on Esperanza Estate. A sickle moon. Some of the cane is still standing, but almost half of the crop is cut. The fields near the overseers' bungalows are desolate, burned and hacked to pieces. If you walked towards the overseers' bungalows you would be able to see forever into the distance. The future is not hidden. But that makes no difference. What has to happen will happen.

A wronged thakur in a room in the coolie barracks removes his pagri and prepares for his own doom, stirred by a terrible sense of duty born out of Rajput chivalry.

He walks out into the night with his cutlass in hand, more certain of what he is about to do than he has ever been about anything in his life up to now. He has to kill a man, and destroy his own future in the process. He has no choice.

Afterwards he vanished into the same cane traces where Sunnariya had gone with her friends. But his story did not end. Because they could not catch him. He had escaped.

And he became the stuff of legend. He would appear suddenly out of a cane field, and ask a poor ahir for some of the milk he had just milked from his buffalo. Or he would appear at a farmer's hut after dark, and be asked to share the evening meal with the family.

Many Indians saw him, but no one reported him.

The only white people he was in touch with were the missionaries.

At first everyone on the estate was told that he would be caught and hanged for murder. But then months went by, turning into years, and the police failed to catch him. Now this was becoming a problem. He was evolving into a hero. So in the end, after a rash of copycat dacoities in the area, the government decided to negotiate with him through the missionaries.

The missionaries managed to persuade the colonial government to give up their demand that he be hanged for murder. They cited the provocation: his daughter had been attacked by the man he had killed.

They also reminded the colonial government that they were under a legal obligation to respect the immigrants' culture. That had been one of the key conditions of the indentureship scheme. That obligation did not end, they said, with simply leaving the Indians' children to grow up without any schools to go to. There were other more positive ways in which they were supposed to respect the Indians' culture. For instance, they were to understand an Indian father's obligation to look after his daughter when the estate and the government had failed to do so.

And the colonial government was conscious that it had a bad track record in terms of not having done enough to curb the excesses committed against the Indians by the estates, which all too often seemed to overlook the fact that the Indians were not their slaves.

There had already been an incident, a few years earlier, where police and British Army soldiers had opened fire on Indians leading a Hosay procession of tadjahs through San Fernando, commemorating the martyrdom of Hussein, grandson of the Prophet Muhammad. More than a hundred innocent pilgrims had lost their lives. Further mishandling of the law and order situation like that would invite a parliamentary enquiry. The colonial government was ultimately answerable to the British Home Office.

But the government could not simply let Mukoon Singh go; that would be sending the wrong message altogether to the community.

In fact, they did not want him around in Trinidad at all.

So the negotiation went on between the government and the missionaries to arrive at the terms under which Mukoon Singh would agree to surrender. And slowly the deal was struck.

Mukoon Singh would have to agree to the one sentence that, for him of all people, was tantamount to death by hanging.

Repatriation to India.

FAST-FORWARD

W HEN KOJO DROPPED A LETTER INTO MY LAP THIS TIME
I wasn't surprised. I was sitting in Dad's Morris chair
again, sharpening my mind for the day on a crossword.
Kojo continued toward the kitchen to get himself some
tea. I could hear his voice in the background trying to
chat up the maid.

This was a letter I had been expecting. It was from
someone who knew my address in Trinidad, and who
even knew some of my professors in Ann Arbor. I had
written to him briefly telling him that I had got an AIIS
grant to go to India, but he would have found out about
it anyway. He was a student my Sanskrit professor
always looked forward to meeting at functions held by
the Indian community in Ann Arbor, to get a different
take on the news out of India.

Nishant. There are a lot of names in Sanskrit that
mean the sun, and his was one of them: the end of the
night. Or more loosely translated, the early morning sun.

Far, far away, but still the centre of our planetary
system.

I opened the letter and read the brief scrawled
message. I was not to worry about arrangements for

my trip to India. His sister was in Delhi and his father was based in Lucknow. He would get in touch with them and make arrangements for me to be met at Delhi airport, and his sister would take me to get my train tickets to and from Lucknow. His father would also arrange for me to join a Public Works Department road inspection tour from headquarters in Lucknow to the eastern districts.

So when was I coming back to Ann Arbor?

Now the sense of countdown accelerated. I quickly wrote out a reply that I was almost done with my recordings and transcriptions and was winding up in Trinidad. I would let him know my arrival date and flight as soon as I had made the bookings.

Then I picked up the phone and called Dylan's mother, my travel agent, and asked her about flights. She said she would get back to me later when it was all confirmed and she would bring me the ticket when it was ready.

I had hitched my wagon to a comet.

I got busy, making lists of all that was left to be done, and who else I had to meet before I departed on the jet stream.

Time to take Sheila up on her invitation to go for a swim at the Sevilla Club pool.

Sevilla Club...

My mother had always shunned what were once whites-only clubs. But Sevilla Club, once the preserve of the estate overlords, had long since been integrated. The rallying cry of Eric Williams's party, which had brought Trinidad and Tobago to independence, had been 'Massa Day Done'.

The day of the white master is over.

There could be no more whites-only establishments in Trinidad. But my mother had been sceptical about the kind of wildlife she might encounter at Sevilla. Her blue eyes and Canadian accent would have protected her. But she was not a part of the white Trinidadian stream. She would not have known anybody there. And she had seen enough of white racism when she married Dad.

Anyhow, taboo things had a way of making me curious.

So that afternoon I found myself with Dylan and his brother diving into the deep end of Sevilla's L-shaped pool while Sheila's two children splashed about in the shallows, with water-wings on their arms.

Then I saw Sheila pull up a lounging chair onto the grassy lawn near the middle of the L and settle down with a glass of something that looked cool and nice. I got out and pulled up a chair next to her.

'So, what news about your heroine? Is it the prince or the monkey?'

I was confused now. What heroine?

'On your tape! You were busy transcribing it, remember?'

'Oh, yes! Right, Saranga. I don't know yet. The story is getting complicated. I have lots more to go.'

A waiter came by and Sheila ordered the same drink for me. Then the kids all came out of the water and wanted French fries, so the conversation between us stalled for a bit.

After a while the kids went off. Dylan's brother had found a bird's nest in one of the bushes near the pool, and wanted to show it to Sheila's kids.

Now we were alone again.

'I told you I got a grant to go to India,' I said. 'Now a friend in Ann Arbor has written to tell me he's going to arrange everything for me. His family is there.'

'Aha! A mystery man!'

'Sheila! Nothing like that! Just someone I know.'

'You never mentioned him before.'

I hadn't. Too many things to sort out there.

I had met Nishant just two days after I first arrived in Ann Arbor, and he had made out at once that I was an Indian from Trinidad. The accent, he said.

Then we just happened to bump into each other everywhere. And all of a sudden I found myself getting pulled into a different current, away from the new crop of students, high above the ground, up to a place where ideas were coming fast and fierce and new songs kept appearing on the radio in his car every week. Where, in the afterglow of the sixties, the world was huge, and with open skies all around us.

Then one evening he had brought me to his apartment along with a bunch of other friends, to meet his aunt and uncle who were visiting Ann Arbor on a round-the-world trip.

Later he told me that his aunt had taken to me, and had gone back and told the family in India that he had found a girl.

But had he, really? It wasn't so simple. Nishant had made it very clear from the start that he was not going to spend his life in the US. He was determined to go back to India. And as far as he knew, there were no foreign wives who had managed to find their feet in a career in India. Someone like me might have a hard time finding work: the job scene in Indian academia was xenophobic.

I thought of the handloom kurtas Nishant liked to wear. India was on the other side of a porous handloom curtain. Once I crossed that curtain to settle in India coming back out would not be easy. Indian salaries did not encourage frivolous travel. You got one chance to go abroad. And Nishant had had his chance.

A purdah, I thought. Like Ajie's orhnis. Woven in the mind. But stronger than a curtain you could touch.

So we persisted in suspended animation. Everyone saw us as a couple, but we were wary of making a commitment. Like we were waiting for something, some sign.

And like a good little Indian girl I went along with that. I think I was also a little afraid that he might be right. Go back to India?

Now, as I was getting ready to make my big exit from Trinidad, and to fly to India alone, a question kept cropping up, first from Ajie, and then from a lot of the old people I talked to.

How will they *treat* you there? How do they look at people like us, who migrated from India as bonded labourers?

'Hey! Penny for your thoughts.' Sheila.

I was back at the poolside in Sevilla. 'Just thinking...In the last installment of the story, the monkey goofed it up royally, and Saranga was last seen going off in a wedding procession with the prince to her new home.'

'And the monkey?'

'The monkey? Well, he was almost in mourning, but stumbling behind on her trail, down but not out.'

'He won't get her!'

Dylan the druid. He had come back and sat down on the grass next to my chair.

'He won't! Don't I have a say in this?'

'Look, friend, you don't know the prince at all. Why you pushing her on to him?'

'Hey! I just said not the monkey! Is only you talking about a prince.'

'Well,' said Sheila, 'lover boy is certainly holding out in the story. There must be something to him that I can't see.' She made a dismissive gesture. And with that said she called out to her kids to wind up.

'Animal charm!' Dylan quipped.

'Magic, Sheila, magic!' I reminded her. 'That's what makes the world go round.'

Now it was getting close to sunset. Sheila raised an eyebrow at me, as if to ask, is that what they call it these days? Then she rounded up her children to take them to the changing room. My cousins also went off by themselves to the men's changing room. And I decided to have a look around, to explore the building.

As I strolled around in my swimsuit through what looked like a covered shed with a billiards table, a man looked up and considered me for a long moment. Sheila had waved out to him, had told me he was an overseer. From Scotland.

'Are you a member here?'

I freaked, and said something or the other and vanished into the women's changing room. I locked myself inside a cubicle and wrapped the towel tightly around me. Then I paused to get a grip on myself. Never again, I told myself. I'm not coming back here!

And then the moment passed.

I changed back into my jeans and tee shirt and came out to meet the others. Sheila was going to take her kids home. Did we want to come over for tea?

No, I thought. I'd better get on with it. Back into dry clothes. I could feel the clock ticking away again. Countdown.

We drove home straight from Sevilla, over beautifully paved roads through fields of arrowing cane. Roads with little twists and turns over gently rolling countryside. I allowed my motor to race a bit. I wanted to dispel the image of the overseer focusing his eyes on me through an alcoholic haze, sizing me up. Deciding if I belonged or not. Like, was I some Indian girl poaching on his property? I let the back wheels slalom into the curves, heard the tires squeal, and noted the grins on my cousins' faces.

Anyway, I would need all the energy I could conjure for a long session with Ajie tonight. She was feeling the window of time beginning to close too.

So after supper that night Ajie filled up a thermos of tea and brought along two mugs, and I picked up a bunch of sikiyé figs, those tiny sweet bananas my mother loved, and we took our places at the drop-leaf table upstairs.

Ringside seats to watch Sada Birij fight his way back from the bottom of the sea!

'Kaahey ke maaney? Arey, hai Saranga, hai Saranga karat, ta chalal jaala. Ta aagey gail, tab okey lagal pyaas.'

Why should he listen? Crying 'Hai, Saranga, hai, Saranga, I've lost you, oh Saranga, I've lost you!' he went on his way. And after a little distance he found that he was thirsty.

So he went to a pond, and when he got there, he realized that

he couldn't drink from his hand, because if he did his hand with
the message on it would get wet. So he had to dip his whole face
into the water, like an animal, to drink.

At that time two women were coming to that pond to collect
water, and when they saw him drinking like that one of them said:

> Arey, na mukhey pani piyo re pyaarey!
> Aa unkar kawana bichaar hai?
> Baalepana se laagi lagana gori,
> Aa kajara sindoorawa haath ji.

> Oh, don't drink with your face in the water!
> What must he be thinking?
> The fair girl's marriage was fixed since she was a child,
> And kohl and red sindoor powder are on his hands!

Kohl and sindoor powder are on his hands, she said, the red
sindoor powder that married women put in their hair parting.
How can he drink from his hand?

Now Saranga's palanquin had gone far ahead, and Sada
Birij trailed behind. And when he went a little bit further on, he
reached a kutiya, a shrine.

Saranga went to her new home. And Sada Birij went to the
shrine. In that shrine there lived a sadhu who could see twelve
years into the future, and twelve years into the past. And he was
asleep. And there was lots and lots of bush growing all round,
lots and lots of creepers all over the house, and Sada Birij cleared
it all away. And when the sadhu's sleep ended, he saw that
someone had cleared away all the bush and overgrowth.

He said: 'If you are my god-son, then come into my presence.
If you are my god-daughter, come before me.'

He let his god-son come before him, and Sada Birij went and
stood there. Then the sadhu asked him: 'Son, what misfortunes

have befallen you?'

Sada Birij launched into the tale, and told him everything.

The sadhu said: 'Listen to me, son. In this region everywhere you look you will only find women named Saranga. Only named Saranga. And I don't know which house you mean, which house your Saranga lives in. This is Dhara Nagari.'

So he said: 'I see.'

So the sadhu said: 'Look, go from house to house as a beggar, and whatever alms you get, go and leave it at the crossroads. Whatever alms your Saranga gives you, bring it here for me. Then I will grant you one wish.'

So he agreed. And went begging for alms:

> *Arey, beta howe Raja Jagadeep ke, re, pyaari,*
> *Aa galiyaan na galiyaan na maangat, ji.*

> *Oh, this is the son of Raja Jagdeep, my love,*
> *Going from street to street begging.*

And he went from lane to lane singing like this, begging for alms:

> *Arey, tera karanawa, hai, re, Saranga,*
> *Maangat galiyaan na galiyaan na bhiccha, ji.*

> *Oh, all because of you, oh, alas, Saranga,*
> *Lane after lane, begging for alms.*

So like this he sang, he begged, he sang, he begged, and when he reached Saranga's door, when he came with the beggar's invocation, 'Jai!', her mother-in-law said: 'Oh, daughter, take a look, there must be a beggar there. Go and give him some alms.'

So she filled up a tray with pearls, diamonds and gems, filled it up, and went out to give alms, and when she reached the door it was Sada Birij. Their eyes met. And they overflowed with tears. Now neither did he take the alms, nor did she give it, their eyes locked as one.

Then from a nearby palace another Saranga was looking at all this. And she saw a crow pecking away at the pearls in the tray. Some he ate, and others just fell. And she saw it all. And she said:

> Arey, Dhara Nagari me muruk na basela koi,
> Aa chatoor basata ab koi, ji.
> Arey, baalepana se laagi lagana, gori,
> Aa naina milaniya hoat hai.
> Aa kaag moti chun-chun khaat hai.

> Oh, there are no fools living in Dhara Nagari,
> Everyone who lives here has sense.
> Your match has been fixed since your childhood, fair girl,
> And now you are looking into each other's eyes.
> And a crow is pecking away at the pearls.

Then he took the alms from her. He took the alms and gave it all to the sadhu. And the sadhu put it away.

And later in the night, when everyone would have eaten and drunk and would be off to bed, the sadhu conjured a snake as a gift for Sada Birij through the power of his mantras. And he told it to go and bite Saranga.

And the snake went and bit Saranga, and all over the town the news spread, that Saranga had been bitten by a snake, she had been bitten, and that she had died.

And the sadhu said: 'Good.'

And he told Sada Birij to go and wait at the burial grounds, to see where they buried her.

So he went to the burial grounds, keeping out of sight. And

he saw the whole funeral, and waited till everyone was gone.
Then he went, and using the sadhu's magic mantras, he got her
body out of the grave. He took her out and carried her away, he
took her to the sadhu's home at night so that nobody would see
them.

And the sadhu brought her back to life. Through the power
of his mantras, he prayed and blew a spell and brought her back
to life.

Then he said: 'Son, keep this box. You should open it only
when you get back home. Do not open it on the road. If you do,
things will go against you again.'

So Sada Birij said: 'All right—'

We ended the session that night on a cliff-hanger: would
Sada Birij manage to restrain his curiosity about the box
until he got home safely with Saranga?

Was he ready to be our hero, or was he still a monkey?

I know what Dylan would have said: A hero? No
way! He's a monkey. Not our class, sis!

I know what Sheila would have said: that the monkey
would have made, perhaps, a good first husband.

Ajie would have smiled at Sada Birij as long as he
didn't try to get out of the story, or out of a Hindi film.
Ajie's reaction to Hindi films always mystified me. She
would chuckle at the high jinks the heroines got up to,
though that was precisely the sort of behaviour she told
me was 'un-Indian'. There was a space for love and
romance and wayward Indian girls, but it wasn't in the
real world.

What did Deeda think? She was the storyteller, though
the ball was up and rolling by itself, and the most she
could do at this stage was be a commentator. But she

was not hiding the fact that she liked Sada Birij. The one always far behind, and the one who never gave up. She was making sure that he stayed in the race.

And I was thinking along a different track. I was intrigued by what the sadhu had said about there being many Sarangas. We had even seen another one of them looking on as our Saranga stared into Sada Birij's eyes and the crow pecked at the pearls she was giving as alms. She didn't sound too happy about finding our Saranga with Sada Birij.

What did the storyteller mean by bringing in this crop of other Sarangas?

KANYA-DAAN

I HADN'T FORGOTTEN ABOUT FIXING SUNNARIYA'S *marriage. But I waited a week before I talked to her about what Mukoon Singh had said just before he disappeared. I thought Sunnariya needed a little time to settle down, to catch herself first. Then I asked her about what was worrying me:*

'Before I go and speak to Janaki-didi, you have to think and tell me. What is your feeling about the boy? Is this something you are ready to do?'

Sunnariya didn't answer the question. 'If Baba said you should talk to her, then you should go.'

I stopped to think. Go slow, I said to myself. She has just been attacked in the cane fields, and now her father has had to run away. I told myself to be patient. 'Okay, I will go. But I just want to know if you are okay about the boy. You ever got a chance to talk to him?'

But Sunnariya would not get into this talk. 'The boy? I don't know him at all. What is the problem?'

I looked at her, and then I shook my head. 'I am trying to give you a little chance to make up your own mind. This marriage is something that is going to be forever. I don't know the boy. But you are all the time with Janaki-didi. I thought you might have an idea.' No reaction. 'What happened, you don't care at all?'

I caught a flicker in her eyes when I said that. But she didn't say anything. I decided to leave things for now. 'All right, we will talk about this later on.'

She just looked at me with her big light eyes, as though she had made up her mind and was waiting for me to stop wasting time.

All the next week I didn't talk about meeting Janaki-didi, and we just went about our business. In all that time I went every day into the cane fields to work, but Sunnariya did not leave the barracks. She sat inside the room and occupied herself with things that needed doing. Sewing. Arranging all her father's belongings. Organizing the cooking area.

She went out Sunday morning to a prayer meeting, in one of the barracks, with other Christians. When she went outside the room her orhni was back in place, almost hiding her face like when I first met her in the depot in Calcutta, and her skirt was hiding her feet.

And all the men in the barracks were sure that she was the most beautiful woman they had ever seen.

I think that when a woman is very calm and still and has sadness floating around her like a perfume, and when she covers her head so that men can't see her properly, when she is aware of their eyes always on her, they will always think that she is very beautiful.

The next time we sat down to talk, before I could say anything, she started: 'Look, Deeda, I don't know what you are worrying about. Baba said it was time for me to get married, and if he has thought about it, I am happy with that.'

I tried again. 'Sunnariya, this is a different country. And your father is not here. The only way for women like us to manage in this place is to hold the wheel for ourselves. Don't tell me you are not glad for a chance to make up your own mind?'

She was going to give the same kind of reply again, but then she stopped. She just looked at me, and then her eyes were like a little child's again.

'Deeda, I am tired,' she said, 'I am tired of everything. You think we can make up our own minds, but the one time in my life I got that idea and did what I felt like doing, something bad happened, not only to me but to all of us. Because of me Baba has had to run away and hide, and I don't want to think about what they will do if they catch him. Now I don't want to fool myself. I was awake when Baba talked to you, before he went, and I heard him. Baba thinks this is the best thing for me.'

'Don't blame yourself for this thing, Sunnariya! You didn't do anything wrong!' Was that what had been going on in the child's mind all this time? That the whole thing was her fault?

She made a wave with her hand to say 'not important'. 'Baba did what he had to do, and now I have to do my part. The people in the barracks still think I am a good girl, even after all the trouble I caused. I don't want that to change. I can't get more than that in this life.'

She was now going to be the daughter Mukoon Singh would be proud of!

And as I looked at her, inside our room with the door closed, she looked back at me and pulled her orhni tight over her head. And then I understood.

All the layers of clothes around her, protecting her like the boat had protected us from the sea on the journey to Trinidad. And I, like a fool, was telling her she could fend for herself. Like telling her she stood a better chance against the storm waves if she jumped off the boat and started to swim.

Sunnariya was going to stay in the boat and let other people find the way for her using the charts her father would have followed. In any case, she had never really wanted to do it any *other way, since the time I met her. She had never looked at boys, or wondered about things like love.*

Maybe she knew she could still find herself at the bottom of the sea after leaving the wheel in other people's hands, but she must have thought it was better to go down with the boat, with the water coming in slowly through the hatches.

I think she had so much faith in her father that she didn't really think she could go down. She was still a child, and thought that if you were a good girl, you would find happiness in the end, the way it happened in the stories I had told her. A beautiful princess would find a prince who would love her. She wouldn't have to do anything, it would happen by itself.

Anyhow, I had made a promise to Mukoon Singh. I must not forget that.

So the next evening after work I went to talk to Janaki-didi.

It was easy: Janaki-didi had always loved Sunnariya, and she could hardly believe Mukoon Singh was really giving his only daughter to her for safekeeping. I think her eyes got back a little bit of shine when she thought of the sagaai and the biyaah in another two years. I didn't want to rush, but I also didn't want to wait longer than that. Janaki-didi didn't waste time asking the boy if he agreed, the way I had asked Sunnariya. He would have to be the biggest fool in the world if he didn't want to marry this girl.

The boy was happy to be getting Sunnariya as a wife. Well, that was not exactly right. It looked to me as though what was really making him happy was the thought of having Mukoon Singh as a father-in-law. Sunnariya was just the bonus.

He and Mukoon Singh had spent many, many evenings breaking bounds to go and listen to the missionaries, and Mukoon Singh was like a hero for him. Especially after he had killed the overseer.

That had given all the men in the barracks some pride, as if they had done it themselves. And what was making him happiest now was being in a position to do something important for his great friend. So he got his mind working, thinking about what were all the things he should do now. To give Mukoon Singh's daughter a good home.

And then I saw that Sunnariya was thinking the same way. She had decided that Janaki-didi was the best mother-in-law she could imagine, and someone she already knew and loved. She knew that for her own peace of mind the person who mattered most was her mother-in-law. The boy was less important.

But I am a storyteller, and I remembered how it used to be in all the stories. Two people in love. And not just in the stories, I realized. In my own life I had seen it.

And here we had two good little children who would never think anything wrong, getting married more to their in-laws than to each other!

Where was love?

I think Janaki-didi in her heart agreed with me.

Anyhow, I told Langoor Mamoo to pass on word to Mukoon Singh that I had done what he had asked. And that we were going to have the sagaai when crop was over. The biyaah would be in two years' time. I also wanted Langoor Mamoo to tell Mukoon Singh that all of us were praying for him, in our different ways.

And I wondered if he would send back a message for me.

The sagaai was a small thing. Sunnariya's brothers helped out and took the place of her father. Janaki-didi called one of the catechists to the estate and they held a prayer meeting in her room. It was the first time I was seeing a Christian ceremony. Everything was different: different bhajans, a different book they were reading from. But at the same time I was surprised that it was so much like a Hindu puja.

After that Sunnariya did not go out to work in the fields. She stayed and helped Janaki-didi during the day, and came back to our barracks in the evening. The estate people agreed to let her work as a khelauni, I think, because they were afraid of what could happen if they tried to force her to go back into the cane fields. I think they were afraid of her brothers, or maybe of her father, or of the other men in the barracks. In any case, Sunnariya never went outside the barracks area after that, and she never went near the cane fields. If she wasn't with Janaki-didi she was almost always in our room.

From time to time Langoor Mamoo would come and tell us that Mukoon Singh was well. But we never met him, and he sent no messages at all. It was as if he had forgotten me.

Even Sunnariya's brothers had to depend on Langoor Mamoo to get any message to Mukoon Singh. The police would have been keeping a watch on them for sure. I don't know, maybe they went and met him. But they never told us about it.

Janaki-didi's two sons used to hear things about him from the missionaries, because the missionaries always had an idea of what he was doing. But I don't think the two boys went and met him.

And then Langoor Mamoo told us one day that he had heard that the government was now saying that they would not hang Mukoon Singh if he agreed to give himself up. They wanted to send him back to India.

But he was still running free. He had not surrendered.

And our life went on, on the estate. One more crop, and then another. Two new sets of migrants had come on the boats from India, and now there were plenty more children on the estate. I was still working in the fields with Acchamma. Now we were both old-timers, and sometimes we were even cutting. And Sunnariya was in the barracks area helping Janaki-didi with minding all the extra children. And Janaki-didi's boy was beating silver under the steps of the estate house and making jewellery.

Then it was time to start preparing for Sunnariya's wedding.

We would sit together in the evenings, Sunnariya and I, and I stitched a lace edging on to her white orhni, and she sat and made all the gathers for the skirt of her white wedding dress, and hemmed it. Then she cut out the blouse that would be the top of the dress, and I helped her pin it to fit. She would sew it up later, during the day.

Janaki-didi used some of her money to buy mohurs, gold coins, for her son to melt so that he could make twelve gold churiyaan, thin bracelets, for his bride. Kalloo and I went and sat outside the barracks to watch him melt his own gold coins in the crucible and pour the molten gold in a bright stream into the mould. Then he milled the gold stick into long wire the thickness he needed for the churiyaan, pulling the wire through smaller and smaller holes in an iron plate. All the children came to watch him do the 'diamond cutting', the final work with the hammer and chisel.

Later when Sunnariya's clothes were ready, Janaki-didi gave her her own channan-haar, her gold filigree necklace, which she had brought across the ocean from Faizabad and kept safely for her first daughter-in-law.

I used the money Mukoon Singh had left with me to pay for Sunnariya's dress and the feast after the ceremony.

We were going to get passes to go out of Esperanza Estate to the little wooden Presbyterian Church in Dow Village, where they would have the ceremony. One of the local ministers they had trained was coming to perform the ceremony. Then after the ceremony in the church, they would sign and register the marriage.

On that day we all went to the church. Sunnariya's two brothers were ready to do the kanya-daan, to give the bride away.

I sat there and watched the afternoon light streaming through the windows, and I watched Sunnariya and Janaki-didi's boy standing there in their bright new clothes in front of the minister.

> *Karo meri sahaay,*
> *Masiha-ji,*
> *Tuma bina kuchhu na sahaay,*
> *Karo meri sahaay.*

> *Be my support,*
> *Honoured Messiah,*
> *I cannot bear anything without you,*
> *Be my support.*

I heard the words of the bhajan and realized with a sudden shock that Sunnariya was now going out of my life. Not completely, but mostly. I was wondering if I was prepared for that.

The minister was talking, first to the boy, and now to Sunnariya. I woke up from my daydreaming and caught the end of what he was saying: '…grahan karti hai?'

…do you accept?

'Mai karti hoon.' Sunnariya's voice.

I do.

I listened carefully after that. The minister was talking again.

'Is aurat ko is mard ke saath biaahe jaane ke liye kaun deta hai?'

Who gives this woman to be wedded to this man?

'Mai deta hoon!'

I do!

The voice rang out from the doorway of the church. The same Khari Boli as the minister! Everybody turned in surprise. Mukoon Singh! In broad daylight! In front of the whole estate!

He walked up the aisle towards Sunnariya, and took his place in the spot for the father of the bride, and the ceremony continued. The whole church was silent in shock. Only Sunnariya looked calm, as if there was nothing strange about it.

He was older. Thinner. There were a few lines around his eyes. But everything else was the same. The pink pagri, the rich strong voice, the bright eyes glowing like the stream of gold that was melted to make the churiyaan. I held my breath to stop my heart from pounding.

From far away I heard the voice of the minister saying the words that finalized the marriage between Sunnariya and Janaki-didi's boy.

And then the ceremony was over. It was time to go and sign the register. Sunnariya turned to look at her father. Her eyes were shining too. But she would not cry. She already knew he was to be sent back.

And for the last time he lifted the pagri off his head and handed it to Sunnariya.

Keep this, he said. Remember me, and never do anything to dishonour me.

And Sunnariya bent and touched his feet, the last time she or any of her children or grandchildren would touch anybody's feet.

And he turned towards the door. I followed his eyes.

Two policemen were waiting for him in the doorway. I knew there would be more outside.

He smiled. And then he came walking back down the aisle, and he stopped in front of me. Stopped and looked at me, and that was first time I saw him look uncertain about anything.

'Deeda. Aayegi mere saath? Jahaj me?' he asked, very softly.

Will you come with me? On the boat?

And time stopped. I couldn't breathe. I couldn't think. Mukoon Singh and me, for the rest of our lives. Sunnariya was married. Now I was free.

Repatriation to India. The same long boat journey. The same between-decks, the coolie quarters. The same waves, the same storms.

But none of that had me worried.

Wait for me, I will come back for you. So this is what he had meant!

Two years now, and no message at all from him. And now like a bolt of lightning from a clear sky, this kind of a test.

I thought of Kalloo, still a child. Who would look after this child if I went back? I could not leave him behind in Trinidad, and I could not take him back now. He would never be able to adjust.

And I knew then that what had grown between Mukoon Singh and me was a part of that time we had had together in the barracks, in Trinidad. India would be a different story: in India I would be just a kahaar, and he would be a thakur. A Rajput.

Would he understand and protect me in India? Would he even see the problem?

And would people there let us be happy?

Then I remembered I had to give him an answer. So I closed my eyes and pressed my palms together in front of my face, though my heart was breaking.

Namaste.

A respectful refusal.

I looked up and saw the sad smile on his face. He was disappointed in me, but he had no reason to be surprised. What he had asked for was not small.

And he turned and walked towards the policemen at the door. His sons went out with him.

He had planned this carefully in advance.
This was his surrender—

In retrospect.

Yes, Deeda had 'blinked'. Faltered at the last fence. But as hard-headed as she might have seemed then, she had not been wrong. She would not have been happy. She would not have been with Mukoon Singh for long, anyway.

Mukoon Singh's trail goes cold after he leaves Trinidad. A strange and spiritless journey it must have been, sailing against all the prevailing winds and ocean currents that had brought us to Trinidad. I don't think he died on the boat, as Ramlal had done. I would have heard about that.

The news from India, after that, came only from Heera Singh and Houri Singh, who had brashly followed their father out of their sister's wedding, to go with him on the boat. Letters and letters, first written to Sunnariya, and then to Nana, written in Kaithi.

At first Nana used to reply, in carefully schooled Hindi. A contact with India!

Their letters all asked the same question: can you arrange for us to come back?

That Nana would never do. Mukoon Singh had been a hero, but his sons were just a big potential problem. Hooligans, that was the word he used. They would have brought the police into his life.

But he collected the letters, and kept them in the great steel vault in our shop where the gold was kept. And then, one afternoon, when I was away on holiday, and he had a premonition of his own death, because he knew things like that, he took them all out and made a bonfire of them. What he had told Ajie then was that he did not want anyone finding these letters after he was gone and trying to follow their trail and make their way back to India.

And there was only one person in the family who showed signs of doing that.

Me.

I was the one who had made the effort to learn Bhojpuri. I was the one who was curious about India. I was the one who was always fascinated by people from India.

It was good that Nana's father and Sunnariya had not thought of waiting for their time to expire before having their wedding. Because their indentureship was not, in the end, for the five years they had expected or the ten years they had ultimately signed for. Esperanza Estate managed to extend their indentureship period until it finally lasted eleven years and five months.

The date on Sunnariya's freedom papers was three and a half years after Nana, her first child, was born.

Nana had been born in the barracks at Esperanza Estate.

CASCADURA

I<small>T WAS BACK TO WORK NOW, AGAINST A MONUMENTAL</small> deadline. I was ready to interview any old person who could give me a flood tide of spontaneous speech in Bhojpuri. But I was inclined towards jahajis. I felt they would have something more precious to tell. And I knew where each one was to be found.

I was just winding up an interview in Spring Village with an old woman, over ninety, who had said she was a jahajin.

Her name was Bhagmaniya, and she told me about having been '*peit me*', in her mother's belly, when her mother had boarded the boat. And she told me about having been born during a storm, while the boat was being tossed on a mad sea.

I kept chatting with her in Bhojpuri after the tape recorder was switched off. So she was a jahajin after all. The easiest way to tell if people were jahajis, I had discovered, was to press stop. If the Bhojpuri stopped too, they were born in Trinidad, and only going through a bit of make-believe. To help a student who would 'fail' if they didn't conjure up the mood and talk Bhojpuri for her. Then, with the tape recorder off, we would be back to reality, speaking Creole English.

With the jahajis, the dream went on.

Sometimes the best things I heard were to be found only in my memory. The tape recorder had already been packed up, but the stream of Bhojpuri had continued. I remembered it all. Though sometimes I would find myself combing through my tapes and notes later on and not finding it. Something I knew a particular jahaji had said. I could remember the moment when it was said. The sight of a very old woman in helpless tears at the memory of something that happened nearly ninety years ago, and me putting an arm around her. Or a quirky insight that went way beyond the topic at hand.

But try as I might, I just wouldn't be able to find it on the tape.

Fyzie carried the tape recorder back to the car. I looked tired, he said, while he had only been skylarking.

Sometimes in our picaresque journey through Caroni with the tape recorder, an old jahaji would send a question his way, try to include him in the conversation. Deeda had tried too, in the beginning. But he would always fend it off. He didn't understand Bhojpuri, he would say firmly, with a smile, and this was not his scene.

Sometimes it took a lot of self-possession to just sit back and skylark, I thought. The world was full of lesser men who could not resist the temptation to muscle in on a woman's work and grab some of the limelight.

Tonight we had earned a bit of a break. I wasn't ready to head home, so we went off to look for a roti-shop.

In our exploration of roti-shops we had come across a lot of other things they served with the rotis. One place offered us sea conches. Another place had made stewed armadillo, known as tatou in Creole. And tonight we were faced with another kind of creature, from the murky swamp, not yet cooked. Did we want to wait?

I looked at the ugly armour-plated fish with the long whiskers on the snout. And I remembered Dad having brought them home once from a fishing trip. Well, not exactly a fishing trip. Nothing laid-back about that desperate hand-over-fist scramble for fish! Dad had brought back a big diesel pump in the car that he and his friends had used for the fishing. They had somehow dammed up a small pond off the swamp and pumped all the water out, and gone in and picked up the fish from the bottom.

They would still have been alive. They were adapted to living in the mud, where the oxygen supply was poor, and they had a habit of coming to the surface anyway to take gulps of air.

Cascaduras. Spanish for hard-shells. Dad had treated it as a French Creole word: *casque-doux*. Which had the opposite meaning, soft-shells!

At that time I was just a fussy child, not ready to eat anything new. Certainly not anything that looked as if it had recently been alive. So I had just stood in the kitchen doorway and watched Dad make another one of his grisly concoctions.

I hadn't eaten it then.

But now I was on a fast countdown, getting ready to leave Trinidad. And I remembered the story about the cascadura: that anyone who ate cascadura was destined to die in Trinidad.

Why not settle the future the easy way? I thought for a moment. Eat the fish and leave it to fate?

But I blinked.

I told myself it was only a rain check.

Fyzie was amused. You're superstitious?

Well, maybe.

There was no other reason to back off. It wouldn't have taken me anything to eat a piece of the fish. I wasn't squeamish any more. But I think I was beginning to feel a tow towards an ocean a good bit larger than the pond Dad had so easily dammed and emptied. It wasn't any place specific that I had set my sights on. In truth there was no place I had ever been as happy as I was those days in Trinidad. I had always found the reality of the outside world bleak.

I think I was just getting back to that time-bomb programmed into my cells that told me that life was not about sitting down and being happy. That that was something I should limit to brief stopovers in port for refueling. I was returning to that thing in my blood that told me that I should always be struggling, moving ahead, and that if I wasn't, I was doing something wrong.

And suddenly now, as I looked at the cascadura, I got a toxic whiff of an old familiar feeling. Of a sense of failure that would overtake me whenever I did not find myself up against something impossible. Of a sense of having let down a legion of soldiers that stood at my back. And I would picture the gleaming hurt in my father's eyes.

The sense of panic that it brought made me stand up at once and start tilting at something big enough to make me confront my limits.

Then the thought came to me that I would settle for happiness one day. But not yet. It struck me that happiness was something you looked for when you retired—pressed stop and sat on that beach in the late afternoon, while other liners and tankers and pirogues plied their way along on the horizon past the breaker line. And didn't feel you were missing all the fun.

Pressed stop, rewound the tape, and just listened to it with a smile. I had never learned how to sit and just enjoy a tape.

Then again, maybe I was at heart a jahajin. I knew I hadn't finished sailing, as much as I had needed this long stay in port to recharge my energy reserves. I was beginning to get a sense of the fine distinction between a long stopover and journey's end. A tiny thought kept emerging out of the clutter in my head, that if I stopped now I was soon going to be staring at a different feeling of confinement.

It crossed my mind that the claustrophobic atmosphere at home, the feeling of stuckness, was almost designed as a spur to keep me going. To convince me that the only way out towards something that made me happy was up. North.

In the sixties, when a lot of Trinidadian families were migrating to Canada, my parents never even considered it. It would have been so easy then. My mother was Canadian. My parents knew Montreal and the Maritimes well. But they had shrugged off the discussion then as frivolous.

I got the impression that there was something about bringing us up in Trinidad that they had wanted, rather than the instant melting pot of North America, where even the dream of continuing the journey would unravel, where my brother and I would simply melt into the crowd and vanish from their sight. Just as they had been happy that I had wanted to go to the Trinidad campus of the University of the West Indies for my first degree, and only then on to Michigan. In Michigan my big selling points had been my background in Caribbean Creole languages, and Bhojpuri.

Going abroad was not an end in itself. It was only a shortcut to empowerment.

Something like becoming Christian in order to be able to jump the cycle and reenter the karmic wheel at a higher point, eyeball to eyeball with the brahmins.

I took a last look at the cascaduras, dead from an overdose of the oxygen they were used to consuming only in tiny sips, and shook my head. Some other time, I said. I had to move on now.

We took ourselves away from the tiny market and back onto the open road.

PASSING THE TORCH

THE REST OF SUNNARIYA'S STORY I ALREADY KNEW.

Sunnariya married my great-great grandfather and returned to living in the Esperanza barracks, as their time had not expired. But she was already out of field labour, and so was he. And his mother, Janaki-didi, was already running a little shop on the estate, and had never worked in the fields at all. The family had joined the aspiring middle class even before their indentureship period was over.

When Sunnariya's husband became a Christian, he took on a first name, or a Christian name, before his original name. John. After the missionary who converted him, John Morton. His original name then became his surname, for himself and for his descendants. Ramesar.

And his brother also took a Christian name, William, and kept his original name as a surname for himself and his descendants. Ramcharan.

Deeda's fears about Sunnariya's husband were not out of place. He did earn, as Mukoon Singh had hoped, and provide materially for Sunnariya. But his true love came out of a bottle. He was an alcoholic. So for a good while it was really Janaki-didi and Sunnariya holding the dream together with sheer will power.

Sunnariya didn't give any sign of resenting this, or of feeling that she had expected something more out of him. In fact, there didn't seem to be any signs of friction at all. Sunnariya's strongest adult relationship was with her mother-in-law, Janaki-didi. And she turned the rest of her attention towards her children. These were the ones who would listen to her. These were the ones she would shape.

Sunnariya had five children, four boys and a girl. And Deeda was there each time for the delivery, to make her walk till the very end, and to hold her hand and steer her through the storm waves.

Sunnariya sent her children to the Esperanza Canadian Mission School, where they learned, among other things, English and Hindi. While she could only encourage their English without actually helping, she took a stronger interest in their Hindi. First of all, she made sure that they would not speak any Bhojpuri at all. That was a *'tooti bhaasha'*, a broken language. Just as Creole was 'broken' English. The unbroken variety was Hindi, the Hindi they were learning in school, which was practically the same as the Aligarh dialect she had learned as a child in India. They were to reply in Hindi even if other Indians spoke to them in Bhojpuri.

The other thing she made sure of was literacy. They would learn the Devanagari script in school, but after school they would go to the moonsie, who had also settled nearby in Dow Village, not far from Esperanza, and he would teach them the old Kaithi script that her father had written in.

And it is this running-hand Kaithi script that Nana later used in his personal account books when he opened his jewellery shop.

When her indentureship period was over, Sunnariya more or less withdrew from the public gaze. And this only enhanced the tales of her legendary beauty. Of the orhni that covered not only her amazing hair, but much of her face too. Of the skirt that swept the floors so that you could never see her feet. All just a memory, because she was not in view any more.

No talk of her golden eyes, so like her father's. Nothing specific any longer.

Nana would sometimes get a faraway smile and conjure for me vignettes of afternoons after school, in Dow Village, of his father busy at home melting gold coins in a crucible to make jewellery, while he and his brothers were busy with silver, learning to make the taabeej used by Muslims and Hindus alike. Learning to mill the silver into sheets, cut out the shapes and solder the edges together, with a coating of borax solution so that the metal did not oxidize when heated. Directing the flame with a phuunknee, a small blowpipe.

And sometimes on a day like that, he would say, his mother would have a visitor who would make her smile again, giggle like a girl, and cover her mouth with her hand. Deeda. They would go inside and talk and talk and talk, and he would be surprised, since his mother was usually so serious.

Sunnariya often came and sat down next to her children at night when they were in bed but not yet asleep. She would stay and talk to them, tell them stories of her father, and tales of Rajput chivalry. And then when they were asleep, she would put out the flame of the lamp, and go away.

But one night, when Nana was thirteen, and Sunnariya was expecting her fifth child, she had come to their bedside and sat for a long time. When the children fell asleep and she was about to put out the lamp, she hesitated. And then she changed her mind.

She must have sat and stared at the golden flame for a long time with her golden eyes.

And then she left the lamp burning and went out of the room.

And Nana remembered waking up the next morning with soot in his nostrils.

That night Sunnariya had gone into labour, and Janaki-didi had gone to fetch Deeda. And Deeda had come. But this time the monster waves were worse. And Sunnariya's boat ran aground in the shallows, on the sandbars that lifted the great waves from the sea bed in that treacherous strait.

Ulta baccha, they had said. A breach birth.

And Sunnariya would have known she was about to go under.

But Deeda did not give up. She sat with her, willing her to be strong, trying to take charge and turn the baby around as wave after wave broke over Sunnariya without bringing any movement. And when nothing else worked she held her hands and hoped for a miracle and waited with her for the long night to end.

And then the eye of the storm passed over them, and the wind died down, and suddenly all was still and calm. Sunnariya's fifth child was born, a boy. And for one bright moment it seemed as if the nightmare was over.

Then the storm resumed, with full force. But Sunnariya, weakened by the night's fury, had no more strength left. And slowly the salt waters closed over her, leaving her newborn passenger alive and safe in Deeda's arms.

Sunnariya was the first in our family to die in Trinidad. As is customary in the Presbyterian Church, she was buried, not cremated. And all the Indians in the barracks at Esperanza, and in Dow Village, came to the graveside to condole with Nana and his brothers and sister, and with Janaki-didi and Nana's father.

Matti ko matti, raakh ko raakh, dhool ko dhool
Earth to earth, ashes to ashes, dust to dust

Sunnariya, the first Janaki at the depot in Calcutta, was returning to the earth.

Soon after Sunnariya died, her husband, always a shadow, went blind and one day he drifted away from home. Vanished, like his hero Mukoon Singh had done before him, never to be heard from again. It now fell to his brother Ramcharan to step in and care for Nana and the other four children. His wife was already nursing Sunnariya's last child alongside her own son. Now Nana knew what he had to do. He dropped out of school and walked to Esperanza Estate to ask for his father's old job, sitting under the steps of the estate house, beating silver to make jewellery for the estate manager's wife. He understood that his mother had passed on the torch to him, and that he would now have to join Janaki-didi in holding the family together. Reading was now something he would have to do at night.

And Janaki-didi is supposed to have said that she had had to wait until she had a grandson to get what she had been hoping for from his father in her old age.

About Deeda I cannot say. Deeda was always the consummate survivor. I never asked her if she had married after leaving Esperanza Estate, and she never told me either. It simply never came up in conversation. But Deeda was not like Sunnariya: Deeda had always known how to take charge of the present and not put off things like happiness.

But her world did seem to shrink after Sunnariya died. Her dreams were smaller. Deeda's indentureship at Esperanza ended a little after Sunnariya's did, and she settled, as most of the other time-expired Indians from Esperanza did, in Dow Village. But soon after Sunnariya died she moved on, following Kalloo to Orange Valley, where he had found a job and a wife and settled down. And she eventually found herself living next door to another jahajin, Rampyari, from a much later boat. There in Orange Valley she lived a peaceful life surrounded by Kalloo's children and their children, coming from time to time to check that all was well with Nana and his family.

Deeda did not try to do impossible things.

As years went by Nana began to feel more and more responsible for his three younger brothers and his sister. At first Janaki-didi tried to cope with things at home, with help from her other son and his wife. And Nana kept working under the steps of the Estate House at Esperanza, and from his bicycle on Sundays after Church, in Couva and Chaguanas markets, making jewellery and saving his money in the form of mohurs. But the pressure was building: Nana needed to find a wife, mainly to do the cooking and help look after his brothers and his sister. So Nana married a thakur girl, the daughter of a man named Pirthee Singh. And from that unpromising start, the need for a cook, came a beautiful relationship, everything Nana had hoped his parents' marriage might have been, but wasn't.

Janaki-didi lived to a great old age. Even Ajie told me about her, and about the little shop she had run in the barracks area of Esperanza Estate. She was still around with her great-grandchildren in Nana's home in Dow Village in Ajie's time. She was a survivor too.

Ajie was Nana's oldest child, the oldest of sixteen. Nana sent her to his old school in Dow Village, Esperanza CM School, and after that to Naparima Girls High School, which was then a Canadian Mission boarding school for Indian girls in San Fernando. And she, too, had her education cut short.

She had come home for the holidays when she was fourteen, delighted with her school report. She had wanted to show Nana that she had topped her class in Hindi.

And then she saw the wedding tent up, and she knew that it could only be for her, and she started to cry.

The girl who had sat next to Ajie in class at Naparima Girls had gone home and talked about her. Pretty and fair, she had said. So Nana had received a proposal of marriage from the girl's parents on behalf of her eldest brother. They were a Christian couple, an ahir man with a kurmi wife, both jahajis. Or Calcatiyas, as they preferred to be called, people who had sailed from Calcutta. And they were very rich, with sugar estates, a cocoa estate, and a lot of property in San Fernando.

It had been an astoundingly fast and steep climb for the old man, my other great-grandfather, but he had started early. His first money had come from selling water to the thirsty cane cutters working side by side with him in the fields, and this money was saved at first in the form of mohurs. Then he began to think bigger. He began lending money carefully to the French Creole owner of the estate he was bonded to, waving aside all offers of repayment. Not in a hurry, he would say. And he sat on the sidelines watching the man get deeper and deeper into debt, and selling off his other assets. And then, when his indenture was over, when he was certain the estate owner could not possibly pay up, he called in the loan. And took the estate—his first.

The next estate he acquired was a repeat of the same story. He had sighted oil sand on the estate, and known it would be useful in the construction work he wanted to get into. He was soon lending money to the French Creole owner of that estate, who was also losing his grip on things.

Nana, with so many other children to worry about, must have been bedazzled at the prospect of such a match for his oldest child.

So for a time Ajie's world shifted south of San Fernando, to one or the other of her in-laws' estates. Two years later, when she was expecting my father, she was brought to San Fernando for the delivery, to one of their homes on Coffee Street. Then on a Sunday morning, when her father-in-law was giving a sermon as a lay preacher from the pulpit of Susamachar Church, next to Grant School, he was interrupted with the news that he now had a grandson. And he broke off what he was saying to announce this good news to the congregation.

My father was named after his father, who in turn had been named after his father, the jahaji standing there at the pulpit that Sunday morning announcing the continuation of his line.

There are bright glimpses of that time down south. Ajie being given a pair of gold bracelets, in place of her elbow-to-wrist armour of silver bracelets, after Dad was born. Ajie learning to shoot with a rifle, and standing on the steps near the kitchen of the old estate house guarding her henhouse from mongooses. Ajie in a peach-pink sari going with my grandfather's sisters, who preferred black, to the premiere of a Hindi film, imported by her father-in-law for the first of his cinema halls. Ajie in the kitchen of the old estate house, making chocolate from cocoa grown on their estate. Dad, as a young boy, riding his horse over the pastures and down to the beach, and then standing in the water and giving his horse a combing.

Nana eventually shifted out of Dow Village. In 1930 he bought half an acre of land in Couva, a town just north of Dow Village, and built what would be the family home. His house, like all concrete houses at the time, was built on pillars, and he completed the first floor before enclosing the ground around the pillars below. So it was necessary for him to build a grand covered staircase in front of the house to reach the drawing room and the bedrooms upstairs. A staircase much like the staircase he had sat under as a thirteen-year-old boy on Esperanza Estate, beating silver to make jewellery.

But Ajie's marriage, like Sunnariya's, was not made in heaven. Ajie had been chosen by her in-laws in the hope that a fair pretty girl would be able to wean their son away from an unsuitable relationship with a woman on one of their estates. And Ajie had gone into her marriage, like Sunnariya, thinking that all it took to manage a husband was being beautiful and being good. Twice she came back to Nana, to get the strength to try again, and twice she went back. And then the third time she came to Couva Nana took a bold decision and filed for divorce, and changed her surname and her children's back to her maiden name.

The old jahaji, my great-grandfather, had spoken too soon, that Sunday morning at Susamachar Church, about the continuation of his line. There was a major parting of ways in store by the time my father was sixteen, which would leave my father carrying only half his name, the first half. Like Janaki-didi, Ajie also left her husband's home and went into exile with her children, but not across the salty ocean. Ajie went back to Nana's home in Couva, where she worked with him after that, running a pawnshop for him and doing the accounts for his shop.

I remember as a child watching Ajie get ready to go out. She would take out a lace orhni from her drawer and wrap one edge around her waist, tucking the two corners into her belt, and then bring the rest up over her chest like a sari, and throw the end over her head. She would pin the orhni to her shoulder with a diamond brooch, and fix it to her hair with pins, and let the other end float over her shoulder and down her back. Then she would open a locked drawer and pull out a pair of heavy gold beras and a gold chain with a rare gold coin as a pendant. And she would put on earrings made by Nana, with exquisite diamond cutting, chisel work on gold that mimicked the effect of faceted diamonds.

I think I made the connection quite early: covering up with a lace orhni came with being in a position to wear expensive gold jewellery. She did not wear her orhnis just to be submissive. Wearing lace orhnis was a powerful statement that she was now light years away from the estate, and forced labour.

When I was a child my standard of beauty was Ajie. Long, long hair that came down to her knees, seen only when she had just washed it, and a kind of stillness and dignity. Nana had always said that her beauty had been her undoing in her in-laws' home. It had caused resentment, though they had wanted her as a daughter-in-law precisely for that.

Sunnariya and Ajie. Two women of legendary beauty with shipwrecked lives. Ajie, who had eventually turned her back on the struggle and lived on into old age, and Sunnariya, who had stayed the course and died young.

Both women had turned their faces away from the present, away from themselves, and looked only to their children to realize their dreams for them.

Like Nana, I was the oldest of the oldest, all the way back to Faizabad. The torch, carried by Sunnariya and then Ajie, had passed on to me. I was programmed, I don't know how, to turn my face away from happiness into the winds of a cold future. I could see the snare, but I still could not escape it. Because it would play tricks with my mind. If I gave up and simply lived, as I often dreamed of doing, my mood would sink below sea level.

I was trapped too.

I was still there in the strait, navigating my own killer waves. It made no difference whether I turned back or forged ahead. The waves would still be there battering at me as long as I remained in the gap. I had to get out.

The only escape I could think of was keeping my head above water and going with the flow. The current I faced in the strait was stronger than me. If I went with this adverse current I could try to turn the corner with it, and the bigger picture would emerge, as Rosa had said. I would have to keep going for now, and live by my wits.

So when I turned my attention away from being trapped, and decided to reengage the big world and get back to Ann Arbor and then to fly on to India, it was not a cool, rational, well thought out decision. It was simply part of the energy of the same storm. It was a continuation, not an ending.

But there would be one difference, I told myself. I was not going to make the next generation sail the high seas for me. The curse had to end.

I was going to pilot the ship out of the storm myself and find it a safe harbour.

'TAKE ME HOME'

I WAS ON MY WAY TO VISIT DEEDA ONE LAST TIME BEFORE
I left for India, as I had promised. This time I had planned
in advance and picked Rosa up after work. We turned
west at St Mary's Junction and headed towards Orange
Valley and the late afternoon sun. There was still plenty
of light in the sky.

As I drove I updated Rosa on the end of Sunnariya's
story, the part that was nowhere in my tapes, but which
I had heard from Ajie and Nana. About Sunnariya and
her children, and how differently life had turned out for
her than it had for Deeda.

'Your great-great grandmother knew the risk she was
taking,' she said. 'She never actually got off the boat. She
kept sailing on through the most restless sea of all. The
middle class! Not an easy trip to finish in one lifetime!'

'I know. All the elaborate orhnis and cover-up,
making her kids speak Hindi, all the stuff of Rajput
chivalry she fed them. How did she do it without putting
everyone's back up? That took some navigation!'

'Well, she died young. That is the easiest way to get
people to like you. Then they can take over and turn you
into an icon.'

'They hardly ever saw her anyway,' I mused. 'And not at all after her indentureship ended. She was already well on her way to being an icon in her lifetime.'

We parked the car and got out. Deeda was waiting for us with Rampyari, on the hammock under the house. But she looked different. She was excited. She was glowing.

I saw the flash of recognition as she looked at Rosa and sized her up.

Rampyari had put a plate of biscuits on a little table in front of the hammock. Some children brought us glasses of sweet-drink.

So I told Deeda that my trip to India was now fixed. A friend of mine was getting in touch with his family, and I would be going to Faizabad and Basti after all.

And then she smiled, and it looked like the sun had stopped descending in the sky, like it had refused to set. She leaned forward as if to tell me a secret:

'Hum tohar sangey chalab!' I am coming with you!

And I seriously stopped and did a fast tally of my finances to see if I could really spring for a ticket for her.

She saw my expression and laughed. Really cracked up. I had made her day.

No-no, she said, when she stopped laughing. Not really coming like that. I am not ready to fly through the air! I am too old!

Then I was curious. What was going on in Deeda's mind now?

She leaned forward again. Are you taking all the tapes?

Of course, I said.

And the story of Rani Saranga and Sada Birij?

Especially that. I want to check if people in India have heard the story too.

All right. You will find the village? Like how I told you? In Basti jeela?

I nodded.

All right, she said. I want you to go to the village with the tape. Somebody will remember Parbati the kahaar, who went from the village with her child, Kalloo, when people were running from the drought ninety years ago. I want you to play the ending of the story. There.

I was going to play the story anyway. But where should I start from? Where did the ending start?

Deeda leaned forward to explain. Start where he wakes up and finds that she is gone. Where he sees the elephant's footprints and follows them to find her. They know me, and they know the story. I am cutting out the middle only.

So now I knew where to stop in my transcription. I wanted to take Ajie's help till the last moment, but I also wanted the magic of hearing it as if for the first time in Basti.

Deeda, like a great river, had long since finished tripping down mountain slopes. Now, after a long, long peaceful run over level ground, she wanted to deposit all the silt she had gathered in the mountains before she rejoined the great ocean at the end of her journey. Like we all did, I guess. But Deeda wanted more, it seemed: she wanted to see her story return first of all to the place she had left. She wanted, through her story, to pass on the news that she was still alive, but in a different universe.

The story could not end with the heroine still in exile. So she was sending back her Saranga, her more fanciful self.

I would be carrying a hitchhiker with me. Had she been waiting all these years for someone like me to give her a ride? Did she know Sunnariya's great-great granddaughter would come for her one day? I suddenly realized that through Sunnariya and Janaki-didi I was Deeda's jahaji. We were like family. I had to be there for her.

So it was settled. She turned her attention to Rosa. I told her about the kind of work Rosa was doing, looking at women who had come on the boats alone.

Deeda nodded and launched into details about the women she had known, about who all had come as widows, who had come with parents, who had run away from hard times, and who had simply walked out of the house. And a kind of woman who never got married at all. All this I translated softly as she spoke, relaying back the questions Rosa had been saving up to ask since the first day she had begun listening to Deeda's tapes.

And as I listened to their conversation the migration came across to me as a story of women making their way alone, with men in the background, strangers, extras. In the history books it had always been the other way around: it was the men who were the main actors. But there was also this unwritten history of the birth of a new community in Trinidad. And it was women who were at the centre of the story.

The best things never did get onto tape.

'I've been thinking about what you said that day,' I told Rosa on our drive back to St Augustine. 'About going with the flow, and not forcing the ending. I've decided to move on after Carnival. But I can't say what I'll do after that.'

She smiled. 'Keep me posted,' she said, 'I think you have a long voyage ahead.'

I dropped her off and turned to head back to Couva. I wanted to finish another chunk of the Saranga story with Ajie that night. But I would leave the ending for when I was in Basti. As I had promised Deeda.

I think Ajie was hooked on the story too. I decided to ask Dylan to make a copy of the tape for her, so that she could enjoy it in real time without having to pause at the end of every sentence and explain to a latecomer.

That night I brought out the tape recorder to the drop-leaf table upstairs for the last time. The other interviews I would transcribe later by myself. This chunk tonight would be my swan song with Ajie.

Rewind. Play.

'...gharey dibiya kholey ke, rasta me na kholbey. Na aisan ta phir dhokha khaybey.'

'Ta okey le gail. Ba okar jiyara na mane, u jaai ke rasta me dibiya khol del.'

...open it only when you get back home. Do not open it on the road. If you do, things will go against you again.

So Sada Birij said: 'All right.' But his spirit rebelled against this, and on the road, he opened the box.

When he opened the box Saranga stood up. Then she walked on, both of them walked on blissfully, blissfully, and her feet got blisters. The poor girl had never walked on the road before. Now she walked on and on.

The sun was very hot, and both of them went and sat down under a tree. And Sada Birij put some cotton wool on her leg as a pillow, and he fell asleep on it. And she kept sitting. Her body was completely covered, but one toe was showing.

Then a king came by on an elephant. When he saw her foot, he thought: 'If her foot is like that, what must her face be like?'

So he went and dropped his whip in front of her. Dropped it. Then he said: 'Oh, could you pick up the whip for me?'

So she said: 'No, I can't get up, because my husband is asleep on my leg.'

So he said: 'Put his head on the ground, and give me the whip.'

So she said: 'No.'

So he tossed his pagri to her. And he said: 'Put his head on the pagri and give me my whip, and I'll go on my way.'

So the poor girl took the pagri, and she picked up the whip and handed it to him. And he grabbed her hand, sat her on the elephant with him and carried her away.

But when he was taking her away, she said: 'Look, I'm not going to your home now. I need twelve years. Then after that you will be my husband. Or else nothing.'

So the prince decided to build a Shiv temple for her. And now there were carpenters everywhere busy building it.

That is where Saranga stayed and waited for Sada Birij to find her.

And when he woke up he said: 'Oh Saranga, I've lost you, oh Saranga, I've lost you, oh Saranga, I've lost you!' Where is Saranga? She's gone.

And he started to walk, and when he saw the elephant's footprints, he followed them. He said: 'She went this way—'

This was the place! I pressed stop and rewound the tape to cue it to just before the sentence where Sada Birij woke up. I had explained Deeda's strange request to Ajie, and she had seemed intrigued, and quite ready to do her bit for Deeda and stop here. She would have her own tape in a day or so, and Dylan would play it for her. The rest of this tape I would have to manage on my own.

Deeda must have a plan. She was steering the story now, and pulling a helpless dreamy lover along with her, leaving him clues everywhere to keep him in the race.

Hard-headed woman.

Or maybe Deeda was just a starry-eyed romantic after all. Still dreaming of a man for whom she might have been everything, instead of a great big hero too busy fighting his battles and thinking about honour to worry about how she fitted into his life.

Or too stuck on making it big to notice little things like magic that made life worth living.

There is always something more romantic in dark-eyed loss than in the over-lit world of success. In what could have been, than in what actually happened.

Deeda had not forgotten her first love.

There were many things they had never had a chance to have together. Among those were disillusionment and acrimony. Something had stayed young and fresh, in her mind at least. It was the salt water between India and Trinidad that had kept them apart.

And Deeda was a realist.

What about the prince? She could have made him out to be a villain. She didn't. What is more, she never really had Saranga say no to him, though she always had the power to hold him off, and to set conditions. And he was, amazingly, quick to give her the time she needed. He didn't just want a trophy.

Now I wanted to get a sense of the prince too. I wanted to see if, in the air of strength and worldly success that surrounded him, I could detect a note of whimsy or magic. Was that what Saranga had been hoping for each time, what made her give him a tiny chance?

The more contrary the story got, the more I could feel Deeda's presence there at the helm. Well, that was where she had always wanted to be, ever since the early days on the *Godavari*, when she had first seen the man up front holding the wheel.

Deeda had seized the initiative and had made up her mind how she wanted to end the story. I would have to wait till India to see what sort of brew she was cooking up to serve me.

ANDA SIKHAAWE BACCHA

Sunday lunches had become a tradition in our house as Dad's brothers and sisters spread out and away from Couva. But they had stopped being a weekly event as they once used to be. A few years ago the driveway would fill up with cars every Sunday, and all the cousins would slink into the house, full of teenage angst and unfinished business with the outside world.

These days the family had to be called if we wanted everybody there.

Ajie was always the one in charge of the kitchen, and she would quietly supervise the making of a feast, with a full Indian menu. But there was always space for a few Creole or North American items.

Since I was leaving to go back, Mom had decided to bake a cake. So I went with her to the supermarket on Saturday, and roamed around the aisles storing up images of fruits and vegetables I wouldn't see in Ann Arbor, while Mom got busy picking up bilingually labelled things for her cake.

It had not been easy for Mom, settling into a big Indian joint family in the Trinidad countryside. The first things that had got to her were all the constraints. Not being able to go out the gate and walk down the street. Not being able to wear the clothes you put on for sports. In fact, no sports at all. Basically, just sitting put in the house. In Trinidad it wouldn't be safe for her to walk on the road, she was told, because she was too 'fair'. She would stand out.

After putting up with this seclusion for two years, Mom had gone out and got a job soon after I was born, leaving me during the day with Ajie. And Ajie would take me into the shop with her and put me in a child seat suspended from the ceiling of the 'cage' she sat in, with all the cash and the vault of gold behind her. And little old ladies from the sugar estates would come and stand outside the cage and stare at me, and when I woke up, they would realize that I was alive. Not a toy! And I got used to hearing them talking in Bhojpuri, and Ajie replying in something almost like Hindi.

Mom became a teacher at Naparima Girls High School, Ajie's old school, and the school where my father's sisters and almost all his female relatives had gone. So during the day she met a mix of Canadian missionary women and women from the new Trinidad middle class, on La Pique hill in San Fernando, and that satisfied her wanderlust.

But she always talked of the old days in Corner Brook, Newfoundland. Of walking all over the town by herself as a small child. Of skis and skates and sleighs in the winter. Of bags of groceries being delivered home in winter on a one-horse-open-sleigh!

'How did your parents let you go around all by yourself?' I would ask. 'Weren't they scared?'

'Oh, no,' she would say. 'It was perfectly safe. It was a small town and I didn't stand out. In Corner Brook I looked just like everybody else.'

So that was it, I had thought.

But I would press her. 'What exactly would go wrong if I went out by myself like my friends do? If I got on a bus?'

'You might get attacked,' she would say, 'or even kidnapped. People might think your family had money.'

It was a short step from those scare stories to making me super-conscious about how different I looked. Making me actually scared of going out on my own.

But I could tell that Mom was looking forward to my going back to Michigan so that I could have the sort of freedom she herself had been missing in Trinidad. Once I was out of Trinidad and Tobago airspace she would cease to worry about my safety.

I thought of our two German Shepherds, locked in their enclosure during the day, and let out to go absolutely wild in the yard at night when the gates were locked. Other people let their dogs roam around the house during the day, petted them and talked to them, and they always behaved well, wagging their tails gently.

Ours would have jumped up and knocked you down if they got loose. I actually remember one of them knocking down one of my little cousins with just a wag of his tail. The one thing we dreaded was one of them getting out of the gate, since they had never developed road sense. One of our champion German Shepherds had got out the gate one night and been hit by a car, and had died with a look of bewilderment on its face.

So my family's faith in my survivor instincts abroad amazed me.

On my first trip to Michigan I had missed my connection at JFK. But my bags had gone on the flight. And they had been waiting for me in Detroit. I had checked them in and taken back my ticket, but not collected my boarding pass.

And then, two days later in Ann Arbor, Nishant had seen me for the first time, surging to the front of a line, excited, just assuming that I could. And he had told me to get back one space, behind him.

I had already sent Nishant my flight details and he had sent me a telegram that he would be waiting for me at the airport in Detroit.

Sunday morning dawned. Mugs of tea waiting, covered, in the kitchen, for us to pick up as we came down. The kitchen would already have been in high gear making lunch by the time I left my room and headed towards the back stairs.

I stopped to look out my window of time.

That was the only place from which I could see clear over the high galvanized fence at the back of our yard. A tall breadfruit tree blocked the view from the window in Mom and Dad's room. Across the rough asphalt road, the Back Street we called it, the mortuary lawns were lush and green. And alien.

We had every imaginable tree, vine and herb in our back yard, even a patch of sugarcane, and Ajie's flower garden full of orchids, rosebushes, poinsettias and potted plants was out there in front. But we had no lawn. A lawn made no sense to an Indian family in the Trinidad countryside.

I went out into the back yard, past the dogs' enclosure, past the breadfruit tree, past the Julie mango tree, past the little patch of Bon Bon cane.

A grey tabby cat was sitting on top of the back fence, sunning itself. I stood quietly watching it.

It sensed me there and turned. Its eyes were the same cool green as Maracas waves. We looked at each other like that for a long time.

Then it got to its feet and stretched. One more look in my direction, and it turned and sleekly jumped off the fence onto the Back Street.

I turned back towards the house for my farewell lunch.

Kojo was sitting on his chair at the back of the living room downstairs, watching a Hindi film on TV and separately listening to Hindi music on his tiny radio. Only Kojo could do that.

And aunts and uncles and cousins were beginning to arrive, and park, each in their favourite spot.

Dylan's mother came and handed me my ticket, and told me to check that she had got it right.

My other aunt, the historian at the UWI seminar, gave me a cyclostyled draft of her own thesis on the migration from India, with lots of little notes in the margin in ink which would be typed into the final version. I opened the book at random and found myself on a page listing the places in India the migrants had come from. The second and third places listed, near the top of the page, were Faizabad and Basti.

Then Dad's voice came from the doorway calling us all to the long table.

It wasn't the food that made the day at our Sunday lunches. There was too much variety, no single focus. It was Dad, in his element like at no other time. Cracking jokes and poking fun at us all, one by one, until we gave up and joined in the fun. Until we sat back and enjoyed the whole stand-up comedy act. It was lethal to try to talk sense at Sunday lunch.

And I came in for a lot of ribbing for looking distracted, as if I was halfway to Michigan already.

'It's a mystery man,' said Dylan, sitting next to me.

'Whaaat?' I burst out.

'He supposed to pick her up when she cross the sea.'

'Whoa! That's a fairy tale! We're talking about me now!'

'Taking bets!' he announced. 'Will she go with the prince or choose the monkey here? Place your money now.'

My jaw dropped. Dylan gave me a wicked look. Then he grabbed his plate and got up to leave it in the kitchen.

'And the winner is...'

And the rest of the room pounced on me.

Later on he caught up with me. 'So what is the answer, really, monkey or prince?'

I gave up. Time to get it off my chest. 'I don't feel right just walking away from somebody who never did me anything wrong. He helped me out with my work, he kept me from going off the deep end when my mind was coming apart. And what am I giving him back?'

He gave me an ironic smile. 'Only partly right, sis. He didn't do you any harm. He couldn't! You would have walked away before he got a chance! But you don't know him any better than he knows you. You think he just gave and gave and gave. Well, that's one way to look at it.'

'And the other?'

'You were just some white princess who came into his life. No different from any other white princess, except that you took him seriously. You gave him the confidence to think that there might be more like you he could get. So now he'll go far. But he'll still never know the real you.'

'And I don't know the real him either, right?'

'No, and you don't want to. It doesn't upset you that he has kids all over the place. It doesn't even threaten you. You're on a trip! Remember that day we ate the fried shark at Maracas? You said something about equal relationships, remember?'

Had I? I had thought it, had I said it out loud?

'"If they catch us they eat us, and if we catch them we eat them."' He shrugged. 'You were looking for somebody dangerous, but who you knew you could handle. You were feeling low and needed that sort of a boost.'

'And why did I need a boost?'

'Because you think you're on the rocks with your prince. He's not budging on something and you're feeling stuck. And he's not someone you feel you can take head on. So you're running away from the real problem.'

'Yeah, the real problem! What I really need is an unequal relationship! I need to get my butt shipped off to India for good.'

What had I just said?

'No,' he said. 'But you need someone with a mind to match yours. Not one of those crossword puzzles you like to zip through. How long would you be able to put up with that?'

'You're right, but the India thing is non-negotiable. And the problem is, I even understand. I think he's now bored to tears with the US, just waiting to get out. He's actually excited about going to India. And I don't want to be the one holding him back.'

'And your Mom and Dad are okay with this?'

I hesitated. 'I never told them. If they knew they would have a fit! India?'

He smiled. 'So you're doing the opposite of your old lady. She's cheating for the monkey and you're cheating for your prince!'

'I guess.'

'Then what is it you're running away from?'

I wasn't sure how to put this. 'I just feel like it's all happening too fast. And it's a life sentence hanging over my head if I go. I'll never get to be myself again. Once I take that step I won't be able to undo it.' And all my dreams, all my hard work to become a linguist would come to nothing.

'Well, at least you get to dip your toes in the river before you decide to jump in. The girl in your story couldn't.'

Then I remembered. 'No, she managed to get herself some time after meeting the prince. She didn't go to his palace, she lived a while by herself in the forest where she was born. But it was borrowed time.'

I sat for some time, and we didn't talk. I could feel a long-range gravitational pull calling me back out of my distant orbit into the centre of all the energy. Everything was conspiring to make me move on. I thought out loud:

'But what do I really want?'

I think he was waiting for that question. 'Magic,' said the young druid. 'That's what you said, remember?

But magic doesn't only come with sizzle, sis, it can be intelligent too. You don't find that too often, but that's the best kind. You won't get bored with it.'

Anda sikhaawe baccha, as Ajie would say. The egg teaches the chick!

'How do you know all this?' I asked.

'Because I'm the person who loves you more than anyone else does.'

And there was nothing I could say to top that.

BOBBY'S DAY OUT

Bobby had called Fyzie and me to watch them put the finishing touches to his band's Carnival float. The bow of a sailing ship, going as far back as the foremast with its sail. It was painted dull brown, to look like wood that had been seasoned in salt water, with bright black streaks painted between the boards to look like the asphalt caulking. The crew would have coal shovels and look a bit like pirates. So it was a hybrid ship, with coal engines as boosters!

Bobby's band was depicting the sea journey the jahajis had made from India. Along with the steel band that supplied the Calypso music, they had added a whole lot of dholaks and tassas for the rhythm. For much of the time it would be only the dholaks and tassas playing, along with some bongos. And the usual spanners striking old brake drums.

The bulk of the band would be costumed as jahajis, wearing dhotis and bright pagris if they were men, and ghangri-jhoola-orhnis in bright colours if they were women. The actual jahajins had worn saris. Well, these costumes looked better in a Carnival band.

The ship didn't have a name. I asked Bobby if he wanted one.

'Why not!' he said.

So I named it the *Godavari*.

The real *Godavari* had been a steamer made of steel, big and ugly, Deeda had said. But this wooden ship looked better.

Then I got busy with a brush and paint and added that finishing touch in clear white letters near the bowsprit.

And Fyzie got busy seeing that the thing moved smoothly on its hidden wheels.

Then I went and bought them a soft toy cat with bright golden eyes, and told them to stick it on the yardarm. For good luck.

So Bobby was another one who had dreams of holding the big wheel. He showed us his costume. He would look a little bit like a pirate too, with a patch over one eye and an admiral's hat. A few of the men in the band would be going in front, pulling the ship on a chain. He alone would stand on the deck. The rest of the band would be down on the road.

Bobby was going first class.

I, however, was not. But I was going. My packing at home happened against a soundtrack of Carnival music, as I put Dylan on the job of recording all the calypsos of the season, and he turned his room into a sound studio. The last few days before Carnival went by in a flurry of activity, as I ticked off all the last things to be done. Then only Carnival was left.

I sat with Ajie in the shop on Carnival Monday, while a sprinkling of jab-jabs, or diables, came by begging, cracking whips and saying, 'Pay the Devil!' while kids on the pavement quickly made room for them, and pretended they didn't 'fraid maas'. No kid wanted to admit he was afraid of the masqueraders.

Carnival Monday was always like that, small time. Made you wonder if Mardi Gras, the next day, would take off.

But it did. Bobby stood at the helm and took charge, with a smile that flashed like a lighthouse beacon. Tuesday afternoon the good people of Chaguanas came out to play Carnival and saw before them a hybrid ship, backed by a hybrid orchestra, taking over the road. And behind the ship was a band full of modern-day jahajis jumping up on the road to music, and sharing the spirit and building up the momentum for some true Carnival knowledge later on. A whole new crop of teenage girls had come out to play Carnival, and all the men were eyeing them and making plans.

Fyzie and I stood on the roadside, part of the enormous crowd, and watched Bobby's *Godavari* sail through Chaguanas. And when the surge had passed, our mood mellowed. We decided we had had enough of crowds. Time to follow another tradition people like Sheila observed every Carnival. We got into the car and headed for Mayaro beach, far away from all the crowds and all the brittle-bright Carnival music.

Down south we went on the highway, and then we turned off to go through Princes Town, and on past Rio Claro. First we went through cane lands, with little siwalas, Shiv temples, then we were going through dense forest, and then we reached the long fringe of coconut groves.

Fyzie drove and I sat, not saying much. Just storing up images, and feeling the bluewash descend upon me.

And soon we reached the Atlantic Ocean. Mayaro.

We parked the car at the side of the road under some coconut trees. We were not alone, another couple had had the same idea. But the place looked desolate. We were far from any houses, or any shacks on the beach.

We sat near the car, under a coconut tree that was leaning out toward the water. Next to us was a coconut, half buried in the sand, with a shoot growing out of it. It could be from one of the trees here, or it could have washed up on a wave from just about anywhere. But this would be the end of its journey.

Out on the horizon an oil tanker passed by, headed north. The same route the real *Godavari* would have taken, after sighting land more or less where we were sitting. I could see the top half of it, the hull was mostly hidden by the sea.

The world was truly round.

I sat and stared out at the water and kept sloughing off my artificial Carnival high, feeling the chug-chug of my engines slow to a crawl, and then die.

Silence. The sound of surf. The wind in the coconut trees.

My mood sank quickly, down to sea level, and then it plunged below the surface. I decided to let it stay there, suspended in the salt water. I did not want to fight the blues off this time, I wanted to wear them around me like a cloak. I was tired of putting on a good face.

Some words were coming through to me in Spanish, a song, 'Alfonsina'. I didn't know the story behind the song, but I did know that something awful had happened. A woman had walked out into the sea, and kept walking, and never come back.

I knew I would never come back.

I had come to take my last look at the coastline.

I just sat and stared at the endless sea stretching before me.

It was an act of will, wrestling with the gloom inside me. Struggling with a part of my own self that just wanted to give up and sink down, down, down. I knew the symptoms, and thinking of doom in every sentence was the clearest sign.

I turned. Fyzie was looking at me. He put his arm around my shoulder. 'I know how yuh feelin',' he said softly. 'I not feelin' so good mihself. Look, you doan have to worry if you change yuh min' later. If you want to come back, jus' come.'

Jus' come. A shy invitation from Fyzie. Something he had never said before.

But could it ever be that simple? Just push my hand inside my pocket and buy a ticket. And walk away from a million little things that would have grown around me to hold me down. Quicksand. When the world turns grey and your own mind slows and sinks, and the will to move is gone. Can you ever return to the bright world you have left? Is there really a place for you in the garden if you cut loose from the real world and try to go back? Can you really play around with a story like that?

Fyzie could. He had walked away easily from many girls, with kids spawned over many Carnivals before this. He did not get distracted by the life on the roadside.

But I was going. I was going for good.

I sat and stared into the muddy grey water near the shoreline and held on tight to nothing at all, deep in the doldrums, as images of this place living on without me played before my mind's eye in vivid detail. As if I had died.

When your mind is below sea level there is one little thing you have to hang on and be ready for: that little flash that is worth all the gloom, that single useable thought. Time passed, and I held on. The sky above me changed slowly, the shadows faded. I waited for sunset. Magic light. I kept my eyes focused on the sea.

Then right on cue the cloud cover parted and a soft whisper of clarity shone out of the oily darkness inside my head and told me that I was exhausted.

And then I could see it, the black tiredness. This deep trough was always the payback for the wave of manic energy. The wave which had banished shyness and let me walk 'brave and bold' into strangers' homes with a bright smile and record all their heartfelt narratives. The wave which had also seen me through the final flurry of goodbyes.

But it was something else too. I was trapped inside a story that had to run its course, and I was fighting with the story, trying to swim against the current. Trying to get out. When I was merely a part of the story, with no independent existence. The story was what had given me the journey I had to make, and I had already come a long way. There would be a resounding echo of emptiness if I exited from the dream.

When you are caught in an undertow taking you to the bottom of the sea you do not try to fight it head on. Your only chance is to go with the current and escape it from the edges, with a tiny change of direction. Hold your breath and save the energy for when you can make a difference. Wait, as Deeda had done all these years.

Now Fyzie took charge, pulling me back from the brink, as he always did. He grabbed hold of me by the shoulders and propelled me back to the car and sat me down in the front passenger seat. Then he got in and took the wheel and started the engine.

'Let we go back Chaguanas,' he said. 'We could reach in time for Las' Lap. Wha' yuh say?'

And we pulled away out of the doldrums and drove north on the Manzanilla-Mayaro road along the Atlantic and turned west after Manzanilla, and made our way back on small roads through miles of little cocoa trees shaded by tall flame-coloured immortelles. By the time we reached Chaguanas the sky had darkened to a rich deep cobalt blue, and lights were on everywhere. From a distance we could hear the sound of steel band music.

I could feel the drums pulling me into sync with a faster tempo, taking me into the music, away from the hollowness inside me, lighting up the dark corners.

We parked the car and went to join the band.

Las' Lap would be at eleven o'clock. Lots of time to conjure the mood and join the jahajis as they jumped up in the streets till the last possible moment.

Bobby called us up to stand with him at the wheel.

I grasped the wheel and held it, for the first time. Where are you, Deeda? I thought.

I decided not to try turning it. A big ship like the *Godavari* knew its own way and rode the currents and the winds and the waves. And I had a huge wave at my stern that knew where it wanted to go. I realized that even holding the wheel like a helmsman I had only so much play in steering my course. There would be many other players with me if I wanted to move in a band. And there were only a few rare moments when I would have the option of changing direction. Most of the time control was an illusion.

I handed the wheel back to the real helmsman and went back into the anonymous crowd. In the dark I looked like everybody else, in perfect camouflage, travelling incognito with a wave of jahajis, the past and the present moving in step. Down the street in front of Chaguanas Market, jumping up to the beat of the same dholaks and tassas that had dragged the *Godavari* out of the doldrums, and powered the engines that had headed it towards the stormy channel, and once again taken it north across the Atlantic doldrums to connect with the trade winds near Trinidad.

As the end drew near the steelband sounds faded out, and now it was only the dholaks and the tassas, like an enormous heartbeat, igniting the fires deep inside the living ship and sending sparks to us to keep us going.

Don't stop, girl, we headin' up to Las' Lap! Just a little more! With one last burst of acceleration I pushed myself to keep moving, down the straits, down the islands, going with the flow, feeling the throb of the engines, heading towards the depot, like a long break-away, grabbing the last moments of the great adventure, until the clock struck eleven and we dropped anchor.

And it was time for everybody to pack up and walk down the gangplank. The long, long ride was over.

Christians would go home with a gloomy sense of the start of Lent. And the whole crowd would go with a sense that the great illusion was over, till next year, same time, same place.

Tomorrow there would be not a trace of Carnival to be seen, not even a song on the radio. And the day after that I would be flying out, back to Michigan.

I dropped Fyzie off and drove home to finish packing.

LIKE ICARUS

THERE WAS NO REASON WHY ASH WEDNESDAY SHOULD wear a watery dismal look, but it did. The sunlight was feeble, and the streets were suddenly empty. It might all have been a dream.

Dylan was up early, and back in school uniform.

I sat across the table from him with a mug of tea while he put away a large plate of scrambled eggs and toast. In between bites he looked up at me, getting a fix on my mood.

'Welcome back to reality!' he said at last, when his plate was empty. 'I heard you were up there steering a big ship in Chaguanas last night. And now you have to fly economy class tomorrow. What a comedown!'

I gave him a baleful look and said nothing.

'So!' he said. 'Had enough of make-believe?'

'No,' I said. 'Tomorrow I get my old role back.'

'And what is that starry role?'

'I get to be Icarus. I get to orbit the sun again, if my wings don't melt.'

He sobered down at once. 'Or you can stop playing any role. Just be yourself.'

'I don't remember what that is.'

He looked squarely at me. 'You are the girl who had the idea of coming and recording the old people. You went in there and made it happen. And you're the one who got a grant to go and look at the scene in India.'

He paused to consider me, and then he continued.

'Just a few hours back you were ready to go and conquer the world. Don't give up your power! Don't forget who you are! Get a grip on yourself!'

I could hear Mom coming down the stairs. She had already had her tea upstairs in her room. Now, with a brief halt in the dining room for a slice of toast and jam, she would be off to beat the traffic north to St Augustine and my old school.

And Dylan would head in the opposite direction, south to San Fernando.

I got busy rearranging my tapes and transcripts. I tagged the tape of the Saranga story in bright red ink, and decided to cue it.

Rewind. Stop. Play. Deeda's voice. '...*uran khatola. Ta u baney lagal...*' I pressed stop.

Uran khatola?

Later, I thought, rewinding again. Maybe I'll ask Nishant.

It was decided that Mom would drive me to the airport. Ajie and Dad would stay back in the shop.

Next morning I brought my bag down to Mom's car. I put my hand luggage and winter coat on the backseat. Then I took a picture of Mom and Dad standing near the open trunk where I had just put my bag. Low angle, thinking to make them stand taller.

The result did nothing to empower them, but it drew attention to the 'child' they were both staring down at

with a stricken expression. Dad stood with his arm
around Mom, as if sheltering her in some way. The picture
caught it all. Guilt at feeling relieved about me going.
The wish that they had handled this visit differently. The
realization that I was going for good.

I kept my smile bright as I died inside.

I tried to think of how they could have been different
with me. No answer.

Ajie gave me a weepy hug. She had seen all her
children go, one by one, across the seas to college, and
for her an old scene was playing out again. Like giving
your daughter away in marriage: it brought you to tears,
but you knew that the time had come.

Then it was Dylan's turn to give me a hug and his
parting shot: 'Ooh sis, this is where I'm supposed to say,
"Boo-hoo, come back soon," but, like, this time, don't.
Don't let me down. See this story through, and give it a
good twist in the tail!'

And Mom and I were off.

As we pulled into the parking lot at the airport I saw
Fyzie waiting for me in a friend's car. Mom saw him too,
and froze. He stayed in the car.

I checked in and went upstairs with Mom to have
coffee. I kept up a bright patter, and we both tried to talk
as warmly and as innocuously as possible. Then she took
a look at her watch, and said it was time for her to be off
to school. I walked her back to her car.

I walked back into the airport with Fyzie, and the
scene replayed itself in the coffee shop upstairs, with more
life and colour, but as warmly and as innocuously as
before. We could have been two old friends who would
be meeting again in a week or so. Fyzie was giving me a

bright send-off. He walked me to the emigration door
and gave me a friendly hug, and a wave.

I walked down the long corridor to the plane, feeling
with each step the hold of the last few months loosening.
A time outside of time was ending.

The plane taxied to the runway, turned to face east
and revved its engines. Then we raced down the runway
directly towards the early morning sun. Icarus, I thought.

The young man at the immigration counter at JFK
asked me whether I wanted to use my tourist visa or my
student visa. He could give me a longer stay on my
tourist visa, he said.

'Student visa,' I said. 'It doesn't matter, I'm not staying
long. I have to move on from here.'

'Where to?' he asked.

'India!'

'There's no problem staying here,' he assured me.

I couldn't believe it. A US immigration officer trying
to get me to stay?

I connected to Detroit, and landed as a different person
in another universe. There, waiting for me at the gate,
was Nishant.

I gratefully slipped into my old role, and let him take
over and get my bag out to the car. We drove on the
snowy highway on the right side of the road back to
Ann Arbor. I switched off and let him talk, giving me an
intense update on all the news from the US, and listing
who we were to meet in the next few days. We would
drop off my bags and I could change and be ready for a
party his research group was having that evening.

I stood at the party wearing clothes I had left behind
in Ann Arbor, and let Nishant drift into the centre of the

crowd. I needed time alone to think. I was bewildered at the compliant creature I had become. I hadn't even said a word about my time in Trinidad! My mind kept drifting back to that other universe, where I had fought for the right to be in charge of my life. Where I had seemed to be strong.

I found myself thinking about Saranga. I realized that I never ever got to see that strong lady actually contending with her prince or his world beyond the few moments when they met, if even that. In the story she was always buying time to think, and looking back nostalgically. Sequestering herself in little dwellings away from the palace. Had she also been afraid, after taking the plunge, that she might lose her footing altogether?

An older man from the group drifted over to me and started asking me about the work I had been doing. My brain came alive, and I found myself talking about all the people I had recorded in Caroni as statistical samples of different age groups. I was back in academia.

Out of the corner of my eye I saw Nishant note, from across the room, that I had managed to look after myself. Then, like two ships moving in the same current, we drifted and eventually found ourselves part of the same group.

Back to life beyond the breaker line.

After the party the two of us went off to a cozy bar and got a table off in a corner. I found myself telling Nishant about Deeda's strange request, that I play the last part of her story in her old village in Basti, to someone who remembered her and her son.

'I think she noticed that I didn't exactly get it while she was telling it to me. So it would be like a first time for me too. That would be part of the magic. By the way, there was a word I didn't understand on the tape. Think you can help me?' I asked.

'You mean listen to the tape?' he asked.

'Well,' said, 'I heard a bit by accident. I got my cousin to make a copy of the tape for Ajie, and then I realized I had to get it back to the same spot, where the ending starts. First time I didn't rewind it enough, and when I played it this word sort of popped out. *Uran khatola.* Mean anything to you? You have a word like this in Hindi?'

He frowned. 'It's a flying cot,' he said.

'A what?'

'An Indian magic carpet. But actually a wooden cot.'

'Cot as in khatiya? The wooden bed frame with a criss-cross of jute string that you put the bedding on? We still have a few of those in Trinidad.'

'Yes,' he said. 'That's one of the words for it in Hindi. That's all? Now you can figure out the rest of the story by yourself?'

'I think so. I knew there had to be some magic trick to get the story to end the way she wanted. So now I know what she's coming with. When I hear the story in Basti I'll be able to follow it.'

It was already almost March, and Nishant felt I should not put off my trip to India. The Indian summer would hit some time in April, and by May the daytime temperatures would be over a hundred Fahrenheit.

So next day I got in touch with the American Institute of Indian Studies and got started. Then I started phoning the airlines to make reservations. Air India, I thought. The girl who did my booking told me exactly what the menu would be throughout the flight. I was so intrigued by this that I decided to stick with Air India.

Nishant had once met the visa officer at the Indian embassy in Washington, an older man, and they had sat for ages and talked Indian politics. Now he phoned him and asked him how to go about getting me a visa. He told him my background, Indian from Trinidad, doing a PhD on the language spoken by Indians in Trinidad. He added that I had an AIIS grant to go to the areas migrants had come from in India.

The visa officer thought a moment. Processing my visa as an AIIS scholar would take time, he said, as much as if I were an American. Why did I want to do all of that? I was only going to be in India a short while, and as a Commonwealth citizen, and an overseas Indian, I could simply come to the embassy, fill out a form and get a visa straight away.

So I flew to Washington DC to get my Indian visa. Then I continued on to New York to catch the Air India flight.

As I waited to board the aircraft in New York I kept hearing Ajie's voice echoing in my head: how will they *treat* you? Or, transposed to the present context, how would the crew and the other passengers view me: as a foreigner, or as some species of Indian? My looks were ambiguous.

And sure enough, the stewardess did ask me if I was Indian.

I told her yes.

She looked at me curiously. 'What caste?' she asked. Caste?

I decided not to give her a list. I just stuck with the one I had grown up with.

'Sonaar,' I said. Goldsmith.

She looked at me completely confused. 'That isn't a caste!'

When Nishant had once talked to me about caste, during one of our long, long drives through the Midwest, many of the labels he had used were completely new to me. They were sub-groups of the caste he belonged to. It was almost the same, hearing other students from India talk about caste. It seemed to me that they were all banias, brahmins and thakurs, and that they only knew about each other and the one or two other small castes that were officially on par with them. But I was certain that my notion of caste was not wrong. Caste was about sonaars, lohaars, kahaars, ahirs, kurmis and chamains too.

There was a big disconnect between what I had seen as caste in Trinidad and what the students I knew from India perceived.

That was what Nana had meant by the caste system. Not just something that defined what we did, but something that assigned us a lower position, below other Indians we no longer saw as better than us in any way.

Nishant had truly scooped up a creature from a different set of origins. Even then I had a sense that he had taken a bold step in sending me alone to meet his family.

I looked at the stewardess as she bent to talk to a couple, up the aisle. She had probably met sonaars in India. If she had ever gone to have jewellery made, she must have. But they would have been background noise, just faceless craftsmen busy in a workshop soldering and polishing and fixing broken things. Not hybrid-looking young women speaking English and travelling alone on Air India.

I decided to keep a low profile.

I looked out the window at the rapidly changing sky. The windows on the aircraft had a framing of painted filigree around them, suggesting old domes. The sort of dome one might expect to see on the little shrine where Saranga was staying at this point in the story.

Or the tops of the spindled legs of a khatiya, a cot, turned on a lathe.

Uran khatola. I smiled at the thought. I looked down at my hand luggage under the seat in front of me. My tapes were there, safe. My tape with Deeda's story was flying with me.

The sky began to lighten, our second sunrise in the space of twenty-four hours. A woman's voice announced, in English and in Hindi, that we would be landing soon, and asked us to fasten our seatbelts. As we came in to land we heard piped tabla music on the overhead speakers. A tiny heartbeat to boost the engines.

And then it was into the bustling turmoil of Palam Airport, edging up to the immigration desk. A grizzly-looking old policeman in a brown uniform sat at the counter waiting, maintaining a dignified reserve, but barely keeping his head above water with all the English he was being made to read. He took my passport and stared at it, deciphering the information he needed, word by word, and curiously reading a lot of extra things he could have saved time by ignoring. Then he took another cautious look at me and stamped my passport.

Then into the baggage area, where the porters were bustling around, with the same faces I had seen in Trinidad, mysteriously speaking Hindi, not Creole.

As I waited for my bag to come on the conveyor belt, I looked at the porters. Their faces were familiar, but their expressions were not. Some of them seemed to have a wide-eyed but blinkered look, as if trying to handle an overload of sensory information. They seemed not to actually 'see' us there. The jahajis who had just got off the boat in Trinidad had had that look too, in the old photographs I had seen.

The only thing I had to declare at customs was my tape recorder. Nishant had told me that I would have to report it and tell the customs people that I would be taking it out with me again when I left. Otherwise I would have to pay duty on it. That took a little paperwork, but no stress.

The rest of my luggage was of no interest to Indian Customs at all.

I wheeled my trolley out of the building and into the early morning sunshine. There waiting for me wearing corduroy trousers and looking a bit different from the childhood photographs Nishant had shown me, was his sister, Manju.

WALKING IN STEP

MANJU WAS ENGAGED TO BE MARRIED LATER IN THE YEAR, and she had brought her boyfriend with her to the airport. To drive the car she had borrowed from her aunt to pick me up, she said. He gave me an enormous smile and took my bag, and we went off to get the little white Fiat.

The drive back from the airport was like a foray into an old Hindi film. Almost the only cars to be seen on the road were Indian Ambassadors and Indian Fiats, apart from a few foreign cars with diplomatic license plates. Nishant had told me to expect this, his eyes challenging mine, daring me to make a gauche comment. But it was still a surprise, and the first time I was seeing a landscape with such starkly different road fauna. I had grown up thinking that India was ahead of us in every way.

Manju lived in a barsati, a tiny flat built on the flat roof terrace of a large house. During the drive she told me how Nishant had managed to persuade their father to let her have her own flat when she was a student. In the beginning she had shared it with another girl.

We climbed the two flights of steps to the barsati, passed all her potted plants on the terrace, and went inside and put the bag down next to a mattress in her living room that served as a divan. Then she announced that she needed some tea and disappeared into her little kitchen.

As we sat and had tea, Manju told me that the two of us were expected for lunch at an aunt's home, not too far away. We would be meeting her father there. He had come to Delhi on work. I would get a chance to tell him about my plans to visit Faizabad and Basti, and any other places I needed to go to in the area. He was going back to Lucknow the next day, so he could find out when an inspection tour would be going to those places.

I must have looked tired, because she told me that I should rest, that they had to go and return the car. I stretched out on the divan, and before I knew it I was fast asleep. And the next thing I knew she was back, and it was time to get ready to go for lunch.

I got ready quickly and we went down to the street. As we stood waiting for a three-wheeler scooter taxi, a man on a bicycle went by, and as he passed I saw on his carrier two monkeys dressed as a boy and a girl, earnest little passengers, squatting on the carrier behind the saddle with leashes around their necks.

Manju saw me staring. 'Want me to stop him? He'll get the monkeys to dance for you.'

So these were the monkeys Deeda had talked about in the Saranga story! And here they were just roaming about the streets of Delhi on the back of a bicycle!

'No,' I said, 'I just made the connection. I've heard about these monkeys in Trinidad.'

Then a three-wheeler stopped and we got in. I listened to her giving the driver directions in Hindi, and made a mental note of the phrases she had used.

A number of schoolgirls were walking along the road wearing uniforms and carrying book bags. Heading for a municipal school, Manju said, where the second shift of the day was about to start.

Most of the girls had their hair oiled and in two braids, with ribbons braided into the last bit. Then the whole braid was looped back and tied near the top of the braid with the same ribbon in a pretty bow, making the braids look a bit like drooping rabbits' ears. I remembered Ajie oiling my hair and doing it like that a few times when I was small, and telling me that was how she had done her hair at school. I remembered thinking that Ajie must have had really lovely hair, if she could get two thick braids even with all that oil in her hair.

And when I got into Naparima Girls High School there had been a lot of Indian girls coming in from the villages around San Fernando with their hair done like that, and I had felt a little inadequate with my short hair.

The three-wheeler paused at a red light, and Manju gave the driver some more instructions, and we were off again. The sound of the little scooter engine and Manju's Hindi brought me back to where I was.

We got off in Panch Shila Park, and walked through the gate to her aunt's house. Manju's aunt was a tall handsome woman with a tinkling laugh, and she had cooked up a feast. And then her father came out of a room, and shook my hand very warmly.

Nobody asked how I was linked to Nishant. But they had decided.

Nishant's father thought there might be an inspection tour to Faizabad and Basti in ten days' time. It would leave from Lucknow, and I could tag along. It would be no trouble making a detour to the village I wanted to visit.

Nishant's aunt called us all for lunch, and I found myself thinking back to the lunch in Couva before I left for Michigan. The faces here were different, and so was the accent, and the meal was served buffet style and quite different from what we called Indian food in Trinidad, but the atmosphere was similar. One uncle was explaining the details of a cricket match to his little daughter, listing who all 'our' bowlers were.

I was looking at the breaker line from the other side.

Later in the afternoon Manju and I sat and planned my time. Since I wanted to do a train journey, I would take the overnight train from Delhi to Lucknow, and then fly on to Patna, where I had to meet some linguists working on the dialects of Bihar. Then I would fly back to Lucknow, and go by road to Faizabad and Basti. Manju decided she would come with me on the train to Lucknow.

The next day we went together to New Delhi railway station to get our tickets.

'I'll get you a first-class ticket,' said Manju.

'Is that what you're getting for yourself?' I asked her.

'No-no,' she said, 'I'll go second class, three-tier. That's how I always go. It's only thirty rupees, twenty with student concession. First class is a hundred.'

'So why am I going first class?' I asked.

'Oh, it's not so comfortable in second class, it's an open compartment, and the seats are not padded. But I like to take the top bunk.'

The top bunk! Deeda still remembered being on the top bunk, and she had asked if they still had two tiers on Indian trains.

'Can I come with you in second class and get a top bunk too?' I asked.

She laughed. 'You'll end up on the top bunk anyhow!' she said. 'Some old person will refuse to climb up, and you will have to go.'

I'd forgotten about that!

I was actually relieved to be travelling with her. I remembered how scared I had been, as a child, at the thought of travelling in India without an interpreter, facing all the Hindi I hadn't been allowed to learn. I knew too much Hindi to be a foreigner, and too little to be an Indian. And I was more nervous about this than an American student would have been. I didn't want to feel like a foreigner, and would rather say nothing at all than be heard making a mistake in Hindi.

So two days later we found ourselves outside the New Delhi railway station on our way to board the overnight Lucknow Mail, taking on a railway porter in his red kurta and white pajama.

Railway porters here were simply called coolies! The word stuck in my craw. I couldn't get myself to say it. The word had been banned in Trinidad ever since Independence. It was a racial slur of the worst kind aimed at an Indian, and it carried the lingering nightmare of the sugar estates and bonded labour. A dark part of our past. And here at the railway station everyone was casually using the word to call the porters. Ajie would have a fit if she heard.

Our porter loaded Manju's canvas hold-all with our bedding onto his head, balancing it on top of his pagri, and then he stood up like the ship of the desert, taking our bags from us and carrying one in each hand. We went up a flight of stairs, over a few sets of tracks, and then down again to the right platform, where the train was waiting. Manju rushed to check the noticeboard outside our compartment to see that our names were there, and that our berths had not been changed.

Then into the chattering crowd inside the bogey, with porters in red kurtas jostling other porters, as everyone negotiated space to put down their baggage, the heavy bags and boxes going underneath, getting chained to the legs of the seats with huge locks, and the bedding going up onto the top bunks for the time being. Then the porters drifted away and the whistle blew, and the train started moving, and the platform outside began to recede.

Manju had said three-tier, but when we started only two tiers were visible.

I asked her about the third tier. She pointed to our backrest. 'This swings up later, when someone wants to sleep. These chains,' she pointed to two chains hanging from the top bunk, 'hold it in place.'

Had they added a tier since Deeda's time then?

A girl sitting opposite us overheard us talking about the migrants' train journey. Her father was with the railways, she said, and she knew a lot about the design of railway carriages.

There was another class, she said, cheaper than second-class three-tier. Unreserved. In unreserved there were only two tiers.

'It makes sense only to have two tiers,' she said, 'since the middle tier is only a sleeping berth for one person. In unreserved you need extra space to carry more sitting passengers, but you don't have anyone lying down. Everyone sits all the time.'

Did she think they might have had three tiers back in the 1880s, I wondered.

She shook her head. 'Having three tiers is something new in Indian Railways,' she said, 'it only goes back ten-fifteen years. A hundred years ago it wouldn't have made any sense to put a third tier. See, in unreserved it has to be cheap. The middle bunk is on a hinge.' She pointed to the hinge behind us. 'And that hinge and the wood for the bunk cost money, and need maintenance. Indian Railways would not spend money to make a bunk they didn't need.'

Deeda had been right about the two tiers.

It was still too early to climb up to our top bunks, so I looked around, trying to get a sense of the other passengers. The girl opposite us absorbed in a Hindi novel, her feet tucked under her on the seat. An old couple talking quietly to each other down the seat from us. A soldier going home on leave with a large suitcase. And down the corridor a group of men sitting around one man who was holding court, cracking jokes that had the others in splits. I couldn't follow all that he was saying, but the accent in Hindi rang through crystal clear. It was Bhojpuri.

We ate the parathas and pickle we had packed for our dinner, and then we got up to spread out our bedding on the top bunks. I stood there looking at the folded sheet and blanket, and the top bunk, with no idea how to get started. Manju came over and arranged my bedsheet and blanket quickly and deftly to cover the bunk.

I put my bag with my tape recorder and tapes up on my bunk. In time the lights in the compartment were dimmed, and the people with the middle bunks got busy lifting the backrests and attaching the hooks at the end of the chains to keep them in place. And the old couple was ready to go to sleep on the lower bunks. It was time for us to go up the ladders to our bunks.

I lay there and listened to the sound of the wheels, and tried to go to sleep, but I wasn't sleepy. I still hadn't adjusted to the time change, and I felt sleepy at odd times during the day, but not at night. So I lay awake, and replayed a fleeting memory of Nishant telling me that it was impossible for a foreign woman to adjust to India. It struck me all of a sudden that I might be taking on that comment as a challenge, and deliberately blocking out all negative reactions to India. Passing another test, like I had been brought up to do.

Was this another test to see how I handled things without him?

Stick to linguistics, girl, I told myself. Don't confuse the work with the bigger picture, as Rosa would have put it. One thing at a time.

Wait till Patna. You'll be on your own there. You'll have lots of time to think.

I must have drifted off to sleep some time during the night, because next morning when Manju called out to me from her bunk, I was fast asleep. The middle bunk was back to being a backrest, and we were pulling into a station. I could hear a voice outside on the platform intoning 'Chai garyam!'

'Last station before we reach Lucknow,' she said. 'We always have tea here.'

She leaned down towards the window and called out to the tea vendor and told him to bring us two cups of tea.

The tea came in little earthenware cups called kulhars. I smiled. I knew that was a word I couldn't pronounce. I had tried, when Nishant had told me about travelling by train in India and tea in kulhars. The type of 'r' that comes at the end of kulhar had been lost in Trinidad Bhojpuri. It had merged with the other 'r', though the jahajis always got it right. My undergraduate thesis at UWI had been about the loss of certain Indic sounds in Trinidad among people who spoke more Creole than Bhojpuri. I had needed help even to hear if people had managed to keep the sounds separate.

We put away our bedding and climbed down to wait. I stared out through the window, at women in the distance, some with the ends of their saris draped over their heads exactly like Trinidadian orhnis, at men wearing dhotis, kurtas and pagris, and at carts pulled by buffaloes in the distance, some loaded with sugarcane just harvested and on its way to the sugar mills. The train wheels and the engine gave the soundtrack to my daydream.

In a little while the train began to slow down, and then it stopped. Lucknow. Suddenly the compartment was filled with railway porters in their red kurtas, all urgently saying, 'Coolie? Coolie?' and wanting to take our luggage.

I followed Manju and our porter out of the station to where her father's driver was parked and waiting for us.

'WHO ARE YOU?'

TWO DAYS LATER I WAS ON A PLANE TO PATNA. IT WAS TO be a quick trip to visit an institute that did research on the dialects of Bihar, and to meet a sociolinguist who had been in class with my professor in the US. What I wanted was a look at the source varieties of Indian Bhojpuri that might have participated in forming Trinidad Bhojpuri.

I made my way from the airport to a little hotel near the maidan, the large grassy square in the middle of the town. I checked in as a foreigner, showing my passport, and I managed somehow to communicate with the reception clerks. The men at the desk spoke some English, and I used whatever Hindi I knew. I was given a room upstairs with a large balcony overlooking the maidan.

A meeting had been fixed for me at the institute that morning, so I got ready in my Trinidadian clothes and went down to find transport. I was, after all, a Trinidadian scholar. The men at the desk found me a cycle-rickshaw, and gave the man directions to the institute.

We were moving along smoothly when the rickshaw suddenly swerved to avoid a dog, and without thinking I shouted out something in Bhojpuri. Maybe it was something about the man's face, maybe I was daydreaming. But the Bhojpuri had come out of me by instinct. The rickshaw-wala stopped, got off his rickshaw and stared at me, bewildered.

'*Kaa bhail ba*?' I asked him. What's the matter?

He shook his head to clear it, and mumbled something about something being wrong with his cycle chain, and he adjusted it and got back onto the saddle, and we continued. He looked back warily a few times, but did not try to talk to me.

I spent most of the day getting the feel of the institute and what they did. It was largely survey work, mapping the dialects of Bihar. I looked through the files of filled-in questionnaries. Bhojpuri seemed to have changed in India, as living languages do, reacting to changes in the political environment. The modern dialects might not be a good point of departure for speculating about the past.

While I went about my work I had to communicate with the other researchers in Bhojpuri: we had no other language in common. Their Bhojpuri was different from mine. In fact, they all sounded different from each other.

When we stopped for tea I asked them how they did not all speak the same Bhojpuri.

'In Bhojpuri the dialect changes every ten kilometres,' an old professor told me grandly.

I had read about this, but I was surprised to find them all so proud of it. The differences between the varieties of Bhojpuri seemed very superficial to me, just variations in word endings, really, and not any real barrier to comprehension. The myriad dialects seemed more like statements of village identity than anything else.

'Isn't there a single urban variety you all speak?' I asked.

It was an odd question for them, used as they were to seeing Bhojpuri as very rich precisely because of all these micro-dialects. I decided to take a different tack.

'What do you all speak to each other in?' I asked. 'What do you write in?'

Hindi. All educated people in Bihar were at least bilingual, they said. Bhojpuri was a language they used at home, or with Bhojpuriyas who didn't know Hindi. Hindi was the middle-class urban lingua franca, and the language used in schools.

Sunnariya had already been there, almost ninety years ago in Trinidad. And I had considered her attitude an aberration, blaming her for the loss of Bhojpuri in my generation.

Bhojpuri in Trinidad was dying fast, giving way to Creole English and Standard English. In India it was fragmenting into smaller and smaller living universes, each too small to wield any real power, without having had a golden age when the dialects had come together and unified the community. Bhojpuri had become 'pretty', rather than important. In India Bhojpuri had never got out from under the thumb of Hindi.

That evening my professor's friend called me home for dinner, and he tried to steer me towards doing a neat little sociolinguistic study of how Bhojpuri had come together in Trinidad. I could see that this kind of cohesiveness would seem exotic in Patna. After dinner I headed for the hotel, to my room, to bed.

Next morning I was awakened at six o'clock by a loud knock on my door. A bright-eyed young man was standing outside my door with a rough twig broom in his hand. He told me he was the sweeper, and that it was time for him to sweep my room. I told him to go away and let me sleep.

Half an hour later he knocked on the door again, and before I could say anything he told me that he would get into trouble if he didn't sweep my room. So I let him in.

As he swept he kept looking up and asking me questions about everything. Where I was from. What I was doing in Patna. How I was travelling alone. Where I was going after Patna.

I answered all these questions briefly, sleepily, in Bhojpuri. My response didn't seem to satisfy him, but he didn't know how to take it further. Then my tea came, and he reluctantly left.

I got ready and went off to the institute again, and after a morning of poring over survey reports and listening to tapes of different varieties of Bhojpuri I was invited to have lunch with the professors and an eminent old man who was also visiting the institute.

While we were having lunch, the old man, who was sitting next to me, casually asked me my caste. My surname was merely my great-great grandfather's first name, and not a caste label, as was common among the higher castes in North India. So my caste was not obvious to him.

I decided to give the expanded version this time. I was a mixture of sonaar, ahir, kurmi and thakur, I said. The first three castes on the list, I learned later, were known as Other Backward Castes. Two of them were actually peasant castes.

The old man's smile froze and in his next question to me all the honorifics were gone. The conversation continued like this for a few minutes, with the other professors uncomfortably trying to address me as 'tē', the Bihari equivalent of 'tu', which had a real sting in the tail.

It felt odder to them than it did to me. In Trinidad Bhojpuri everyone called everyone else 'tu' all the time, except for the jahajis, who used 'tõ', like Hindi 'tum', for the first five minutes until they felt they knew you better. There was simply no honorific beyond that.

But in Patna there was a third: 'rauwaan', with the same meaning as Hindi 'aap'. In Patna it was 'rauwaan' that went with the English I spoke, my foreign look, and my affiliation to the University of Michigan, not 'tē'. Worst of all, 'tē' did not befit a linguist who knew Sanskrit. The linguists around the table were very uneasy talking down to another linguist.

Then the old man took a decision.

'You are a linguist,' he said in English, 'and for us a linguist is like a brahmin.' Then the honorofics were back and everyone else relaxed.

I inclined my head politely, and smiled. But my thoughts were far away, far across the salty ocean with Nana, who had distanced us all from the Bhojpuri of the sugar estates and bided his time till the end of his life. Waiting for the day when brahmins from the Bhojpuri heartland would have to recognize his descendants as their equals in learning. I had brought one long meandering journey to an end.

Next morning the same sweeper was back outside my hotel room at six, and with him was a painter.

I let them both in and after a fast job of cleaning, the sweeper explained to the painter where I was from, and told him that I spoke Bhojpuri.

The painter put down his brush and his pot of varnish and started asking questions about Trinidad, where exactly it was, how it was that we had gone there, what might be the salary of a painter in Trinidad, and how it was that he had never heard about the migration to the West Indies. They both stayed with me while I had my tea, asking me questions and giving me interesting bits of information about their villages, things I would not learn from the newspapers, they said.

I got ready quickly after they left. A team from the institute was going for fieldwork that morning to a village close to Patna. I would tag along.

The village was close to the highway, and had a primary school. After the institute researchers were done I asked if I could record some of the children. I had never in my life heard a child speak Bhojpuri. All my good interviews in Trinidad were with old people at sunset, when the day's work was over.

The children came and sat. Most had their hair neatly oiled and the girls' hair was in braids, except for a couple who had shoulder-length hair in pony tails. They started to recite for me things they had memorized in Bhojpuri.

Wait! I said. Not poems! Just talk to me, tell me about school, your friends.

The children instantly switched into Hindi. Two girls, sensing what I was after, consciously put the right Bhojpuri endings to the words in their Hindi stream of thought, inventing on the spot.

They could probably have told me old stories in Bhojpuri. Maybe even made up new stories. But Bhojpuri was alien to the present-day real world things I was asking them to talk about. School and friends their age were part of a life lived in Hindi. I was back in Sunnariya's home in Dow Village ninety years ago.

That afternoon I came back early from the institute to rest a while before I went out again for the evening.

After a little while there was a knock on my door.

I opened it. An older man stood there and introduced himself as the hotel cook. He had come, he said, to find out why I wasn't having any meals at the hotel. Was something wrong with the food?

I let him in. Soon a few of the hotel staff came in and joined him, and they sat in a line opposite me wondering how to start. Then the cook came to the point.

Who are you? the cook asked. Are you with the government? You are educated. How is it that you can't speak Hindi but you speak Bhojpuri and English?

Part of the answer was obvious, from his interest in me. I was a Bhojpuriya, like him. In Delhi I might come across as a foreigner, but here in Patna I was not a stranger. What made no sense to them, though, was the hybrid look, the strange Caribbean clothes, and an educated Bhojpuriya not knowing Hindi. Whatever my schooling, it had not been in Bihar, or anywhere else in North India.

I started to answer the question and something seemed to click inside the cook's head as he heard me speak in a Bhojpuri strangely devoid of Hindi words. His eyes widened.

I've heard someone speak like you, he said, in my village! But she was very old. The oldest woman in our village. I think we all used to talk like you, long ago.

He had heard about the migration to the sugar plantations abroad. I did not have to tell him. He was only curious about which of the colonies my family had gone to.

For years I had had to listen to people from India telling me that we had 'lost' our culture, and lost our language, implying that the only way to find it again was to turn back to a dismal past and submit to the inequality of the India we had left. But what was slowly becoming clear to me on this trip was that India too had 'lost' something in all these years, if moving on could be described as loss. Now we were no longer together, but we were in step, on parallel tracks.

The India I saw was not moving towards being the North America I knew, but the India of the 1970s and the Trinidad I had known as a young child were a lot alike. I could see it in the man holding court on the train exactly as Dad did, with the same teasing sense of humour, and I could see it so easily in the children I had met only that morning in the village near Patna. Their school uniforms, the mix of long and short hairstyles among the girls, the slackening hold of Bhojpuri on the school-going generation.

I thought of the tiny tugboat going ahead of the *Godavari*, towing it until it was safe for it to start its own engines and make its way down the Hooghly through the treacherous swamp to reach the global waters. I smiled. The jahajis as an advance party going ahead of an enormous subcontinent? I looked at the men sitting with me in the room and suddenly imagined I could see them all in jeans, bantering with me in English with Creole accents, and with Toyotas parked downstairs.

That was why the Indians I had met up to now had all looked so unfamiliar. I had been looking at the wrong people.

And another thought suddenly struck me: where were all the women? Wherever I went in Patna, with linguists at the institute, or here in my room in the hotel, I was always the only woman in the group. The other women I met, in the evenings in their homes, were mostly silent, shy, in the background. The face of the Bhojpuriya community in India seemed to be male.

No wonder Rosa's findings about women migrating alone had seemed so bizarre to the Indian men in her audience, even in Trinidad. The female energy released in the migration must have come as a shock. Just as Bhojpuri had come out from under the thumb of Hindi in the migration, and evolved into a lingua franca in its own right, women had emerged from seclusion and silence, and fixed their eyes on the big wheel that steered the boat. I had always felt uncomfortable when people from India put on a patronizing expression and told me that Bhojpuri was a 'sweet language'. Now I grasped the unthinking put-down in those words, and what it was that had made me wince every time I heard them talk like that.

Languages too could wear orhnis and be beautiful.

I conjured in my mind the faces of the other linguists I was in touch with, who were doing research on Bhojpuri in Guyana, Mauritius and Suriname. All women!

And then a cynical thought flashed across my mind screen: was I looking at radical change and empowerment, or just another one of the devious meanders our course so often took? That just as seclusion from the workforce and hiding under orhnis were actually a step up from forced labour in the cane fields, in the modern world where successful men wanted to be engineers and managers and earn big money, linguistics occupied no pinnacle, but was simply a field of study where women like me could keep ourselves busy doing fine embroidery, as it were, and not knocking at the citadels of power. That excluding women from linguistics was an issue only in the tiny closed world ruled by brahmin men.

I shook my head to dispel the thought. I didn't *want* to be an engineer or a manager. In linguistics I could sail the open waters.

Suddenly I thought of Saranga, the lady who had taken the first plunge across the watershed. Out of idle curiosity I asked the men in my room if they knew *Rani Saranga ke Kheesa*. They did. So I decided to ask them about the scene in Dhara Nagari where the sadhu had said that there were many Sarangas. Had I misunderstood what he was saying?

No, they said, there were many Sarangas in the story, and the young woman who had seen our Saranga and Sada Birij looking into each other's eyes had been another Saranga.

What was that all about? I asked.

The cook didn't know. But he was firm about one thing: there were many Sarangas. He had just never given it a thought.

No, said one of the others. Not just many Sarangas. *All* the women in Dhara Nagari were Sarangas!

Then I remembered. What Deeda had said was 'only named Saranga'. And it made sense. They had all left worlds behind them when they went as brides to Dhara Nagari. Like our Saranga they had all crossed a watershed. They were like Deeda, like Sunnariya, like

Janaki-didi, like Acchamma, like all the women who had come to Esperanza, and to all the other estates.

The Sarangas in Dhara Nagari were jahajins! Of course! Dhara was a word that meant stream. A river, a flow, a current! A watershed.

And like the jahajins they were not all alike. Some had come to terms with their new lives, begun to chase new dreams, laid the past to rest. And there would be some who looked back at what they had lost.

Deeda was like our Saranga. Deeda had crossed the kala pani and become a different person, though she had kept wondering about what she had left behind. But the person she had been back in her village was gone. Like Saranga she would even look different now. If she came back people would stare at her and ask: 'Who are you!?'

And who was I? I was the one who would take her home. Tomorrow I would be flying back to Lucknow, and in another day or two I would start the last lap of my journey with Deeda to the end of the rainbow.

RAINBOW'S END

By THE TIME I GOT BACK TO LUCKNOW THE ROAD TRIP TO
Faizabad and Basti had been finalized. Nishant's father
was the engineer on the inspection tour. He would be
checking progress on a bridge near Faizabad, and
another bridge beyond Basti. Manju had decided to come
with us too.

So we set off a day later in an official white
Ambassador, Manju and her father and me sitting in the
back, and his driver and chaprasi, his personal assistant,
going in front. The chaprasi put on his saafa, his fancy
uniform turban, and that made it visibly an official trip.
Then we made our way to National Highway 28 and
headed east to Faizabad. Manju's father announced that
the distance to Faizabad was 130 km, and that the trip
would take about three hours.

As we drove towards Faizabad the landscape begain
to look more and more like the Caroni landscape in
Trinidad—mango trees in flower, rice fields, sugarcane
fields, and a sense of more greenery. The only unfamiliar
thing was the density of human habitation. Small fields
abutted other small fields, and there were little homes
everywhere. The sense of distance that I was used to in

Caroni, of seeing across large fields of rice and sugarcane with hardly a house in sight, was not there. I remembered the times I would catch sight of a light in one solitary house in the distance after sunset, across rice fields or cane fields, or near the mangrove of the Caroni swamp. That would be an alien sight here.

Just before Faizabad we turned off the highway and headed towards a small bridge under construction. Labourers were everywhere, and as our car drove up I could hear a few voices saying, '*Sahib aa gaye*', the boss is here. Manju's father got out with the driver and chaprasi, and leaning forward intently with his hands clasped behind his back, he paced back and forth across the little bridge, questioning the engineer on site.

Then we continued on NH 28 to Faizabad, and went straight to the Public Works Department Rest House, where a big lunch was waiting for us. We took our bags out of the car to our rooms. We would be staying the night, and driving on to Basti the next day.

The servants in the Rest House were called 'bearers'. Suddenly I could see Deeda's parents, a rauniyar kahaar and a dhodiya kahaar, bearing a palanquin on their shoulders.

After lunch we sat a while in the garden outside. It was an L-shaped garden, in front of the Rest House and around one side, and it was mainly a neat manicured lawn with very fine durva grass, or doob, as Nana used to call it. All around the lawn, like a fringe, were pots of dahlias in bloom, like tall sentinels, yellow, red and pink. In smaller pots there were other flowers. Double marigolds, orange and yellow. Pansies. Snapdragons. It was the sort of garden we would not have called 'Indian' in Trinidad. It had a lingering feel of imperial rule.

Nishant's father asked me if I knew where my family had come from in Faizabad. I was stumped. A street address? I searched the memory banks in my head for a lead. Then a word came up, the name of a town that Dad had once tried to teach me how to pronounce properly. Nana had been telling me that his father, Ramesar, and his father's brother Ramcharan were not strictly from Faizabad. They had been from a place called Ajodhyapur. I remembered Dad getting me to say 'dhya', and not 'dha', and seeing that I got the 'u' in 'pur' right.

Was there any place they knew by that name in the area? Ajodhyapur?

Manju's father's eyes widened. Ayodhya! You are from Ayodhya!

I was stunned! The *real* Ayodhya! I had never done the obvious thing and transposed the 'j' to 'y' and made the connection. I had only been told Ajodhyapur was a small town near Faizabad. Were we from the real Ayodhya?

It was only 6 km from Faizabad to Ayodhya: they were considered twin cities. We drove there that afternoon in the white Ambassador, and I began to understand the meaning of the word kutiya that Deeda had used in the Saranga story. Most of the houses we passed seemed to have little shrines in front. Ayodhya was known as a city of temples.

The driver took us through a neighbourhood where one might find sonaar families. I tried to imagine Janaki-didi, Ramesar, Ramcharan and little Ramlal walking these same streets almost a century ago, thrown out of their home by Janaki-didi's in-laws and forced to walk to Faizabad, where Janaki-didi and her sons, with nowhere to go, signed up as girmitiyas bound for Trinidad. They would have been part of a sea of humanity in similar distress, ripe for recruitment. They would have been practically invisible to a government officer moving through these same streets.

And here I was, more than ninety years later, coming back in a Government of India white Ambassador, the first of our family ever to be coming back. It meant nothing, and it meant everything.

A story could not end with its heroine still in exile, I remembered. I was bringing another long journey to an end. I was back in Ayodhya in place of my great-great-great grandmother, Janaki-didi.

The sun was setting, and we turned back towards Faizabad, to the Rest House, ready for a good night's sleep, before continuing onward to Basti in the morning. I fell asleep that night and dreamt I was Deeda.

The next day was a beautiful spring day with a magical light in a sky the same cornflower blue as on the day I went to tell Deeda I was going to India. The deep green durva grass and the yellows and oranges of the dahlias and marigolds were all so vivid that I could almost hear them as music in my ears. We sat on the lawn and had breakfast in a little world of our own oblivious of the real world outside the garden.

Then we got into the car and settled in for a shorter trip. According to Manju's father it would be 80 km further east on the same NH28. A little over two hours.

The highway meandered towards the north, and then we were crossing a river, and a sign told me it was the

Ghagra. The driver saw me in the rear-view mirror reading the sign and told me that the other name for the river was Saryu.

By now I was alert to the y-j connection. Saryu had to be Sarju in Bhojpuri, or Sirju, as it was spelled in Trinidad. Langoor Mamoo! He should not remain in exile either. I had no idea if he was connected to this place, but I imagined he must be. He had been recruited in Faizabad too. I smiled at the thought of Langoor Mamoo, who had travelled with Deeda and Janaki-didi all the way to Trinidad, and even to Esperanza Estate. He could easily have run away from Esperanza like Mukoon Singh, but he never had. He had stayed close to Deeda and Sunnariya, and kept them in touch with Mukoon Singh.

We stopped at the PWD Rest House in Basti. Manju's father went on with the driver and the chaprasi to inspect the bridge that was a bit beyond Basti. They would be back in time for lunch, after which we would drive on to Deeda's village.

I checked my tape recorder and put in some brand-new alkaline cells I had been keeping especially for this trip to Deeda's village.

The driver got directions to the village, and we set off. We turned off the highway, and drove what seemed like a long distance, then the driver stopped and asked someone on the road again. We were close. Turn left after another kilometre, we were told, and the road would take us straight there.

There is a sharp difference between villages on the highway and villages deep in the countryside. Schooling, modernity and Hindi reach the villages near the highway first. Away from the highway time moves more slowly, and the secluded villages show stronger ties to the past.

We parked the car and the driver went to find the village pradhan, the headman, to tell him that the Chief Engineer for bridges wanted to meet him.

The pradhan came out curiously, and when he saw the white Ambassador with the chaprasi in full official headgear sitting in front, he sent his men to go and get khatiyas for us to sit on. Then we sat together, and the chaprasi explained in Hindi that I was doing research on the dialect of Basti, and that I wanted to meet an old person in the village who remembered a kahaar named Parbati who had left with her son Kalloo more than ninety years ago.

The pradhan looked doubtful, but he said there was one very old man in the village, and he was a kahaar. He sent his men off to find out if this old man knew anything about any Parbati or Kalloo. It suddenly struck me what a strange thing it was to expect to find anyone now who would remember Deeda. It had been more than ninety years! I began making contingency plans to do a bit of recording with any old person I met.

Then the pradhan's men came back, and coming behind them was a bewildered old man, very thin and very stooped, walking with the help of a tall stick. Well over a hundred, I thought. The old man sank down into a squat in front of the pradhan, his knees nearly touching his chin.

I suddenly remembered the two little monkeys I had seen the first day in Delhi with Manju, squatting on the carrier of the bicycle, with their knees up under their chins. The old man was squatting there like a trained monkey, ready to perform as he was told to.

Then the pradhan told the old man that I wanted to hear him sing.

Before I could do anything to stop him the old man broke into singing, squatting there, in a fine strong voice. When he stopped, the pradhan leaned forward, probably to tell him the next song he should sing.

This was not what I was here for.

The pradhan caught my expression and leaned forward with his hand raised, to stop the singing. The old man grimaced and flinched back from the expected blow.

I remembered this scene. Where had I seen it before?

The old man, now confused, began to sing again, and the pradhan again leaned forward with his hand raised.

And the next thing I knew I was up on my feet, standing between the two of them, looking down at the old man.

> *Tumhe ta laagey lakari, re, pyaarey,*
> *Humein laagey kareja-kheenchey hunkari.*

From far away I heard my own voice singing the words of Saranga's song.

> Blows are falling on you, my love,
> My heart is tight with pain.

The old man stared up at me and his jaw dropped. Then something seemed to click, and he smiled faintly and continued the song:

> *Arey, humein ta laagey lakari, re, rani,*
> *Aa tum karo mahaley-beechey bhoga ji.*

Yes, blows are falling on me, queen,
And you are living well in a palace.

I turned abruptly to the pradhan and spoke to him in my Trinidad Bhojpuri. *'Ehi burhwa se hum maangi baat karey!'* I want to talk to this old man.

The pradhan stonewalled. We could talk right here, he said. He had arranged tea, and it would be coming soon.

I looked around helplessly. Now Manju's father came to my rescue. He leaned towards the pradhan and explained, in hush-hush tones, that I was an Indian from abroad, and that I had come to talk to these old people about their relatives overseas. So the pradhan reluctantly agreed.

Manju's father, the driver and the chaprasi stayed back and kept the pradhan occupied. Manju and I followed the old man to his hut with the tape recorder. When we reached he rounded up a few young boys and got them to bring us a khatiya to sit on, and Manju and I sat with the tape recorder between us.

I told the old man that Parbati, who we called Deeda in Trinidad, had asked me to play the tape of the end of Saranga's story for him, since I was coming to Basti. The voice he would be hearing on the tape was hers.

He nodded.

As I pressed play, the VU meter needles jumped, and two boys sitting behind us gave a start. I paused the tape recorder and explained to them that we were running on battery power now, and that the needles were showing how much current was flowing. At the moment we had full power: I pushed the tiny button that tested the batteries, and the needles surged all the way to the right.

They sat behind the khatiya and said they would keep their eyes on the VU meters for me to make sure that we had enough power.

The old man pulled up a tiny stool and sat close to us. I released the pause:

'Aa jab i uthal, tab "Hai, Saranga, hai, Saranga, hai Saranga." Kahaan ba Saranga? Na ba.'

And when he woke up he said: 'Oh Saranga, I've lost you, oh Saranga, I've lost you, oh Saranga, I've lost you!' Where is Saranga? She's gone.

And he started to walk, and when he saw the elephant's footprints, he followed them. He said: 'She went this way.'

And then he saw a big group of men at work. So he stopped there. And he asked for work there. So they gave him work, but he had disguised himself with a false beard, moustache and wig. And he asked for work, so he got it.

Then he sings, and he works, saying:

> *Arey, beta howe Raja Jagadeep ke, re, pyaari,*
> *Sada Birij mera naam, ji.*
> *Tera karanawa, hai, re, Saranga,*
> *Dhowe intiya aa rori ji.*

> *Oh, this is the son of King Jagdeep, my love,*
> *My name is Sada Birij,*
> *All because of you, alas, Saranga,*
> *I am washing bricks and gravel.*

The old man was singing Sada Birij's song along with

Deeda on the tape in his strong rich voice.

Now he sings, and he works. So the other workers say: 'Listen, you just sing. And we'll work.'

And the poor man sings, and they all work. And when the sound of his voice reaches Saranga's ears, she sends for him.

When he saw Saranga, then, man, he was suddenly more full of love than a thousand men! She said: 'Be quiet! Or the two of us will get into trouble!'

She said: 'Listen, you go, do your work slowly, and I will give an order here that they should go and tell the prince that we need a big piece of sandalwood.'

So he said: 'Okay.'

So they got her the sandalwood, and there were many carpenters working there, and she called them and told them to make an uran khatola. So they started to make it. And she told Sada Birij to go and watch them and learn how to fly it, how to land it, to learn everything. And by the time it was ready he had asked and learned about everything he had to do.

So she said: 'Good.'

Then when it was ready, she sent for Sada Birij and a barber, and she got him a good haircut and a shave, got him a proper bath, and then she said: 'Tell the prince to send his sister. Now I am ready to come to his palace.'

So they said: 'Okay.'

I looked at the old man. He was staring intently at the tape recorder, his eyes shining. He looked up and saw me looking at him, and then he noticed Manju next to me. After that he kept looking at me and Manju as he listened to Deeda's voice on the tape.

Now the sister came, and the three of them sat in the uran khatola, and he flew the plane and he made five rounds over the palace, he circled five times, and people below kept watching, thinking, 'Now it will land, now it will land', and he flew the plane away and then they were gone.

Now the old man was smiling. He knew the end of the story. More than ninety years had just vanished. He was young again.

I glanced at the hand-luggage tag on my tape recorder bag.

And when the plane flew away, it went and landed outside his own house.

The old man nodded, smiling.

Then his mother came out to meet them, and she took her son and daughter-in-law with her into their home.

Then came Deeda's happily-ever-after line, the way she ended all her stories:

'Itana hum jaanila!'
That is as far as I know.

I waited a few minutes for the reverb from the story to die down inside my head. All of a sudden I felt lighter than air. The old man sat too, willing the dream to go on.

Then slowly we came back to the other world, to the natural sounds around us.

The two boys behind the khatiya looked up from the VU meters, and inclined their heads. They had done their job. I reached out and pressed stop: the bridge across two great oceans to Deeda's little house in Orange Valley disappeared.

And then the khatiya we were sitting on was back to being just a wooden cot, and Manju was back to being Manju. But the old man was not the same old man who had sat looking helpless at the feet of the pradhan. There was a shine in his eyes now.

Parbati had reached out to him, after all these years.

I looked around. The chaprasi was standing there, waiting to carry my tape recorder back to the car. I packed up my tape recorder into its bag and he took it from me. Then Manju, the old man and I got up together, and in one instinctive Trinidadian gesture, I gave the old man a hug.

From Parbati, I said, Deeda.

Then it was time for this other Saranga to go. I took a last look at the old man standing outside his hut, the hut where Deeda had packed those last handfuls of parched rice along with the sattwa powder and an extra sari long, long ago. The hut where Kalloo had been born, after Deeda had walked and walked, like her mother-in-law had told her, to make the child come faster.

I turned to go with Manju and the chaprasi, through the tiny village, past the pradhan still sitting on his khatiya, back to the car. The day was nearly over. The sun was setting, and on its way to the other end of the rainbow, to Trinidad, to Orange Valley. For Deeda a long, long night was finally coming to an end.

Manju and I got in the backseat next to Nishant's father and the chaprasi sat in front with the tape recorder. The driver had already turned the car, and now he started the engine and we headed back to the Rest House.

Tomorrow we would be driving back to Lucknow together.